THE COMPLETE CASES OF
HORATIO HUMBERTON, VOLUME I

J. PAUL SUTER

THE COMPLETE CASES OF

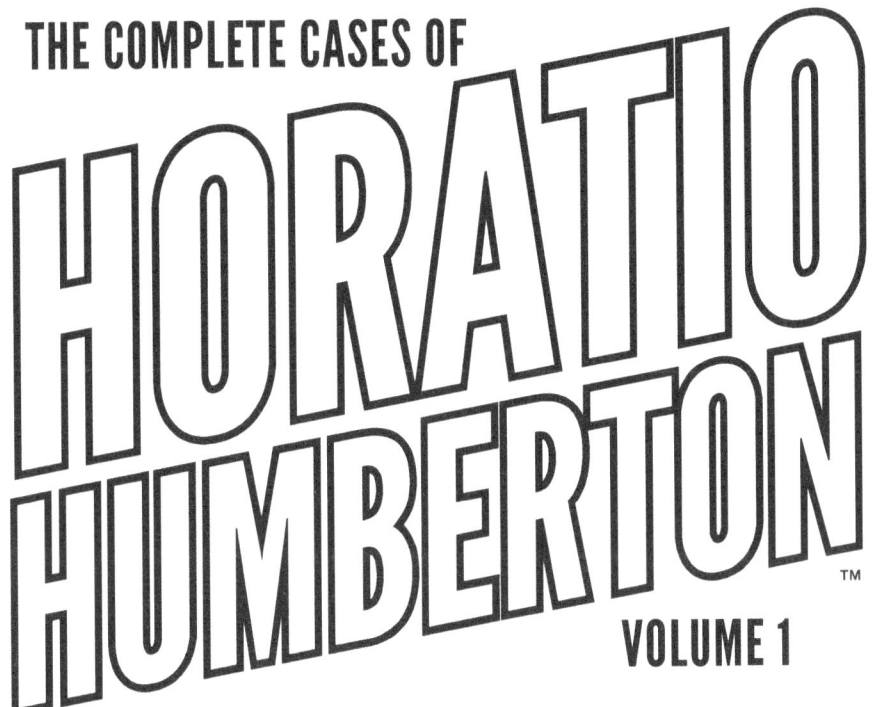

HORATIO HUMBERTON™

VOLUME 1

J. PAUL SUTER

PRIMARY ILLUSTRATOR
JOHN FLEMING GOULD

STEEGER BOOKS • 2019

PUBLISHING HISTORY

"He Talked to the Devil" originally appeared in the November 7, 1925 issue of *Flynn's* magazine. Copyright 1925 by The Frank A. Munsey Company. Copyright renewed 1953 and assigned to Steeger Properties, LLC. All rights reserved.

"The Angel of the Damned" originally appeared in the July 1932 issue of *Dime Detective* magazine. Copyright 1932 by Popular Publications, Inc. Copyright renewed 1959 and assigned to Steeger Properties, LLC. All rights reserved.

"Eyes of the Dead" originally appeared in the September 1932 issue of *Dime Detective* magazine. Copyright 1932 by Popular Publications, Inc. Copyright renewed 1959 and assigned to Steeger Properties, LLC. All rights reserved.

"The Werewolf Horrors" originally appeared in the February 1933 issue of *Dime Detective* magazine. Copyright 1933 by Popular Publications, Inc. Copyright renewed 1960 and assigned to Steeger Properties, LLC. All rights reserved.

"The Mill of Horror" originally appeared in the August 15, 1933 issue of *Dime Detective* magazine. Copyright 1933 by Popular Publications, Inc. Copyright renewed 1960 and assigned to Steeger Properties, LLC. All rights reserved.

"Seconds of Doom" originally appeared in the September 1, 1933 issue of *Dime Detective* magazine. Copyright 1933 by Popular Publications, Inc. Copyright renewed 1960 and assigned to Steeger Properties, LLC. All rights reserved.

"About the Author" originally appeared in the July 1932 issue of *Dime Detective* magazine. Copyright 1932 by Popular Publications, Inc. Copyright renewed 1959 and assigned to Steeger Properties, LLC. All rights reserved.

TABLE OF CONTENTS

HE TALKED TO THE DEVIL

THERE WERE FEW COOLER BURGLARS THAN SQUINT REILLY, BUT HE WITHERED AT THE SCENE IN OLD CALLOWAY'S STUDY

CHAPTER ONE
A DESPERADO'S FEAR

NOT BEING an imaginative man, Patrolman John Manders paced his nightly beat on the River Road untroubled by ghosts from the forgotten past of the neighborhood. Conscientiously he tried the door handles of ancient warehouses and ship supply stores. That these same buildings, though fallen to a lower estate, had once been mansions of Cleveland's aristocracy was no concern of his. He was interested in their present security. He walked slowly, incuriously, swinging his night stick.

Approaching the old Calloway residence he glanced up at Verdaunt Calloway's oddly barred study window. He always glanced up. The lighted window assured him that Calloway had not yet gone off on another of his harebrained trips to the ends of the earth. All was as usual. Leaving the yellow circle beneath a street lamp, which was fighting the rapidly rising fog from the river, Manders plunged into the darkness in front of the Calloway place. He intended to try the handle of the front door and pass on to the warehouse just beyond. But he perceived unexpectedly that all was *not* quite as usual. A drunk leaned against the next lamp-post, on a line with the warehouse.

Manders hurried forward and tapped the drunk on the shoulder. He could not see the man's face distinctly—night and the fog prevented—but being of a kindly nature he felt well-disposed toward the unfortunate.

"One o'clock in the morning, my boy," he said good-humoredly. "Time for every man that don't have to go out to be in bed. Tell me where you live and I'll help you on your way."

The man's response was immediate. He whirled about, threw both arms around the patrolman's neck, and burst into tears. Manders, catching one flash of his flaming red hair and thin, eager face, recognized him. It was Squint Reilly, one of the coolest burglars in Cleveland. Reilly never touched liquor.

Manders was no novice. In the very moment of recognition he took the proper precautions. He ducked, and with one hand forced himself loose from Reilly's embrace. With the other he drew his gun.

"Got you covered, Reilly," he announced calmly. "One funny move and I'll bore you!"

The burglar backed, or rather staggered, against the lamp-post. He was still sobbing. He spoke in an unsteady, thick voice which was scarcely understandable.

"For the love of Heaven, get me away from here! Call the wagon, but get me away first!"

Manders stared at him in amazement.

"Did somebody shoot you?" he demanded.

Reilly shook his head and began to sink down the post. After brief hesitation the patrolman searched his prisoner for weapons, then supported him with one arm, keeping him covered with the revolver in the other hand. The burglar evidently was trying to stand, but his legs would not support him. He was shivering violently.

"Is it a fit you're having?" Manders suggested in bewilderment. "You're not drunk, are you?" Then, as sudden

He gave me one look before I had sense enough to run for my life.

enlightenment came to him—"I'll be hanged if the man ain't in a blue funk! Are you frightened of something? Is that it?"

The red-haired man nodded and repeated his request to be taken away.

"The call box is at the corner. Come on," invited Manders.

The burglar came. He still required support, but, as they proceeded, he regained some of his self-control. When they reached the patrol box he was able to stand, but he was white and shaky. He tried unsuccessfully to speak, and smiled weakly at his own effort. At length he found voice to answer the policeman's questions, though his tones were uncertain and thick.

"Sorry to make a fool of myself, officer," he said, with a show of dignity. "I never did it before, this way. But I seen something that took everything I got right out of me."

"What did you see, Reilly?" the policeman inquired, with something of the tone one would take with a frightened child. It struck him as queer that he should be talking thus to one of the most desperate characters in the city.

Reilly looked fearfully up and down the street, and answered in a whisper:

"I seen the devil!"

To the extent of two steps, Patrolman Manders gave ground. He almost forgot to keep his prisoner covered—almost, but not quite.

"Did you say the *devil?*" he demanded, with the suspicion of a chuckle.

"That's what I said," Squint Reilly retorted, showing a trace of resentment. "If you don't believe me, go see for yourself. He's up in old Calloway's study."

Manders scratched his head. He did it absent-mindedly, with the butt of his revolver, but his prisoner took no advantage of the opening.

"What the hell *did* you see?" the policeman persisted, with growing heat at the unprecedented situation. "You seen something all right, but I don't get you on that devil stuff."

Squint Reilly stiffened, with the air of an honorable citizen whose word has been outrageously questioned. At the same time he glanced toward the end of the street, which had just been enlivened by the entrance of the police patrol. He was recovering from his shivery condition.

"I told you what I seen," he asseverated coldly. "I seen the devil. If there's a devil, he was up in Calloway's study. If there ain't one, I seen him anyway. I could tell you something more, but I won't. Climb in through the kitchen window, the way I did, and have an eyeful."

"Look here, Reilly, tell me about it?" the policeman urged; but the burglar shook his head.

"I've talked all I'm going to to-night. Put me in the wagon, and go have a look—see."

To the wagon crew, when they had pulled up at the street lamp, Manders told of the situation, with a grin and a sage shake of his head.

"Reilly's gone cuckoo all right, but I'd better rout old Calloway out and see if the place has been entered. One of you guys come along."

Squint was hustled in, and the patrol rumbled on its way. Accompanied by Patrolman Clark, a young policeman with a mental quickness which promised better things for him in days to come, Manders mounted the broad Calloway steps and rang the bell. He rang it again and once again, with an insistence which set its echoes pulsating through the lofty rooms within.

"We're wasting time. Come around to the kitchen window, where Reilly got in," suggested Clark.

"Where he *said* he got in," corrected Manders, with dignity. "I think myself he acted cracked. We'll find everything O.K."

"No harm in trying," persisted the younger man.

He led the way, to the resentment of Patrolman Manders, who took pains to elbow past him into the little alleyway on which the kitchen faced. Thus it was the policeman on the beat who received credit for discovering an open window in the rear of the Calloway mansion.

"Follow me!" Manders directed, officiously, vaulting through the window without delay, to make sure of maintaining his position as leader.

"I'm with you," announced Clark; then, stopping abruptly: "Whew! Oh, Lord!"

Manders also had stopped, choking and sputtering in the heavy smell which swept thickly into their faces.

"What is it?" he exclaimed, coughing.

Clark was sweeping his flashlight around the broad kitchen.

"It's coming through that open door," he answered. "Hall door, I guess. Come on, let's go."

Manders's hesitation had forfeited the leadership for him. He could not pass Clark without rushing forward with dangerous speed. No one could tell what might be ahead in the darkness. It was well known in police circles that Calloway, the eccentric, had connected electric lights only in his study. The darkness in other parts of the house—in which anything might be lurking—could be quickly relieved only by the flashlights. So Manders reinforced Clark's circle of light with his own, and contented himself with following where the younger man led.

Clark progressed down the hall, though not without exploring every suspicious corner with his flash as he approached it. Some of them required close examination before they could be approved as harmless. For Calloway, an enthusiastic ornithologist, had filled his mansion with stuffed birds from every clime. Manders wondered whether the choking smell could come from any of these, but he scouted the idea as unlikely. While his mind was still upon that subject there was an echoing crash above stairs.

"What's that?" cried Manders. Clark lifted his voice in a stentorian, "Hey!" But there was no response.

"Take it on the run. Something's wrong up there!" urged the younger policeman.

He rounded the corner of the broad staircase, but Manders pulled at his sleeve.

"The smell has about stopped!"

His companion halted, with one foot on the lowest stair.

"Must have stopped when we heard that crash," he surmised. "Come on, old man! Have your gun handy!"

Calloway's study was at the head of the stairs. The door, not entirely shut, permitted a spear of brilliant light to stab the blackness of the hallway. The two policemen climbed swiftly but cautiously toward this chink. They reached it almost together—their rivalry no longer due to jealousy, but to the comradely determination of each not to let the other face danger alone. Clark's hand pushed open the door. As he jumped aside to avoid a possible ambush Manders's revolver, held steadily, covered the doorway.

They might have spared their precautions. No one was in the room. No one who could have ambushed them. Manders turned weakly and looked at the younger man; and as he looked he saw the blood drain from Clark's face and leave it white.

It was Clark who spoke, in a whisper, the one word: "Murdered!"

"Murdered and torn to pieces and the place wrecked!" supplemented Manders, and he added vindictively, "We'll get that Squint Reilly for this!"

CHAPTER TWO

H. HUMBERTON, NECROLOGIST

A FLY adulterated the ointment, as far as getting Squint Reilly was concerned; which was that Squint, being an undersized man, of much greater nerve and cunning than physical strength, could hardly have torn to pieces the decidedly muscular Calloway. The police held

Reilly, but only because they had no one else to hold, and after several days of as blind an investigation as he had ever made, Detective Clyde, in charge of the case, determined late one afternoon to solicit the help of a friend of his who was not really a detective at all; not, at least, by profession.

Clyde had not far to go.

Within four blocks of the Central Police Station, in a foreign district of the city, he stopped before a somber establishment with a store front, the broad windows of which were curtained in chaste green. There were a number of other stores in the block, but this was the only one which did not display its wares in the windows; and the omission was perhaps commendable, for in gold letters set against a background of stippled black, just above the doorway, appeared the legend, "Horatio Humberton, Necrologist."

Clyde had argued with his eccentric friend, Ho Humberton, that one of his calling, especially in a foreign district, would do well to call himself merely an undertaker; but the necrologist had invariably shaken his gaunt head.

"The word is inaccurate," he demurred. "I do not 'take them under.' I merely stand at the top and turn the handle that lets them down. Besides, the term 'Necrologist' is more consonant with the dignity of the profession."

There was no convincing Humberton. By the time he opened his lips on any subject all arguments pro and con already seemed to have been weighed in his mind. So the good-humored, but rather heavy and slow detective had given up the attack. He was thankful enough to have a friend who, however mediocre his success in his bread-and-butter profession, had attained reputation among the police as a student of crime.

Clyde knew just where to find the necrologist. Passing through the somberly furnished reception room he merely inquired, "Is he in, Sade?" of the attendant brunette—who had risen with a professionally sympathetic smile when the street door opened—and proceeded along a narrow side hallway toward the rear of the building. Four doors opened from this hallway. A neat brass plate on the first proclaimed it to be the chapel; the second, also carefully labeled, was the embalming room; the third, the morgue. The stocky detective passed them all unhesitatingly, in favor of an unmarked fourth door, which he opened with a jovial:

"Business good, Ho?"

He had perceived the proprietor of the establishment immediately upon opening the door, but it was only because he knew where to look. A stranger would have seen merely a pile of more or less dusty books, heaped in the middle of the small room because there was no accommodation for them on the already crowded shelves with which the place was lined. Clyde knew that the pile of volumes concealed Humberton's desk. In addition, he was sure that the thatch of neutral, straw-colored material seemingly left at the summit of the pile by some careless maid, was not the tan dust cloth it appeared to be, but the top layer of Ho's rather untidy hair.

The light of a single bulb, decending from the ceiling, played strange tricks with that hair. But none of the tricks deceived Clyde. He expected to see the thatch lift, and a long, spare face with a prominent nose appear beneath it; and he expected, also, to be regarded with a pair of incredibly thick, horn-rimmed glasses, before an answer was returned to his query. Nor was he astonished at the explosive bitterness with which that answer came.

"Damned poor!" replied the necrologist. "How many patients do you suppose I have in the morgue just now?

One! And if he hadn't been killed in a building accident a block away I wouldn't have him!"

The detective chuckled.

"You sure wouldn't," he agreed. "And I guess no other morgue would, either."

Humberton rose to a long, lean height, which seemed to make him dominate the bookish company, like their presiding genius. He permitted a bored yawn to escape unchecked.

"That's the irony of it," he observed ruefully. "I walk down the street and what do I see? People! Hundreds of them! And every one a possible account on my books. But they are all so vulgarly healthy. One has to blow them up or hit them with a brick to make them into cash items. And the law won't permit that. It might have been done in the Middle Ages, when they had real personal liberty. But not now! Not now!"

"Things may not be so bad as you think, Ho," Clyde comforted. "I have a job for you right now."

His friend fixed him keenly through the thick spectacles.

"Necrological?" he demanded.

The detective shrugged his shoulders.

"I'm afraid not. The coroner called in Smith & Hogan before I had a chance to swing it your way. I was thinking of detective work."

"No time for it," Humberton declared promptly. "Too busy. You see those?" He waved his big hands toward the piles of books which hemmed him in. "There are seventy-two books on Egypt. I am going through them profession-ally. When I finish I shall know more about embalming than any one else. I expect to add modern methods to ancient knowledge, and do better work than the Egyptians. When you die, Clyde, have your wife bring you to me. I'll make you last forever. I'll do such a good job that she can keep you around for years if she wishes, without your becoming unpleasant. No odor. No shriveling. Everything nice and sweet. I'm right on the trail now. You wouldn't have me turn aside for detective work, would you?"

"Sit down again, Ho." Clyde was used to this sort of reception. He never looked for prompt acceptance when he brought a job to Humberton. But his friend's ability, when he did turn to detective work, was worth a little pleading. "Sit down till I tell you," he coaxed. "You might as well hear about it, anyway, while you rest your eyes."

The tall necrologist complied; whereupon Detective Clyde, balancing his own considerable weight on a seat improvised from half a dozen books—for the chair behind the desk was the only one in the room—proceeded to set forth the details of the mystery, so far as known. Ho Humberton sat quietly, his glasses fixed on the detective's face, and did not interrupt till the story was finished.

"So you are holding Reilly for the murder?" he commented then.

"We thought that best, Ho."

"Reilly is of an excitable, nervous temperament?"

"Not on your life! Ordinarily he's an iceberg—a professional burglar, and one of the coolest eggs in the city. Something of a runt, but his head makes up for his body. I don't think any one else would have tackled that eerie place of Calloway's."

"And after committing an impossible murder, this cool burglar left the house empty-handed, to round out the evening by weeping in a policeman's arms?"

Clyde blew his stub nose to hide a grin of satisfaction. He had induced the preoccupied undertaker to pick out the obvious flaw in his theory, which was the first step toward obtaining help from the remarkably keen brain behind the eccentric exterior.

But Ho Humberton was not yet won. He gazed somberly at Detective Clyde's florid, expectant face, and shook his head.

"I'm not so sure, Clyde. You come at an unusually bad time. I am just running down a clew which may change our whole understanding of the use of bitumen in Egyptian embalming. But—a murder—"

He crooned the word thoughtfully, with a vacant stare at his books. Clyde knew then that the battle was won. He would never regard the books so if they were not losing. And so it proved, for the necrologist rose, abruptly.

"I will return with you," he said. "On the way you can tell me more. I should like to see the burglar this evening. And Calloway's room, by all means."

He put on the broad-brimmed hat which was as characteristic of him as his glasses or his long, scrawny neck, and in a few minutes they were walking up the street, through the last sunlight of a spring day.

"Did you know Calloway, Ho?" asked Clyde as they threaded their way through various groups of foreign children, some of whom smiled up at the necrologist. However sardonic his thoughts toward their elders, the younger generation invariably liked him.

"Not personally," he answered. "I knew him to be the last representative of a very old family. He was also one of the two or three most distinguished ornithologists in the world, and an able chemist besides."

"That is more than we knew—that about the ornithology," admitted the detective. "We learned it since he was killed. I don't suppose a man on the force ever read any of his books, though he must have written them by the dozen.

Of course, we all knew him well enough by sight. He was the biggest man I ever saw. I'd have backed him against a gorilla in a wrestling match. That *would* seem to leave Reilly out—wouldn't it, Ho?"

"Distrust self-evident inferences," counseled the necrologist sententiously. "Tell me more about Calloway."

"There's precious little to tell—but that little is queer stuff. Calloway was an odd sort of bachelor. When he was in town, he lived absolutely by himself, though he had a big house, and was rich enough to afford plenty of servants, if he had wanted them. Once a week a woman came in to clean for him. He took his meals at a restaurant, and sent his washing out. When he left town he would simply lock up the place and go. If thieves broke in, well and good—not much of what he had was in their line, anyway. Up to that point you might call him merely queer. Now comes the strange part."

He paused. Though the undertaker, walking beside him, was silent, he did not take his eyes from Clyde's round, cheerful face. The detective continued:

"Calloway has a steam yacht—a clipper of a boat, with bushels of speed in her. That was what he went in when he took trips. They were long trips, mind you—he would be gone for a year or more at a time. No one seems to know where he went, and we can't find out where the yacht went, either, when he was in town. It lay in the river just long enough to land him at his private wharf. Then it would steam out again. We've traced it through the Welland Canal, out into the Atlantic; and of course we suppose he had some arrangement with the captain when he was ready to use the boat again. But that's just guess work—we don't *know* a thing. All we really know is that Calloway came back in the steam yacht one night about four months ago, and that the boat left before morning; and that he's dead now—dead and torn to pieces."

Though an expression of horror might have seemed in order, Horatio Humberton smiled—the smile of a connoisseur to whom members of the human race did not become of interest until they had ceased to walk about.

"Was the body really in that condition, Clyde?" he asked with a note of satisfaction in his voice.

"I'm not overdrawing it a bit, Ho. It had been torn to pieces—little pieces."

"Ah, well! I suppose there will be some commonplace explanation. You are sure the burglar believes that he saw the devil?"

"He came out of the third degree without changing his story."

The necrologist sighed.

"Of course he is mistaken. Yet I should have liked his opportunity. There is always a chance, Clyde, that the most improbable story may be true. And the devil—granting his existence—would be a stimulating personage to meet. He would be far less of a bore than the average-clergyman."

CHAPTER THREE
WHAT REILLY SAW

SQUINT REILLY twitched a little from time to time as he spoke, and manifested an occasional tendency to turn his head sharply, as if some highly undesirable visitor might be standing just behind him. This oddity of manner was the more noticeable, since the man whom it affected clearly did not belong to the nervous type. He was by no means stolid. The daring little gray eyes, coupled with a sensitive mouth, revealed his high-strung temperament.

But he spoke coldly and precisely, and his manner in the presence of the chief of police and a selected staff of detectives remained unabashed. He met Ho Humberton's gaze with a look equally keen, though it squinted slightly. Probably his wishes had not been consulted in arranging the interview; but he glanced amusedly over the crowd in the chief's office, to which he had been brought, and acquiesced as graciously as if he had been chief, instead of a prisoner charged with murder.

Humberton opened the examination briskly. At this sort of thing he was as much at home as any professional on the force; moreover, he was secure in the knowledge that the professionals themselves welcomed his cooperation.

"Now, Reilly, if you're willing to talk, I think you can begin where you entered the kitchen window. Tell me everything. The more trivial an experience seems, the more likely it is to be a really important thing that is being overlooked."

The prisoner nodded cheerfully.

"I'm willing to talk all right, sir. This thing has kind of got me going, and I'd like to get to the bottom of it myself. You know I came in at the kitchen window. I left the kitchen door open behind me when I got to the hall. Right away, then, I noticed a smell—an awful smell. It was like bad meat. It almost knocked me down. I thought first it came from something in the hall, but when I'd sniffed around a bit, I found it didn't. It was coming down the stairs."

"How could you be sure of that?" Humberton interrupted.

"There was a breeze blowing down the stairs, sir, and it blowed the smell into my face."

The burglar hesitated, and looked down at the carpet between his feet, until his visitor commanded impatiently:

"Go on."

"I was thinking of something I didn't tell the others—one of them things you mentioned that don't amount to much. While I stood there at the foot of the stairs with the smell in my nose I was sure in my own mind there was a dead body lying around somewheres—one that had been lying dead a long time—and that was where the smell come from. You know the feel you have when a dead man's in the house? Well, that's how I felt. And then somebody upstairs began to talk."

The necrologist nodded comprehendingly.

"You're a type of man who might be sensitive to such an impression," he conceded. "I take it you didn't *see* any one dead?"

"I just felt that way, sir. Then I saw a light at the head of the stairs, that seemed to come from an open doorway, and I heard Calloway talking. He was saying, 'Back! Back!'—just like that, over and over. He must have said it four or five times while I was climbing the stairs."

"You went up anyway?"

The prisoner wiped his forehead. Despite Humberton's rather caustic manner, he had a faculty, when he wished to exert it, of making men open their minds to him. An observer might have been interested to note how the shocked condition of Squint Reilly's nerves, previously almost concealed by his unusual self-control, was beginning to come to the surface.

"It took all the guts I've got, sir, but I went up. That queer feeling I had made me afraid to be alone. I thought Calloway was up there, and I wanted to get to him. He wasn't talking as if he was mad. His voice was kind of low, but it had an odd ring to it that had me clean puzzled."

"When I got to the doorway, there he was standing in the room, with his back to me. He was a whale of a man, with great, broad shoulders. He was saying, 'Back! Back!' and edging himself toward the door, but it was a big room, and he had some way to go yet. I said, 'Mr. Calloway!' but he didn't take no notice. So I stepped inside. And—and—then I saw who he was talking to."

He stopped. Ho Humberton's lean face was a study in concentration. He was alert to catch the meaning of Reilly's every gesture and expression as the tale was told.

"Whom was he talking to, Reilly?" he inquired softly.

The prisoner shivered, involuntarily glanced behind him, and whispered:

"It was the devil himself, sir!"

"How was the devil dressed?" the necrologist pursued, studiously unstartled.

"I can't rightly say he was dressed at all, sir. Whether he was or not, it was the way he looked at me that I went by. He give me one look before I had sense enough to run for my life—and no mortal man ever give another one such a look as that!"

"Tell me exactly what the devil looked like," prompted Humberton; but Reilly shook his head.

"I'm afraid I can't, sir."

"He had horns?"

"I can't say he did, sir."

"You say he was not dressed. Was his skin red?"

"If was more like some dark color—brown, maybe; what I could see of it."

Humberton received the implication eagerly.

"You couldn't see much of him? Why was that?"

The prisoner looked puzzled. He thought silently. Suddenly he brightened.

"Why, it must have been because his wings covered him, sir."

For a moment the undertaker was nonplused; but he recovered, without changing expression.

"You say that he had wings, Reilly?"

"Great wings, that went right down to his feet," was the unhesitating reply. "They looked like—like bat's wings; and they fairly covered him."

Swiftly Humberton altered the direction of his questions.

"What was he doing?"

"He was coming forward, sir, real slow, crowding Calloway toward the door. He had his eyes on Calloway, except when he give me that one look. They was awful eyes, with red rims, sir."

The undertaker pondered in silence. Suddenly he shot another question toward the prisoner.

"How big was this devil you saw, Reilly?"

"Bigger than Calloway, sir. That was one of the things that scared me—that and his eyes."

"You mentioned a smell like bad meat. Did you notice that in the room?"

"Yes, sir, it was worse of all in there. If I hadn't been so scared at the other things it might have turned my stomach."

The necrologist rose.

"One question more, Reilly. We are all theorists, more or less. Probably you have your theory of how Calloway met his death. What is it?"

"The devil tore him to pieces!" Squint Reilly answered with conviction.

"Thank you." Humberton glanced around the circle of detectives. "Thank you all, gentlemen, for not interrupting this examination. Such forbearance is remarkable. I think, Clyde, you and I together will go to the Calloway place. Reilly, you'll notice, is entirely won over to the super-naturalists. Well, the supernaturalists may be right; and we may be able to prove them so!"

CHAPTER FOUR
A DESPERATE ORDER

A FINE drizzle necessitated constant use of the windshield wiper as Clyde, with his necrological companion, drove his small car through the night traffic of Superior Avenue. On the slope of lower Superior, beside the Old Viaduct, a mist from the Cuyahoga rose to contribute whatever unpleasant constituents the drizzle lacked. River Road differed from the nearby river itself, chiefly in the fact that it was paved with rough cobble stones, instead of sooty water; also, in the character of the predominant smells. Whereas the Cuyahoga on rainy days always emphasizes its innate quality of stagnant dampness, River Road discriminates. On that part of it where the gray ghost of the Calloway place waited, ominously, a near-by hide warehouse advertised itself with the breeze or without it, though its insistence gave way on certain shifts of the wind to the sulphurous vapor from the River Furnace.

"Any excitement, Brannigan?" Clyde inquired, returning the salute of the policeman on guard as they drew up at the curb.

"Not a bit, sir."

Humberton climbed stiffly out of the machine with the assured bearing of one whose plans are laid, and who is confident of carrying them through.

"We'll take the same route as Reilly," he observed, glancing up at the gloomy mansion.

Clyde, standing beneath the street lamp, nodded understandingly.

"He was arrested under this lamp, Ho. The kitchen window is around at the rear, in that little drive. I've got my flash light."

It was necessary to detail Brannigan to open the window from the inside, after which he retired again to his sidewalk patrol, shutting the doors behind him. Humberton climbed in, agilely, and immediately walked toward the hallway. He was fumbling for the knob before the detective, following with his flash light, enabled him to open the door.

"You certainly don't waste much time," Clyde commented. "Calloway must have been a queer chap, Ho. He had the house wired, but didn't connect the lights anywhere except in his own study. You'd think most of his carryings-on wouldn't stand the light, eh?"

Humberton did not reply, except to request the flash light. He threw its circle of illumination on the polished rail of the broad staircase they were ascending, and once directed it upward to the door which stood ajar at the head of the stairs. Even the cheerful detective hung back somewhat as they approached that lighted study, in which a man, strong and vigorous above his fellows, had been torn to pieces. But to Horatio Humberton the scene of the crime, however grisly, was merely a factor in his investigation. Though a slight degree of excitement showed in his manner, it was the pleasurable excitement of the hound on the trail. He unhesitatingly pushed the door open, and stood looking with keen interest into the spacious study.

The room had been luxurious; silken window curtains, chairs of Spanish leather, a beautifully carved table, a bookcase filled with rich bindings. But the curtains had been torn down and trampled. The leather of one of the chairs was scored, as if with a knife. The table had been hurled so violently against the bookcase as to shatter its glass. In fact, one table leg was actually tilted up, displacing half a dozen books on the bottom shelf. Yet the window on the same side of the room as the bookcase was unbroken.

Everything—literally everything, it seemed—was soaked with blood. There was blood even on the high-molded ceiling.

Humberton looked about him with amazement, craning his long neck to take in all the details.

"It looks like a physical impossibility for any one to have done such a thing," he said at last.

The detective nodded.

"Jones and Swanaka, two of our best plainclothes men, said very much the same—but they don't credit Reilly's story."

"Have Calloway's remains been positively identified?"

"Yes; from the scraps of clothing attached to them, and from a ring with his name engraved on it. Such of the scraps as could be left are lying about the floor, as you see."

Humberton looked about the floor with interest, and at length picked up one of the larger scraps.

"Do men wear leather suits in this age?" he asked softly; then, turning to Clyde: "I should like to take these scraps of leather to my study. I'll return them in the morning."

"I'm authorized to let you take anything you wish, Ho, as long as you agree to return it. I don't mind saying that we're banking a lot on you in this case. We've fallen down several times lately, and if we don't solve this thing the newspapers will ride us pretty hard."

With the scraps carefully piled on the table—they were bits of leather, obviously different from the small pieces of a pair of soft slippers which could be distinguished among them—the necrologist continued his investigation. He turned first to the broad window.

"Heavy iron bars," he ruminated. "Are the windows in any of the other rooms barred?"

"None of them," the detective replied promptly.

Raising the window, Humberton tried to, shake the bars, one after the other. They were rigid. He regarded them thoughtfully.

"They have not been in there long—the cement is new. Had Calloway been expecting a visit from something of violent strength—something, say, that came through the air—he might have installed such bars as these. With the door shut, the window is the one entrance to this room which a visitor of that sort would have forced."

"But nothing came that way," the detective objected.

"Obviously not. Was the window open when the police arrived?"

Clyde nodded, and Ho Humberton smiled.

"I thought so," he observed cryptically.

He bent over the slash in the chair, examining it carefully from various angles. When he straightened his voice had taken on an unusual ring of excitement.

"Whoever made that cut not only removed a good deal of the horse hair stuffing, but took it with him! Now, Clyde," he continued, "I wish to make an experiment on you."

"Anything you say," agreed the detective readily.

"Stand in the middle of the floor. Close your eyes and remain still for a moment."

The stalwart officer obeyed, with an expression of perplexity on his face.

"That's enough," the necrologist declared after a few minutes. "What were your sensations, Clyde? Anything out of the ordinary?"

The detective pondered, then shook his head.

"I can't say they were."

"Very well, Clyde. Thank you. Possibly Squint Reilly and I are more highly strung—or more imaginative—than you. He mentioned his impression that a dead body lay somewhere in the house. I myself have a curious mental reaction—coming possibly from the subconscious mind—but it isn't nearly so definite as that. I merely feel as if there were something in this room that is not at all obvious."

"The devil, maybe," suggested Clyde with a grin.

Humberton acknowledged the thrust without a smile.

"Possibly," he agreed, absent-mindedly.

Stooping as he spoke he slowly crawled around the tilted table, with the flashlight playing on the under surface of the polished top.

"I thought you'd do that, Ho," Clyde observed with another grin. "You'll notice four fresh scratches on the under side, farthest from the bookcase. We found them, but we're counting on you to tell us what they mean."

Humberton stood up, dusting his knees.

"In the morning," he directed, "you will ascertain where the cement for the window—also the bars, if possible— were purchased. You may be able to find the man who performed the work; though I suspect Calloway did that himself. It looks like an amateur job. And there's something else—did you say Calloway had been buried?"

"The coffin is in a vault."

"That simplifies matters. Have it weighed to-morrow."

The detective started violently, and stared with blank incredulity at his companion.

"Have *what* weighed?" he demanded.

"The coffin," Humberton returned calmly. "You needn't open it. Merely weigh it as it stands, and report the weight to me. I suppose the coroner did not, by any chance, request that?"

"He certainly did not!" the detective confirmed emphatically.

"Ah, well! I have the advantage of being a necrologist— which is the next thing to medical training. As I recall, the present coroner is a politician, not a doctor."

Somewhat to the dissatisfaction of Clyde, who felt that a night's work, however interesting, should end before morning, Humberton insisted on a tour of the house, by flashlight, before he was willing to leave. They wandered through one ghostly room after another, all furnished heavily in the fashion of fifty years before, with the addition of the strange birds and small beasts, stuffed and mounted, from far corners of the earth. These, it might have seemed, would have been fair quarry for burglars. Perhaps their uncanny character, with the difficulty of sell-ing them except to museums, explained the immunity from depredation which the old mansion had enjoyed from all save the daring Squint Reilly.

Though the necrologist examined each room with care, he passed on without much interest until, in a little partitioned inclosure of the attic, they came upon a ladder ascending to a trapdoor in the roof. This the necrologist ascended, while his companion, muttering impatiently, followed.

It was a broad, flat roof, with a huge chimney at each end. Ho Humberton strode about it rapidly, pausing a moment to look at each chimney. The roof of the next building, a warehouse of equal height, adjoined at the south end. He stepped across to this roof, also, while Clyde waited in somewhat disgruntled silence.

"This would have been easier in the daytime," the detective suggested, when Humberton rejoined him.

"Have your men been over it in the daytime?" the undertaker demanded.

"Every inch of it."

"What did they find?"

"Nothing of consequence," answered Clyde. "Have you found anything?"

Humberton was walking slowly toward the trapdoor leading back into the house. For a moment he ignored the question. At length he asked irrelevantly:

"What is the name of the policeman on guard here?"

"Brannigan," supplied the detective.

"Ah, yes, Brannigan. Tell Brannigan to keep his revolver ready in his hand. Not his pocket—his hand. If he should need it, the need will be instantaneous. Delay will be almost certainly fatal."

After which unsatisfactory utterance he sank into a thoughtful silence, which Clyde's excited queries failed to penetrate.

CHAPTER FIVE
AN UNEARTHLY MURDERER

"**I SUPPOSE** you'd like me to drop you at the parlors, Ho?" Clyde suggested when he and his companion were back in the machine. He was mindful of the fact that the necrologist resided in a little apartment just above his place of business.

Humberton came to the surface of a sea of thought, and looked speculatively at the detective.

"Do they lock the stenographer's office at the police station?" he inquired.

Though the obliging police officer started, he rose to the occasion and answered in the negative.

"Possibly we can get what we need there. I shall require— let me see—a box of clips; a Hotchkiss fastener; some Dennison labels of assorted sizes"—he paused, still looking at Clyde, but obviously with no personal interest in that mystified individual—"a bottle of glue might be handy, also; and a sponge with which to moisten the labels. Can you think of anything else we shall need?"

The final question rather nettled Detective Clyde. He permitted the flavor of his emotion to creep into his voice as he answered:

"Seeing that I haven't the least idea what you want all those things for, Ho, I can't!"

"We shall need them in piecing together the scraps of leather," Humberton informed him, with a calm stare through the thick glasses.

"To-night?" roared the detective,

Horatio Humberton continued his train of thought.

"It'll be somewhat of a new experience for me; probably for you also. Yet I believe we should finish before sunrise. That will give us a definite starting-point for the day's investigation. I really can't think this problem through without knowing what sort of leather clothing the murderer wore."

Though Clyde's hope of a comfortable bed and at least a few hours of sleep had been brutally shattered, his professional curiosity went far to console him. He stepped on the gas again and whirled up to the station.

"How do you know it was the murderer and not Calloway who wore the leather clothing?" he inquired, with one foot on the running board.

"The pieces of leather are larger than the scraps of clothing, and the blood on them is merely incidental. They aren't soaked in it," explained Humberton briefly. "I shall wait here until you return."

Considering the heterogeneous nature of his errand, Clyde was back in remarkably short time.

"Did fairly well," he announced. "Found everything except the bottle of glue, Ho; and even that's not a total loss, for I ran across a tube of the stuff in the chief's desk."

The necrologist nodded, absently, and neither spoke again until they drew up before the darkened undertaking parlors. The brunette in charge and the one professional assistant never awaited Humberton's presence to carry on the regular functions of the business—such as closing up shop promptly at five. When he was not to be seen they took for granted his absence on some eccentric errand; and they were usually justified in their assumptions.

Humberton lingered uncertainly a moment in the reception room.

"I'm not really sure of the best place to do this," he observed at last. "We need a broad, flat surface. One of the slabs in the morgue might answer, and the light there is fairly good. You wouldn't mind that patient of mine on the next slab, Clyde?"

"I most certainly would!" the detective answered without hesitation. "Nothing doing on the morgue, Ho. Ab-so-lutely nothing doing!"

The necrologist sighed.

"Then I suppose it will have to be the embalming room. Perhaps, on the whole, that may be even better for our purpose. The light is excellent, and I've a broad work table."

"Listen, Ho!" The big police officer let his voice sink to a confidential tone, though there was unlikely to be any one within earshot. "You said that fellow in the morgue was the only stiff you had around, didn't you?"

"That is the fact, I regret to say."

"You're sure there isn't any—any patient you've forgot, lying in the embalming room?"

"Quite sure. Jack wouldn't forget, even though I did."

Clyde was satisfied that Jack Porgy, the level-headed assistant, would be unlikely to forget; but he nevertheless shook his head ominously.

"Well, if we find anything like that lying around when you turn on the light, I'm off this job till morning."

When the embalming room was lighted, however, Clyde's apprehensions were quieted. He still looked around him, uneasily, at certain furnishings of sinister uses; but

Humberton went directly and callously to the large table in the middle of the room and dumped his package of leather scraps upon it.

"How are you going about it, Ho?" asked the detective.

"*We* are going about it," corrected the necrologist calmly. "You'll sit here at the table. As I match pieces together you will connect them. Try the stickers first—they should permit a smoother effect. As you finish pass your completed pieces to me, and I'll endeavor to match them with others."

Clyde sighed and set to work. Connecting the first few scraps was slow business, but the stickers held. Within half an hour the detective, with fingers somewhat more expert than at first, was speeding to keep up with his partner. For Humberton manifested uncanny precision in his phase of the job. Working silently, he had spread the grisly bits of leather over a good portion of the table.

They appeared hopelessly unrelated. But he attacked them with a kind of intuition. More than once Clyde paused a moment to marvel at the certainty with which the necrologist's bony hand darted out, like a robin after a worm, to capture an unlikely scrap at the far side of his pile—unlikely until he matched it with its veritable brother a yard or more away.

"Do you spend part of your spare time piecing together dissected puzzles, Ho?" the detective inquired, facetiously; but he received no reply. Horatio Humberton, concentrating intensely, seemed not to have heard the question.

Humberton was breathing heavily, with an excitement unusual for him. As more and more of the blood-stained scraps came together into their original form something exceedingly strange was taking shape. The leather clothing which the murderer had worn was not like other clothing. It would have been too large for even such a man as Calloway. It was rounded and awkward. It had no sleeve holes. It seemed an ungainly strait-jacket, with leather fastenings instead of buckles.

The detective, his facetious vein entirely gone, shivered as he fastened the last of the larger built-up sections. Though many pieces were missing, enough remained to picture the original as it had been.

"Ho," he said, almost in a whisper, "this wouldn't fit a human being!"

"The murderer was not human," Humberton replied briefly.

"Good Lord!" "Clyde stared. "You don't credit Reilly's devil story, do you?"

"I believe that Reilly told the exact truth as he saw it."

"But—"

The necrologist interrupted him.

"I'm not trying to evade your question, Clyde. You asked whether I thought it was the devil that killed Verdaunt Calloway. I do not!"

"What was it, then?"

Thoughtfully regarding the huge leather patch work they had constructed Humberton ticked off one point after another on his long fingers.

"Let's use what we know, Clyde, and see where that knowledge leads us. Calloway was killed by something of incredible strength and ferocity. We can call that fact number one. And we may go further from that premise and say that nothing human could have produced such results. To strengthen this conclusion we have fact number two, the leather clothing. It is not such clothing as a human being could have worn. Suppose, then, we accept Reilly's story for the remainder of our description, which is that of a huge, non-human creature, with red-rimmed eyes and wings. You'll note that this clothing—or covering—might have been worn by such a winged creature."

"*Is* there any bird of that size?" Clyde demanded desperately.

"I think not."

"Then as near as I can get to it, Ho, you are working out a theory that Calloway was killed by something that doesn't exist."

Humberton shook his head.

"We have not yet reached our conclusion, Clyde. We are merely working toward it. There is nothing more of importance to be done to-night. Perhaps we shall both be the better for a little sleep."

To this the detective readily assented; but as he held open the door of the embalming room for Humberton to go first, the necrologist suddenly changed his mind.

"Go upstairs and put up in my bed, Clyde. I'll crawl in beside you when I'm ready."

When his guest had gone Humberton proceeded to his crowded study and snapped on the light there. He turned to one of the great bookcases and brought several weighty volumes to the desk. Before he closed these wearily, with a puzzled shake of the head, the sun was shining in the outside world.

CHAPTER SIX
AWAITING THE DEVIL

HORATIO HUMBERTON, stalking stiffly into the front door of his establishment later that morning was astonished to find Detective Clyde calmly awaiting him, in the most comfortable chair in the reception room.

"I thought maybe the devil had carried you away," the detective observed. "Sade said not; and she seems to have the right of it. Or maybe you escaped."

"I've been in the public library ever since it opened," the necrologist explained. "And I've got the information you wanted. As far as I can see it don't mean a thing."

Humberton led the way to the study, dragging a small chair along with him from the reception room for his guest's accommodation.

"Now, Clyde!" he invited, when they were seated.

"As to the weight of the coffin," began the detective.

"Ah, yes—the weight of the coffin! I meant to drop in at Smith & Hogan's myself for that, but I completely forgot."

"Well, I didn't forget," Clyde chuckled. "You asked for the weight of the coffin. I got that. It's here in my pocket, if you want it. But I asked Smith, too, for the empty weight, and subtracted it. The difference is one hundred and seventy pounds."

Humberton beamed through his heavy glasses.

"Very well done! *Very* well!" he commended. "Did you think to learn Calloway's approximate weight?"

"Working it out from his height and general size, at least two hundred and fifty—at the *very* least. He was a giant, you know."

"Can you account for the discrepancy?"

"Well, practically all of his blood was out of him," the detective suggested doubtfully.

"About seven and one-half per cent of the body's weight is blood. Call it twenty pounds. That leaves two hundred and thirty pounds. We have sixty pounds left to explain. Can you do that?"

Clyde shook his head.

"I'm afraid not, Ho. It has simply disappeared."

"Along with most of the stuffing from a padded chair that stands in Calloway's study. It seems, Clyde, that the murderer had an unusually large appetite, and one for very unusual viands. I don't recall any of the carnivora that would care to dine on horse hair."

"It's got me," sighed the detective. "The window bars are about as much of a puzzle, too—though I did have some luck in finding the firm that sold them. The third place where I inquired was Collier & Huntington's, and that was the one. They sold the bars and installed them. It looked like an amateur job, because it was done in such a rush.

"A man called at their place in the evening and insisted that the bars be cut and installed that night. He took the workmen to Calloway's house and stood over them while they did it. All that is fairly clear. But what I can't understand is why it was done the day before Calloway returned to town, and why the order was given by a stranger who was *not* Calloway!"

Humberton gazed at him thoughtfully.

"Try this," he suggested. "Assume that the stranger was one of Calloway's employees aboard the yacht. As soon as the boat touched America, this man was sent ahead by train to prepare the barred room, so that it would be ready when Calloway arrived. Does that fit the facts?"

The detective nodded, though with an air of dissatisfaction.

"Why was it done?" he objected. "Calloway wanted those bars in place before he got there. A blind man could see that. Half a dozen people at Collier and Huntington's could swear to it, too, for the man who called there paid a big bonus to have the work finished that night. But why? That's what I can't understand, Ho."

"Iron bars are intended for one of two purposes," said the necrologist sententiously. "Either they shut something out, or they keep something in. We know that nothing entered through the window—unless it did so before the bars were placed, which is unlikely. What remains?—that Calloway brought something with him which the bars were designed to imprison. In that case, the thing, whatever it is, may be still in the house."

"I'd say that's impossible, Ho. When it comes to straight thinking, you've got us all beaten at the post. Our men are willing to admit it. But as searchers, we're not so bad. We've been over Calloway's house from cellar to attic. We've looked under everything and into everything. We've taken measurements, and accounted for every cubic foot in the place. If anything is hiding there, it's invisible, that's all!"

"Something *is* hiding there; and it *is* invisible," declared Humberton.

For a moment Clyde glanced at the gaunt undertaker; then he smiled.

"All right, Ho, I'll bite. What's hiding there?"

"I don't know."

Humberton rose and walked about the study with the sober, rather saddened manner he fell into when thinking profoundly. He stopped at length, and met the detective's gaze frankly.

"I'm sorry, Clyde, I'm not trying to speak in riddles. If I knew the nature of the thing lying in wait in the Calloway mansion, I'd tell you. It is something which our present scientific knowledge does not realize as being in existence.

My reading at the library has demonstrated that. Farther than this, I have been unable to go."

"How do you know it's there at all?" Clyde demanded.

Humberton squinted through his thick spectacles, as if trying to visualize something before his mind's eye.

"The thing which Reilly saw," he returned slowly, "which wore the leather suit we pieced together last night—which was strong enough to kill an exceptionally powerful and heavy man and tear him to pieces—"

He paused, with a quizzical smile, and the detective nodded understandingly.

"I get you, Ho. A thing like that, if it was running around loose—or flying around—would be pretty apt to be noticed. And if it isn't anywhere else, then it must be in the Calloway place."

"That is one indication—a rather strong one. Another has to do with the rug on the floor of Calloway's study. Do you recall the kind of rug, Clyde?"

"Wilton," answered Clyde promptly.

"Genuine Wiltons have a curious property. They will keep impressions almost indefinitely. For example, the leg of the table, which had been buried in the bookcase, had made a semicircular impression on Calloway's rug. At first, I missed the meaning of that; but the fact itself remained in my mind. It's very significant, Clyde, and I recommend it to your consideration, as further proof of the presence in Calloway's house."

The detective scratched his head.

"I don't get it, Ho."

"Later you will. The need just now is for action. Return to the station and get half a dozen of your best men. Four of them should have rifles, as well as revolvers. Proceed to the Calloway place, and have the bars removed from the study window. I'll join you there in about two hours."

Clyde was turning to go, but he paused at the study door as the necrologist added:

"One thing more, Clyde. I expressed my belief that the murderer of Calloway was not the devil."

"You did?"

"I'm not nearly so sure of that. Bring men who are not afraid to meet the devil, if necessary. They may have the pleasure."

Clyde waited, possibly surmising that this remark was intended to be facetious; but Humberton dismissed him without a smile.

CHAPTER SEVEN
THE MONSTER APPEARS

THE DAY, true to form as an exponent of Cleveland weather, had turned from sunshine to a gray, clinging drizzle. Along the river banks the minute drops of water had a penetrating quality all their own. The Cuyahoga flowed with just perceptible movement in the rear of the ancient warehouses, and behind the Calloway mansion, fouling the foundations of them all; and it seemed that the river's ghost, but a degree less material than the river itself, hovered stagnantly above the neighboring streets.

Humberton strained his eyes keenly through the windows of the taxi—which he had engaged at the expense of the police department—but, despite his watchfulness, he pulled up before the Calloway place before perceiving the little company of policemen grouped on its wide stone steps.

"We're here. Ho," sang out Clyde's cheerful voice.

Humberton climbed out of the machine and shrugged his way to them through the rain.

"Let's go inside," he said tersely.

"Say, Ho," Clyde suggested when they were in the broad front hall, "if we're going to hold a council of war, hadn't we better step into the kitchen for it? I don't like the idea of being just downstairs from Calloway's study."

Silently, Humberton led them through the narrow side hallway, between the grotesquely posed birds and small beasts, to the kitchen. When the others had followed him there, he shut the door, and regarded his assistants appraisingly.

The picked police squad were big men, all in uniform, except some who, like Clyde, had been promoted to the plainclothes division. The chief of police—of the tall and rangy type—was one of the party. He had quietly put himself under the necrologist's orders as a private. Manders and Clark, who had started the case, were among the uniformed force.

"The bars?" queried Humberton, looking inquiringly at Clyde.

"Out. It wasn't much of a job. We dug 'em out by the roots."

Humberton singled out two of the plainclothes men who were armed with rifles.

"You men stand guard across the street," he directed. "If anything comes out of this house—anything that isn't human—shoot it. Don't hesitate—shoot! If I'm making the right guess, we may be dealing with a deadlier peril than anything this generation has ever faced."

"Just what *is* the peril, Mr. Humberton?" the chief of police demanded as the men looked at one another with sobered faces.

The tall undertaker answered frankly.

"I don't know. I don't want to put my guess into words, without proof—it is far too wild. Yet it is the only one, of all the theories I have considered, that seems to fit the facts. There may be no danger at all. But, on the other hand, the danger may be extreme. You'll agree with me that we should take no chances."

One of the men, nudged by a half grinning companion, put a question.

"Is it the devil, sir, like Reilly said?"

Him, also, the necrologist answered seriously.

"Call it that if you wish. It may be the only real devil the human race has ever known—the demon which persists as a race memory, and haunts our dreams. You saw how it affected Reilly—and he's a cool man. I'm not trying to frighten you, but I want to be sure that no man goes on with this who is likely to fail in a pinch. Any one of you who wishes may drop out right now."

There was a moment's silence; then Clyde said:

"I think you can count on us, Ho."

"Very well. Two of you men with rifles go upstairs and batter out the upper panels of the study door. We may have a chance to shut the door and shoot through the panels. You, Manders, stay at the bottom of the stairs, to guard against surprises."

The policemen designated sprang alertly to their tasks. Though mystified, they were not cowards. Humberton led the others slowly to the foot of the staircase, which they had scarcely reached when the sounds of battering from above ceased, and the two men with rifles descended.

"Panels both out, sir," one of them reported. "They were old and rotten."

"We must clear the furniture from the study. Two of you can do that. The others will remain on the upper landing."

When they had reached the top of the stairs the chief of police and Clyde themselves assumed the task of removal. Methodically, the various articles were lifted through the doorway; chairs first, then the table, which was carefully disengaged from the lower shelf of the bookcase. With these out of the way, they rolled up the rug, and removed it. As they performed the work, Humberton stepped from side to side of the study, closely scanning every detail of walls and floor, with the aid of an electric torch. He shook his head, and muttered impatiently. The thing he sought was not apparent.

"Shall I move the bookcase?" Clyde inquired.

"Try it," the necrologist suggested with a smile.

It was a four-section case, of standard design, with a drawer in the base and, apparently, not very heavy. The stocky detective grasped it with one powerful hand at each side, and strained.

"The darned thing's nailed to the floor!" he exclaimed.

He said no more. As he gave another vigorous pull, the bookcase swung out in a wide circle, knocking him as flat as if a locomotive had struck him. At the same instant that whole side of the wall between where the case had been and the window opened like a clam shell.

"Out of the room and shut the door," Humberton shouted frantically, choking in the suffocating stench that suddenly filled the room; and, in that moment, he, too, was felled by a tremendous blow, which flattened him against the wall, on top of the prostrate Clyde.

There was an impression of mighty wings. They appeared and were gone. A giant presence swept through the room and out at the place where the window bars had been. Two sharp reports greeted it from the street. Outside a cry of fear and horror went up.

The necrologist recovered himself almost instantly and, rushing to the window, leaned far out of it, staring fixedly into the rain-dimmed sky. At last he staggered back to the hallway. He was so shaken that, even as he leaned against the wall, his legs gave way under him. But his eyes were bright. He was saying softly to himself:

"It was so! It was so!"

"Let's follow it!" one of the policemen shouted vaguely; but the undertaker shook his head.

CHAPTER EIGHT
A "REAL" BAD DREAM

MY CHAIN of reasoning was fairly good, fairly good. Yet its one weak link almost proved the end of us."

They were gathered that evening in the cluttered study—Humberton's favorite spot for expounding his cases; and since there was hardly room enough to place chairs for the chief, for Clyde, and for Patrolmen Clark and Manders, who were present by invitation, Humberton had hospitably arranged a small pile of books for each of the two policemen to sit upon.

The detective seemed inclined to disagree with an important part of his friend's pronouncement.

"I'll grant it was a good chain all right, but I don't get that about the weakness," he declared.

"The chain itself was simple," the necrologist went on. "There was nothing to it. Really, all we needed to reason our way through it was the bizarre nature of the murderer. Given that, we could be sure he wasn't at large. Multitudes would have seen him. You convinced me, Clyde, that he was not in the Calloway house; but you failed to measure the warehouse next door, which Calloway also, owned. That was the weak link in *your* chain." He smiled at the detective, his eyes looking large and benevolent through the thick glasses.

"But for that weak link, Clyde, you would have found the false wall, leaving room for the prison in which the murderer was confined. I surmised it, from my journey over the roof. And the semicircular mark on the Wilton rug in Calloway's study indicated that the bookcase must be the door to this prison. You recall that I mentioned this mark to you?"

The detective nodded without speaking.

"I should reconstruct the tragedy somewhat like this." Humberton ran his fingers through his pale hair, and closed his eyes. "For some reason—we shall never know *what* reason—Calloway opened the prison in which the murderer was confined, and let it out; or perhaps it came out in spite of him. One guess is as good as another. It broke the harness which confined it—or else the harness was already broken—and slowly advanced on him. We have Reilly's story to help us there. You remember? Calloway must have been a brave man, for he kept his head, and commanded that terrible thing to go back into its dungeon. Perhaps he might have succeeded, if Reilly hadn't happened in to distract the creature's attention. Who knows?"

He held up a thin hand as the chief seemed about to interrupt.

"One moment—we'll finish the scene. After the tragedy the murderer stepped back into his prison. Maybe he became afraid. His weight upon the threshold started the automatic mechanism. The bookcase swung into place with a clang which the policemen heard as they entered, and the table, wedged into the lower shelf, left the semicircular impression with its leg upon the rug.

"I suppose Calloway had had the prison prepared long before, with the hope that he might capture such a creature as this. Probably the carrion meat he fed it had been drugged; though, I suppose, on the fatal night, the effect of the drug must have worn away. All this was part of my chain; but the weakness was there."

"I don't see it," the chief of police confessed.

"You don't?" the necrologist chuckled. "I shouldn't have mentioned it. It was simply this—that I looked for a secret spring to operate the bookcase. I didn't foresee that Calloway, being an immensely powerful as well as an ingenious man, had found something better than the spring arrangement. He had arranged that the bookcase should move when pulled squarely by some one of unusual strength. You duplicated Calloway's manner of opening the prison, Clyde—and it opened. And the terrible creature, with the effect of the drugged meat upon which it had been feeding largely worn off, came out. I'm glad we had the bars removed. It was a safeguard—and it seems to have saved our lives. We lost the murderer, but we are here ourselves."

Humberton leaned back in his chair, beneath the single light bulb, his finger tips together, and a half smile on his face.

"Do you suspect what it was?" he asked of the company in general.

All of them shook their heads. Clyde spoke.

"I dropped in at the library on the way over here, Ho, to read up. As far as I can find, there isn't any such creature."

"The books are right; and yet they are wrong." The necrologist looked about him with enjoyment of the mystification in each face. "The thing we saw doesn't exist—to the orthodox scientific mind. No more than the new process of embalming I am working on will exist for them, even though they see it. It's a racial memory, as I said, Clyde, do you ever have bad dreams?"

The detective was too startled to reply at once; but Humberton went on, regardless:

"Dreams are a heritage of the entire human race—a memory heritage. We remember these terrible creatures in our dreams. In the time when they walked the earth, countless aeons ago, they impressed their terrors upon us to such an extent that our subconscious minds have never forgotten. We've kept them in our dreams—and our religions. For what are the demons with which man has tormented his mind but our dim memories of these things that once lived on the earth? That's why I surmised that this thing *was* the devil. Do you begin to understand?"

"We *saw* the thing! What has memory got to do with that, Ho?" Clyde expostulated.

The necrologist smiled.

"You should read more, Clyde—fiction, works on mysticism—they're all helpful. Modern writers have peopled far-off lands with some such creatures. What we proved to-day was that the mythologists and the novelists are correct. Somewhere on the earth—I don't know where, and it may be we never shall know—Calloway found such a creature. He must have found a place where prehistoric conditions still persist.

I should say that it was, probably, the giant flying lizard—the most terrible enemy of the human race that ever existed. You can find its bones in some of the museums. It had a wing spread of not less than twenty feet. Thanks to the genius and daring of that eccentric scientist, Verdaunt Calloway, you and I have looked upon it in the flesh!"

"But how did he get it here?" Clyde demanded.

"You have my suggestion—that he fed it drugged meat. He must have brought it in a specially built cage on his steam yacht. Probably he had the leather suit, or straitjacket, waiting—that covering which the creature broke when the effect of its drug wore off. If we ever find the yacht and its crew, we may learn some of the details. We might even journey to the land from which the creature was brought. Or if it succumbs to wounds and drops into some inhabited country, we may yet have opportunity to examine it at our leisure. That's for the future to decide."

All five were silent; the members of the police, perhaps, trying to reconcile their views of the impossible with what their eyes had seen; the necrologist, as seemed from the intent expression of his face, following through some interesting ramification of his theory. Had the others tried to guess what ramification, however, they might have shot wide of the mark; for when he spoke, the point of his remarks had nothing to do with the science of detection.

"This is how it winds up!" he said with some bitterness, looking at them reproachfully through his strong glasses. "I solve the case; and who gets the patient? Smith and Hogan!

"I want it understood," he continued, turning to the chief, "that the next time I solve a murder mystery I am entitled to attend the murdered man in my professional capacity!"

THE ANGEL OF THE DAMNED

IT HOVERED THERE—BATLIKE, HORRID—GLOWING WITH POISONOUS, TWISTING FIRE. AND BEFORE IT, GROVELING IN ECSTASY, THE THING WHICH ONCE HAD BEEN A MAN. WHAT DID IT MEAN? WHAT AWFUL MESSAGE FLAMED FROM THAT HELL-PIT ANGEL'S EYES—THE ANGEL OF THE DAMNED!

CHAPTER ONE
MOONLIGHT—
AND A DEAD MAN

HORATIO HUMBERTON rose from his chair in the book-cluttered study at the rear of the Humberton Funeral Parlors, and shook an admonishing finger under the prominent nose of Dr. Sigmund Bensen, Curator of the Tate Archaeological Museum.

"You are playing with fire, Bensen," he declared. "This thing, into which you are going so scoffingly, may be real. So far, you have not been hurt. Be thankful, and let it alone."

A moment before, Dr. Bensen's straggly gray beard had been a silky and docile adornment to his intellectual face. At Humberton's words it seemed to bristle. He had been sitting upon a nicely balanced pile of books—the study's usual hospitality to visitors, since there was seldom more than one vacant chair to be found at a time. The pile sprawled into a hcap, as he too stood up.

"Real?" he roared, in deep bass. "Such rot real? I tell you, Humberton, the whole history of Spiritualism has been one long tissue of lies. Frauds and dupes—that's what they are. And as for the 'spirits'—when you lay a man in his coffin, he has just one more engagement this side of oblivion—an engagement with the worms! *Spirits!*" He laughed, sardonically, and rearranged the books. "My sole object in joining Weekoff at his seances has been to expose the whole business. I mean to show him the truth."

As he sat down again, Humberton smiled—a slow smile, which barely lifted the corners of his large mouth. He helped himself to a long, black cigar from the box before him on his work table, and blinked rapidly a few times

"Do you mean this thing came to life—grew up, and throttled them?"

behind his thick glasses as the potent smoke began to curl upward. But he did not speak.

"How many people have you buried?" the curator demanded in a moment.

"A few," his host replied, modestly.

"You've had dead bodies here—a good many of them lying around, at one time or another, eh?"

Humberton nodded. "Two in the morgue now," he volunteered.

"Very good. Then this ought to be a ghostly place, if there ever was one. Ever see a ghost here? Ever see one anywhere else?"

The tall necrologist smiled again, and looked at his watch. "Half an hour before midnight," he announced, cheerfully. "How far is Weekoff's house from here?"

"How far?" Bensen's heavy brows lifted. "Why—twenty minutes walk, perhaps. But I haven't asked you to go there."

"You are going to ask me. Why didn't you remain at Weekoff's this evening?"

"How could I remain? No one was there."

"Yet you had been invited to a seance?"

"I had. He has them every Wednesday evening—my assistant, mind you—my right hand at the museum—a man who preserves the scientific attitude in all other directions—yet he believes this rot. I have been going with the idea of awaiting the favorable moment, then exposing the thing completely—so that he can't fail to see through it. But I feared to act prematurely. I—"

"Precisely. You went into the house and found no one there?"

"I couldn't go in. The door was locked—everything dark."

"Now we are progressing. Really, Bensen, you are insufferably hard to pump. This is a cool night—yet when you came in a few minutes ago you were sweating. You've been glancing behind you at the hall door. If I ever saw terror in a man's eyes it was in yours when I answered your ring. What happened to you at Weekoffs?"

The curator shook his head, with a touch of defiance. "Nothing!" he snapped.

"Tell me about it."

"There's nothing to tell!"

FOR A moment, the eyes of the two men met; Bensen's a trifle bloodshot, Humberton's gently humorous behind his thick lenses. Then the pile of books was scattered again. The curator had rolled sidewise.

Humberton's reaction was calm and almost automatic. He knelt beside the unconscious man, pushed him over upon his back, and unbuttoned the rather tight collar. He was fumbling behind the row of books on a lower shelf for a bottle of ammonia when the front door of the undertaking establishment slammed. Footsteps approached down the long hall. Presently, the bluff voice of Detective Clyde, of Central Police Station, addressed him from the study doorway.

"I'm on late trick tonight, Ho. Remembered I had a key to this place, and that you're always late, too. What's this? Murder—or just one of your regular patients?"

Humberton looked up into the round red face of his official friend who was filling his pipe and staring down with interest at the man on the floor.

"This is Curator Sigmund Bensen of the Tate Archaeological Museum," the necrologist informed him, crisply.

"The hell you say! What happened to him. He's alive all right."

"I rather think he has seen a ghost."

"No!" Clyde built himself a pile of books, with the deftness born of frequent visits to his friend's study, and sat down, puffing at the pipe. "Don't hold the ammonia too close, Ho. Illegal to suffocate him, even if he is crazy. Does he say he saw one?"

"On the contrary, he denies it." Bensen's eyelids were fluttering. Humberton set down the bottle, and regarded him closely. "But his protestations are just a trifle too emphatic. There, Bensen! Don't try to get up yet. Lie on the floor with this book under your head. You'll be perfectly fit in five minutes."

The detective was grinning. "Pick out a soft book, Ho! Any objection to my horning in on this? It's been a quiet day. A little excitement would make me sleep better."

Bensen sat up abruptly. His head moved slowly from side to side. As his dull eyes rested on the detective, they lighted up with immediate recognition.

"Detective Clyde!" he exclaimed feebly.

"Sure! Hardly thought you'd remember me, professor. Didn't know you, at first. I helped out a few years ago, Ho, when they had some junk stolen from the museum. Ho tells me you've been seeing things, sir."

Helped by Humberton on one side and Clyde on the other, the curator rose to his feet, and sank with a sigh into his host's arm chair. He smiled, apologetically.

"I fear I've made rather an exhibition of myself. I have had a severe shock—so severe that I've been tempted to fence with words instead of telling my story. I started out tonight to attend a spiritualistic seance, Mr. Clyde—a thing in which I take no stock, whatever."

"All the spirits they ever have at those places come in bottles," the detective agreed.

"Exactly. My friend, Weekoff, who conducts the seances, has been experimenting with 'elementals', so-called—a supposed lower order of spirit, of evil tendencies, which never has been incarnate in flesh."

The detective's red face was an absolute blank; perceiving which, Humberton inserted an enlightening word. "Imps, Clyde," he prompted.

"Oh—imps! Sure! I've heard of them. Go on, professor."

"Of course, such things are figments of the imagination. Yet the imagination can be decidedly terrifying—as I have had reason to learn tonight. I was delayed in starting for Weekoff's, so it must have been all of eleven when I reached there. The place was dark. Nothing extraordinary in that—they darken it for the seances. But I hadn't expected the front door to be locked."

"So you went around to the back?" Clyde suggested.

"I did. You must understand, gentlemen, that Weekoff lives in a small cottage. From the window of the back door one can see through to the front."

THE DETECTIVE seemed to sense that something important was coming. "Is there a window in the front door?" he demanded.

"There is not. I looked in from the rear, gentlemen—I looked in—"

Humberton was standing at the archaeologist's left. He leaned forward expectantly. "What did you see, Bensen?" he prompted.

"Something—something—looked out at me. Merely—looked out." The curator wiped his high forehead. "It was imagination—of course. Don't ask me to describe it. Certain things are beyond words. I am not easily upset Humberton, but this had such an effect upon me that I could think of nothing but to come here. You'll pardon me? I will go now."

"Just a minute, Bensen," Humberton put in. "Did you realize at the time that it was imagination?"

The curator shook his head. "I was too much overwhelmed."

"Clyde—" the necrologist turned to his friend of the official force—"I have known Dr. Bensen quite well for some years. He is a scientist; also a materialist. I have never credited him with much imagination. Are you too tired to stroll out to Weekoff's house with me?"

"You mean he really saw an imp?" The big detective was trying not to grin.

"Mean that some imps do not come directly from hell. Weekoff's house may be worth looking into."

The curator rose. "I am quite in command of myself again, gentlemen. No doubt conditions weren't right at Weekoff's; they went to some other house to complete the seance. There were three of them—Johnson, another assistant at the museum, and Tyler, who works in a bank. A very small circle, but Weekoff preferred it so. We need hardly go out there at this time of night."

But the detective had caught Humberton's eye. He was pushing the study door open.

"It's a fine night for a walk," he observed. "Nice and cool and crisp. I've been spending the last eight hours tailing a bird who never stirred out of the same speakeasy he went into for lunch. Give me a chance to uncramp my legs."

"I tell you what I saw was imagination! There are no such things as 'imps'—as you call them."

But the necrologist had shrugged himself into a long overcoat, and perched a high-crowned soft hat on his head. He helped Bensen on with his overcoat.

"You feel equal to the walk?" he inquired, solicitously.

"Certainly. The air will do me good. But I tell you—"

Humberton snapped out the light in the study. "Take Dr. Bensen out, Clyde," he requested. "I'll join you after making sure the morgue and the embalming room are locked up for the night."

A FILM of snow lay on the sidewalk outside. The curator walked carefully, meanwhile enlightening Detective Clyde as to his views on the unreality of spirits—a position with which the detective heartily agreed. Clyde was not deterred, however, from seizing the first opportunity— when Bensen was lecturing them learnedly on the reasons behind 'Poltergeist' phenomena—to put a rather paradoxical question to his friend.

"What did you mean about imps not coming from hell, Ho?" he inquired, guardedly. "Where in hell would they come from?"

He received small satisfaction.

"I merely wish to find out what he saw," the necrologist replied.

"Well, any man that imagines he sees something fierce enough to make him faint must have a bad mind," was Clyde's reflection.

Paced by the long strides of Horatio Humberton, the walk to Weekoffs street was brief. The necrologist himself made it mainly in silence; though when Bensen pointed out the little cottage where the seances had been held, he glanced up at the moonlit sky and put an abrupt question: "Was the moon out when you were here before, Bensen?"

The archaeologist hesitated. "I believe so," he concluded.

"Then it must have shone on the rear door of this cottage?"

"No doubt. I was too much perturbed to observe."

"Front and side window blinds down," Clyde remarked, with professional briskness. "Is that usual, professor?"

"Always, when there is a seance. The so-called 'spirits' perform best in the dark."

"They would," the detective growled. Now that they were at the scene of action, he was taking charge. "Might as well go round to that back door where you saw—whatever it was you saw."

"It was nothing—merely imagination."

"Sure! Then we'll see whether my imagination is working good, too."

As they walked down the narrow brick path to the rear of the small house, Humberton brought up the rear, peering, with the painstaking care of a near-sighted man, at the dwelling itself, the picket fence to the left, and even at the trailing vine along the fence. He was thus the last to arrive at the tiny, square back porch. Clyde already was looking through the window in the door.

The detective stared fixedly for several long seconds. His hand slid into the side pocket of his coat. He brought forth a flashlight, and, without taking his gaze from something within, leveled its beam into the interior of the kitchen.

At last he turned to the necrologist.

"Come up here and have a look, Ho," he said, coolly. "Imagination didn't get into this so big, after all. Moonlight did—moonlight and a dead man."

CHAPTER TWO
DIGITS OF DOOM

WHATEVER COULD have been said about his imagination, pro or con, Detective Clyde was proficient in the more material details of his profession; for instance, in breaking down a door. His substantial shoulders struck the rear door of the cottage, and it trembled. Twice more he hurled his weight against the panels, and a sharp snap resulted.

"Both of you keep back!" he growled. "This part is my job. Come in when I tell you."

Flashlight in hand, he stepped into the little house. The door swung idly behind him. Without hesitancy, the tall necrologist, coolly disregarded his instructions, and entered almost at his heels. He was in time to see the first revelation of Clyde's flash, as the circle of light embraced a sprawling body, just beyond the kitchen sink at the left.

The detective glanced over his shoulder at his friend. "Couldn't wait, could you, Ho? Suppose there had been a bozo in here with a gun!"

"In that case, I might have been in time to provide you Christian burial," Humberton retorted, calmly. "Shall I call Bensen in? Bensen, can you identify the dead man?"

"Just a minute—there ought to be electricity in this place." Clyde swept his flash along the wall. "Here's the button. Now, professor."

The curator had remained on the lowest step, in meticulous observance of Clyde's instructions. He responded slowly. When at last he forced himself to look at the body on the floor, his breath came sharply, and he quivered with emotion. But he did not speak.

"Well?" demanded the detective, with a touch of impatience.

"It is Weekoff."

"That's this spiritualist guy—the one that worked for you?"

The archaeologist nodded, silently.

"Well, let's see if we can figure out what killed him. We won't change the position of the body. I'd rather wait till the coroner comes for that. But maybe we can tell something just by giving him the up-and-down."

"If you don't mind, I will not touch him. I have a deep-seated fear of the dead. Even mummies, which I occasionally am called upon to handle in the course of my work, fill me with horror."

"Yeah?" The detective had paused to light his pipe. "To tell the truth, I don't like to chum round with 'em, myself. Humberton here would sooner take a dead one for his little playmate than he would you or me. But I didn't have you in mind, professor, when I talked about examining this fellow. You can just stand back and watch. Ho and I— where the devil is Ho?"

The necrologist was not in the kitchen. Clyde, who had knelt beside the body, stood and looked about him. His eyes rested on the lighted doorway to the next room.

"He's lighting up the other parts of the house. Not a bad idea, at that." He raised his voice. "Everything all right, Ho?"

Humberton appeared in the doorway. His somber, rather heavy face, betrayed more emotion than was usual with him.

"Possibly we had better call the coroner at once, Clyde," he suggested, soberly. "And I think we should request Dr. Bensen to step into this room. The seance appears to have been held in it. Two of the participants are still present."

The big detective started, as if stung. "Do you mean they're dead, too?" he demanded.

"They are."

"Come on, professor." Perhaps a certain ill-timed flippancy had been perceptible in some of Clyde's remarks. That was one of his failings. If so, it was gone. His mouth clamped shut in a grim line. His blue eyes reflected the horror in those of the curator. As he stepped into the room where Humberton stood, he grasped Bensen by the arm and half forced him along.

"I want you to identify these bodies, too—if you can," he said.

IT WAS not a large room. Part of it was taken up by the cabinet—evidently a home-made job, built of wall board— which stood in a corner. The side of this cabinet farthest from them, and facing a small bedroom at the left, stood open. Clyde's rapid glance swept the place. He moved toward the cabinet.

"One minute." Humberton turned to the curator. "Before you look, I should like to ask a question. Is it usual Dr. Bensen, for more than one person to occupy a cabinet at a spiritualist seance?"

Bensen shook his head. "Certainly not," he emphasized. "The medium occupies the cabinet. The theory is—"

"I know." Humberton nodded and led the curator around the corner of the little enclosure. "First—even before you identify them, Dr. Bensen—notice the position of the bodies. Is there anything in your knowledge of spiritism to explain that?"

Clyde pushed the open section of the cabinet a little farther. Light streamed in, from the chandelier in the middle of the room. It revealed the bodies of two men. They sat back to back in two straight-backed chairs—and they were bound tightly to each other and the chairs, with ropes around necks, waists, and ankles.

The curator recoiled, with a cry of horror. "That's Johnson!" he cried. "He was married only a month ago. How can we ever tell his wife about this? She wouldn't have a thing to do with these seances. She warned him against them—I happen to know that because he told me. My God! And the other one—" He leaned far over, visibly fighting his repugnance. "Yes—it's Tyler. He worked in the Commercial Bank."

"You have not answered my question," the necrologist reminded.

"No." Bensen shook his head, weakly. All the violence he had shown an hour before, in his visit to Humberton's study, had vanished. "I know nothing of this. Sometimes they tie the medium—but never, so far as I have heard, to anyone else. But of course, I am not a spiritualist. My knowledge—"

"Possibly my information is more extensive than yours," the necrologist interrupted. "I have studied the subject. Under exceptional circumstances—for instance, where experiments with two mediums have been tried—the two might have been bound together. Were both of these men mediums?"

The curator turned slowly from contemplating the bodies. He met the nearsighted yet intense scrutiny of Horatio Humberton, and shook his head again. "They never had the slightest claim to mediumistic power—if there is any such power. I have heard Weekoff talk of that. They felt rather keenly about it."

"Was Weekoff himself a successful medium?"

"I am told so." Horror still trembled in the curator's deep voice. "You understand that I don't believe in the thing, at all. But they say Weekoff was unusually effective in raising 'elementals.'"

"Imps," supplemented Clyde, half to himself.

"Precisely. And in physical phenomena, too. Perhaps you noticed some broken dishes on the kitchen floor. They might have been broken in some such way."

"They had been swept to the floor from the end of the sink nearest the body," Humberton commented. "I see a telephone in the front room. Suppose you call the coroner now, Clyde."

The tall necrologist busied himself in a rapid survey of the contents of the room. Bensen dropped into a chair—one from which the bodies were hidden by the cabinet—and buried his face in his hands. Presently, the detective's heavy voice became audible from the next room, as he telephoned.

EXCEPT FOR the cabinet and half a dozen chairs, the room in which the seance had been held was nearly bare of furniture. Evidently Weekoff—a bachelor, living alone—had taken his meals in the kitchen, for there was no dining table. A tambourine lay on the floor, just at the entrance to the cabinet. In one corner, a stand supported a cheap vase, empty of flowers. Three of the chairs were in the middle of the room—one of them overturned. Three others had been ranged in a line against the wall. Bensen sat on the chair nearest the front room, in this line, and as he rocked backward and forward, with hidden face, an occasional dry sob shook his broad shoulders. Humberton glanced at him once, but said nothing.

In his methodical examination the necrologist paused at length at the stand and the vase. "Haven't the 'elementals' a habit of breaking things of this sort?" he inquired.

The curator looked up. "Weekoff mentioned that vase to me only today," he returned. "We had an argument—rather a warm one, I fear. I was trying to dissuade him from this seance—as I always have tried to do. One of the minor points I brought up was the damage done his furnishings by this senseless phenomena—or charlatanism, or whatever it is. Less than a month ago, quite an expensive vase of his—an antique—was smashed to bits. He told me this afternoon that he had replaced it with a cheap vase, so that the 'elementals' could indulge their destructive propensities at less expense to him."

Humberton nodded thoughtfully. He was unobtrusively studying the depressed face of the museum's learned chief.

"Suppose we assume that these 'elementals' really exist," he said, slowly. "We can do that for the sake of the discussion. You have never had any experience with them, yourself?"

"Positively not!" The reply came with something of the curator's former vehemence.

"But no doubt Weekoff has told you a good deal. Would you say he regarded them as dangerous?"

"At times. According to his belief they were mischievous, to say the least. Some of them I think, are classed as distinctly evil spirits."

"Would they do a thing like this if they could?"

"They are the devils of old-time legends. No doubt they would."

Clyde reappeared at the doorway to the front room. "Got a nice break, Ho. That's the beauty of having a real, honest-to-Jake doctor for coroner instead of a politician. Dr. Sollerby had just blown in from a case. Hadn't taken his shoes off yet. I told him about things out here, and he said he'd be with us in ten minutes. No waiting till morning for him! Now, you take the coroner we used to have— that lazy loafer—"

The detective stopped abruptly. Humberton's long, thin hand had slipped into the vase, and when it came into sight again, with the swiftness of a juggling trick, something small and red and very curious appeared between the necrologist's forefinger and thumb. This in itself might not have halted Clyde's characterization of the former coroner. But the behavior of the little curator was curious, too. He rose slowly to his feet. His breath came in gasps.

"The Angel of the Damned!" he whispered.

"What's that?" Clyde took a step into the room. "Look's like a funny angel to me—the kind I'd not care to meet in a dark alley! Maybe that's a real clue! Let's see it, Ho."

But Humberton had placed the little figure gingerly on the stand.

"I think we shall do better not to handle it, Clyde," he suggested. "My own fingerprints will appear at the very top and nowhere else."

"That's right. Sure! And I'm supposed to be a detective! We'll stuff some paper into the vase and take it that way for our finger print department to play with. But that angel stuff—did you say 'angel,' Dr. Bensen?"

THE CURATOR sank back into his chair. Perspiration appeared on his forehead. He seemed unable to turn his eyes away from the queer little image—the figure of a flying creature, about three inches high, with spread wings and outstretched arms, made entirely of cut, red stones, bound together by minute settings of gold.

"You haven't heard of it?" he asked.

Humberton, too, had been staring at the image. He was kneeling by the stand, to examine it from all sides. At Bensen's question he nodded. "I have read about it a number of times," he returned. "Very valuable and very old. As I recall, it is owned by the wealthy collector, Wallis Reddington."

"It was," the curator corrected. "For some time it has been the property of the museum."

"A gift?"

Bensen nodded. His self-control—apparently shaken by the discovery of the tiny image—was beginning to return.

"A gift in anticipation of death, I think. Mr. Reddington is a very sick man, and has been for some time. A year ago, I was called to his bedside, and he gave me that jeweled statue—called 'The Angel of the Damned'—together with the necessary papers conveying its ownership to the museum. I have kept it in one of our strongest cases until I could persuade the Museum Board to put through an appropriation."

"For a special case?" the necrologist prompted.

"Also a special watchman." The curator sighed. "There are drawbacks even to gifts. That little object is enormously valuable. You could group together half the exhibits in the museum, picked at random, and it would outvalue them all. Unless Mr. Reddington takes account of the fact, and leaves us a sufficient annuity in his will, his gift is likely to burden us. It must be guarded. It—"

Abruptly, his voice trailed off.

"Good Lord, what am I doing?" His hand swept over his forehead like that of a man waking from sleep. "I'm taking it for granted, Humberton—taking its presence for granted. How in the name of sanity did it get here? Is it at the bottom of all this? Did someone try to steal it? It could easily be resolved into its component stones. They could be sold for an enormous sum. But why didn't he steal it? Why is it here?"

Humberton was still on his knees at the stand. He had picked up Clyde's flashlight, and by the help of a pocket microscope of his own was examining the curiously built-up image with painstaking care—remarkable care, considering the fact that his long hands never once touched it.

"Possibly, when we can answer your question, we shall know who killed these men," he returned soberly. "I feel the need of more data—facts concerning this Angel of the Damned, as you call it. Tell me about it, while we are waiting for the coroner. Why is it called that?"

"Have you looked at its face?" the curator fenced.

Humberton nodded. "Devilish!" was his appraisal. "The hands, too, are like claws. I notice that while the remainder of the image is built up of separate stones, these parts are exquisitely carved. The Lord would never own this sort of angel."

A faint smile relieved the pallor of Bensen's countenance. Isn't there a Lord of Hell?" he suggested. "Both name and image come down to us from medieval times. The thing was used for purposes of witchcraft. No doubt of that, at all. It is supposed to have the power of calling up familiar spirits."

"Then it might have its place in a seance?"

The curator started. "Yes!"

"Could Weekoff have borrowed it for that purpose?"

"He had the keys."

Humberton rose slowly to his feet, dusted off the knees of his trousers, and, with hands in pockets, gazed down reflectively at the little image.

"Are the gold mountings, which connect the stones, of medieval workmanship?" he inquired, presently.

"The whole thing is medieval."

"Meaning that it is how old?"

"Perhaps seven hundred years."

"I seem to recall, Bensen, that you are an expert, yourself, in this sort of work—the mounting of precious stones and the like."

The curator smiled again. As long as he kept his eyes averted from the cabinet, and from one still, sinister foot which it did not quite hide, he appeared master of his nerves.

"As a lad in Sweden I served apprenticeship to the jeweler's trade," he said, with a touch of pride. "It is still a hobby with me. I have mounted many precious and semi-precious stones in the museum, where the old mountings were falling to pieces."

"Take this little image." Humberton nodded toward the figure on the table. "I see you can speak as an expert. Would you say that the mounting is as old as the cut stones?"

"Not quite. Of course, I examined the Angel pretty carefully when it came to me. I estimate the mounting to date back not more than two centuries. One can tell by the style."

THE FRONT door opened and closed. Clyde, who had been listening in silence to the conversation, turned expectantly.

"Hello, doctor! Glad you didn't wait to knock—I unbolted the door for you. Step right this way."

Dr. Sollerby, the coroner, was fat. That would have been anyone's first impression of him. With the unobservant, it might have been the only impression—a huge, flabby mountain of a man, slow in movement, ponderous of voice, wheezing like a locomotive. The unobservant might have missed his remarkably steady gray eyes; also the straight, alert line of his mouth. The eyes now appraised the room while he took in the company with a comprehensive nod.

"Glad to see you, Humberton. Suppose you take the bodies to your morgue when we get through here. Three of them, you say, Clyde? Nice of you to wait for me. I shan't be long." He was on his knees at once behind the cabinet, working silently.

Clyde nudged his friend and whispered: "That's one of the things I like about him, Ho. The other bozo used to talk all the while he was giving a stiff the once-over. When he got through what he really thought was nobody's business till after the inquest. Sollerby shuts up till he's done. Then he spills it."

Soon, the big coroner rose, and trudged heavily into the kitchen. In a few minutes, he was back.

"Got any ideas, Humberton?" he inquired, cheerfully. "I notice you generally hit the cause of death pretty close. It seems fairly obvious in these cases."

"A blow on the head for the man in the kitchen; strangulation for the other two," the necrologist suggested.

Dr. Sollerby nodded. "That's about it, I guess. You carry a microscope sometimes. Got one with you now? I want a better look at the marks on the necks of these two in here."

With the little instrument—and Clyde's flashlight, which the detective proffered—he knelt again beside the bodies.

"Come over here, Humberton. Take a glance at these marks. Anything funny about them?"

The necrologist did as requested. In a moment he looked up. His eyes met the keen gray ones of the coroner, fixed on him questioningly. Sollerby smiled.

"Damned funny, don't you think so? If it was a pair of hands that strangled those fellows, then the hands had six fingers, besides the thumb—steel fingers, judging by the abrasions. Not only that, but as far as I can tell without measuring, the finger marks are spaced exactly the same on both necks. That's not natural."

Humberton did not reply at once. Instead, he rose, and walked over to the stand on which The Angel of the Damned still stood. He knelt beside the little figure, and examined it again through the microscope.

"Look at these hands, Sollerby," he said. "And you, too, Clyde."

Sollerby took the glass, and knelt by the figure. Before he could speak, however, the curator seemed to come out of a lethargy.

"Seven fingers to each hand," he volunteered. "That is characteristic of certain medieval images used in the black arts. It dates back to ancient Egypt."

The fat coroner straightened, suddenly. "You haven't any kind of measuring device handy, Humberton?"

Horatio Humberton shook his head, with a smile. "Your eyes are good, doctor," he returned. "I thought no one but myself would see that point. It is odd, isn't it? The marks on these dead throats seem to be spaced exactly the same as the claws of the little image!"

Detective Clyde started. "Do you mean this rummy thing came to life, then grew up and throttled them?" he demanded.

The necrologist shrugged his shoulders. "I wonder!" he said.

CHAPTER THREE
CULT OF THE DEMON

THE GROUP which gathered the following evening in Horatio Humberton's study, beneath the swinging electric bulb, was rather odd in its make-up. It included the coroner and Humberton, also the necrologist's hearse-driver and general right-hand man, Ted Spang, whose sleekly smoothed, glossy black hair and sharp, alert features contrasted strongly with the obese Dr. Sollerby, who sat beside him. The other member of the party was small, dark, and unmistakably Jewish. His curly brown beard constituted the only adornment of that character among the four of them. The outstanding fact concerning the group, however, was that though its members had come together to discuss an atrocious crime, no police officer appeared. The absence of Detective Clyde fairly cried for explanation.

Sollerby seemed to feel this. When Humberton had shut the door into the corridor and had carefully bolted it, the coroner put his thought into words.

"Clyde coming?" he asked.

The tall necrologist smiled. His fingers toyed with the tiny Angel of the Damned, which stood before him on his work table.

"I requested Clyde not to come," was his reply; then, before any exception could be taken to his remark: "Sollerby, to what extent are you bound to keep within the letter of the law?"

The fat coroner looked perplexed. "Why—to the same extent as you or any other good citizen."

"To the same extent as Clyde?"

"Hardly." Sollerby's keen eyes flashed the ghost of a smile. "I'm not a policeman. I might stretch a point, now and then, in the interest of justice."

"I wish you to stretch it tonight. Before the evening is over, we may plot a violation of the law. Clyde, being a city detective, would be bound to report that impending event. How about you? You still have time to leave."

Coroner Sollerby was a man of deliberation. He slowly fished a cigarette from his pocket, passed the package to Ted Spang, and lit up while thinking the thing over. At last he came to a conclusion.

"Go ahead," he said. "I'm not the coroner, tonight—I'm just a doctor. If you kill a man and ask me to sit on the remains, I'll turn back into the coroner."

The necrologist nodded his satisfaction. He leaned back in his swivel chair, with the jeweled figure in his hand.

"Pretty little thing!" He held it up to the light. "See the red gleam in the heart of those stones! Red for blood! By the way, Sollerby, I am not sure that you and Mr. Isaacs have met. Have you ever pawned your watch?"

The stout coroner shook his head.

"Then you have not met. Mr. Isaacs is the squarest private banker of my acquaintance. He is also an expert in precious stones—an expert unhonored and unsung in the seats of the mighty—whose judgment I rate a trifle higher than that of any jeweler in the city. He knows the history of stones—their psychology. Am I correct in saying that this figure, Mr. Isaacs, has no psychology?"

"None," the little Jew replied, quietly and very decisively.

"Neither has it any fingerprints of value. Clyde reported to me, when he was kind enough to lend me The Angel of the Damned, that headquarters could make nothing of it. Too many prints have been imposed, one upon the other. We must use the figure in a different way."

The coroner nodded, absently. "While I think of it—" he interrupted—"I mustn't forget to tell you this. I dropped into the morgue this afternoon and went over the bodies carefully—while you were out. Odd feature about the two in the cabinet. I checked it in a number of ways—there's really very little doubt. Both of them had received terrific blows on the head before they were strangled. Understand—they were still alive when the strangling took place. But I don't think they were conscious."

"What killed them?" Humberton inquired.

"Both causes, probably. Either by itself might have been enough. The combination made a sure job of it."

"Were they tied together before death?"

"Oh, yes."

THE NECROLOGIST rose lazily and stood in apparent contemplation before the well-filled book shelves at his right. His eyes traveled upward and came to rest at a row of corpulent volumes on the topmost shelf. He pulled the swivel chair over, mounted it with painstaking care, removed the pair of books at the left of this top shelf, and from the space behind them produced a ponderous tome, which he dusted with his sleeve as he resumed his place at the table.

"Here, gentlemen—" he gazed at his auditors with the peering benevolence of a pastor about to address his flock "—you see one of the gems of my library. It is a first printed edition, written in medieval Latin, of Julius Servetus' *magnum opus* on the Cacodaemons, or Evil Spirits. Some of the most curious treatises on the care of the dead are couched in that tongue, so I have made myself familiar with it. You've never taken it up, Sollerby, by any chance—as a hobby, perhaps?"

The fat coroner shook his head.

"You might do worse. Just now, for instance, you'd be interested in a certain chapter of this book—the one dealing with the fallen angel, Beltonus, known as The Angel of the Damned!"

The three others reacted variously to this startling item. Sollerby's eyes opened rather widely, and he sat very straight in his chair. The little Jew turned his gaze sharply to the tiny, bejeweled figure, now set upon Humberton's table, as if that might explain the reference from Servetus. Ted Spang blew a smoke ring. Emotion seldom found a toehold in Ted's mind.

"The worship of Beltonus was one of the many obscure cults of the middle ages," the necrologist went on, didactically. "Not much is known about it. For instance, not even Servetus can explain the symbolism of the bound worshippers, trussed together two by two and back to back, which characterized the secret rites. The demon had seven fingers counting the thumb as one. He took possession of his sacrifices (can't you guess this, Sollerby?) by throttling the victims. Servetus hints at the exact manner of this death, but the language there is obscure—something about fingers of steel—I can't quite make it out. The point seems to be that Beltonus himself, materialized by certain infernal rites, appeared and claimed his own. Sometimes, he merely came. On other occasions, he killed. His worshippers seem to have taken their chances on that. He was always dangerous."

"Where did they meet?" the coroner inquired.

"Deep in the darkest and most lonely recesses of the woods. And of course at night."

"Well—" the coroner grinned, "—it's a darn good thing I'm not superstitious. I don't recall whether you saw me do it, Humberton, but I fished a blotter out of my pocket last night before we left that house, and used it to take an impression of the claws of your ugly little image. No—I didn't gum up the fingerprints; I held it with my handkerchief. This afternoon was harder. If you ever tried to take an exact impression, to scale, of fingerprints on the neck of a corpse, you know. But I got them. Not only that, but I used what I got as the basis for some interesting figuring. Mathematics always was my dish."

HE WAS slipping a fat finger into each pocket of his vest, in turn, then into his coat pocket. At length, he stood up ponderously and tried the pockets of his trousers. Sitting down, he grinned again.

"Left the figures at home! I'm always doing some fool stunt like that. But I can tell you what they showed. In the first place, suppose I choked both Mr. Spang here and Mr. Isaacs to death—"

Ted Spang merely turned his head, with languid interest, toward the speaker. The little Jew started, perceptibly.

"—I should undoubtedly leave some marks on their necks. Would the marks coincide? That's the point. Would the distance from the mark made by the forefinger to that made by the middle finger on one neck be exactly the same as on the other? And so on? I ask you!"

Horatio Humberton silently shook his head.

"Certainly not! One never picks up two things in succession with quite the same spacing of all the fingers. Try it some time. A precision instrument, with a micrometer gauge, such as I used this afternoon, would show a difference somewhere."

In the heat of his remarks, the stout coroner had let his cigarette burn down too far. The glow reached his finger. He dropped the butt, ground it beneath his heel on the floor, lit another cigarette, and when it was puffing to his satisfaction, resumed.

"Point Number One! Allowing as well as I could for the difference in size of the two necks of these murdered men, the distance between finger prints seems to have been exactly the same. In other words, they seem to have been strangled by a pair of seven-fingered hands which had no lateral movement between the fingers, as human hands have. Can you explain that, Humberton?"

"Not yet."

"I did some pretty delicate work with the prints on my blotter. Used a pantograph, and extended them out until they reached the same scale as the neck prints. When I did that, they corresponded exactly. That is Point Number Two!"

"Which brings us to Clyde's suggestion that the image came to life and grew up."

"Darned if it don't!" the coroner agreed, cheerfully.

"Perhaps—" Humberton glanced at the black-letter book on his table "—we might profitably give a little thought to the supernatural angle. I am no more superstitious than you. The fact remains, however, that these men had met with the deliberate intention of trying to communicate with certain intelligences not yet recognized by science. They were particularly interested in 'elementals.' Now, 'elementals'—granting their existence for the moment—are evil and mischievous spirits of sub-human intelligence. They are not spirits of the dead. They have never been clothed in flesh, at all. If there is a vestige of truth in the thousands of stories of demons and hobgoblins that have descended to us from an earlier day, it seems likely that these things were 'elementals.' To come down to cases, Beltonus would have been one."

Sollerby's eyes twinkled. "Go on," he said. "This is getting good!"

"What does the presence of the Angel of the Damned indicate? We don't have to go over to the supernatural to theorize about that, do we?"

"This fellow Weekoff stole it from the museum, to see whether he could put on a Beltonus meeting," the coroner suggested.

"I think so. Perhaps 'borrowed' would be as accurate as 'stole.' He seems to have been trying to duplicate the conditions of those dark orgies of the middle ages. He may have known the very incantations they used. According to Bensen, Weekoff was quite a learned man in these matters. He and his friends sought to raise Beltonus, let us say. Or they were experimenting, to learn whether such a thing— if it ever had been done, at all—were still possible. And Beltonus came!"

"That's not your solution of this case, is it?" the coroner demanded.

"Perhaps not." Humberton smiled. "I am not a materialist. I believe in ghosts—to a certain extent. It might be the solution—but for one very disquieting fact. That fact changes the whole complexion of our inquiry. It is the reason why I brought Mr. Isaacs here. It explains the question I asked you at the outset, too, Sollerby—whether you object to violations of the law. When we have settled this point, with all that it implies, I fear we shall no longer be respectable citizens. Isaacs, let me hand you the image."

THE LITTLE Hebrew rose and received the proffered figure. He stood thoughtfully a moment gazing at it in his hand, then sat down again. A quizzical smile played about the corners of his mouth.

"Isaacs, is that image a good example of medieval workmanship?"

"Very good workmanship." The private banker nodded emphatically to reinforce his appraisal. "The man who executed it is a master. Very good, indeed. I should say—but not medieval."

"Go on," Humberton requested. "I want both Dr. Sollerby and Ted to know as much about it as we do. We are all in this together."

"Someone with the original figure for constant reference has made a copy," the Jew went on. "An excellent copy! Binding the stones together with the gold bands was simple, but this face! These hands! The work is marvelously done. Marvelously—but for all his skill, the artist who did it missed the precise medieval twist in the gold. You see, gentlemen—"his mild brown eyes lighted with the enthusiasm of the expert "—every age has its own peculiarities. The zeitgeist—the time spirit! No other age can quite duplicate it. Always there is a difference somewhere. I see that difference here. I can't explain it to you. Yet it is present."

"And the stones?" the necrologist prompted.

"Good, commercial imitations. I saw the originals a number of times in Reddington's collection. I know how good these imitations are. These stones are not rubies, at all."

"I don't get this!" the coroner exclaimed. "How closely did you have to examine that figure to know it was a fake, Mr. Isaacs?"

"Not very closely. Does a poultryman have to sniff more than once at a bad egg? I am a poultryman. This is my egg-"

"All right—isn't Dr. Bensen a poultry-man, too?" Sollerby pursued, accepting the metaphor.

"Oh, yes, indeed!" Isaacs smiled, ingeniously. "I am quite a vain man, Dr. Sollerby. I hold that only one person in this city is more expert in precious stones and jewelry than I. Dr. Benson is that person."

The coroner's keen eyes swung swiftly to Humberton's face. What he saw there enlightened him. He grinned.

"Gets better, doesn't it?" he commented, dryly. "Excuse me if I seem a trifle dumb. I've got it now. You're trying to tell me that Bensen knew all along this figure was a fake, but for some reason he wasn't saying anything. What was that reason?"

Horatio Humberton's long hand slipped into the pocket of his coat and brought out a huge bunch of keys.

"The keys of the Tate Museum," he explained. "They were on Weekoff. Clyde was kind enough to lend them to me without asking questions. Mr. Isaacs here, also Ted Spang and I, intend to break into the museum tonight. These keys will be a great help. I am not asking you to go with us, but I do request that you keep our little expedition secret. There is a chance—just a chance—that my theory might be wrong."

"Your theory? You think—"

The tall necrologist nodded, solemnly. "In my mind, it has almost gone beyond surmise. Everything points to one conclusion. Dr. Bensen is the murderer!"

"But why should he do a thing like that?" Sollerby flung the words almost defiantly.

"Because those he killed knew too much."

"What did they know?"

"I am going to the museum to find out," Humberton answered.

CHAPTER FOUR
THE MUSEUM MURDER

WHAT THE Humberton Funeral Parlors gained from their proprietor's repute for learning they perhaps lost in other ways. For one thing, he might, with decided worldly advantage to himself, have devoted more time to building up business for the parlors. Business was bad. It never had been very good. In consequence, the limousine, skillfully driven by Ted Spang, in which the necrologist himself, with Sollerby and Mr. Isaacs, sped toward the Tate Museum, undoubtedly ranked with the shabbier funeral equipages of the city.

It being night, the party could not observe the car's moth-eaten upholstery. But every roughness in the pavement emphasized that the springs were not what they once had been; and some annoying mechanical trouble, lightly characterized by Ted Spang as "a bit of piston slap," made conversation difficult.

These minor discomforts troubled Humberton not at all. He devoted the trip to the museum, which lay well toward the outskirts, to an exposition of his reasons for suspecting Dr. Bensen. His voice was strong and clear. Dr. Sollerby, who had insisted on being one of the party, was not anemic, either. So most of the dialogue was theirs. Mr. Isaacs' speaking tones tended toward the quiet and refined. He listened.

"If he did it," Sollerby objected, in stentorian accents, "why did he come to you? Why did he court investigation?"

"What better way of disarming suspicion?" the necrologist retorted. "There was every chance that one of his three victims might have mentioned to someone else that Bensen was going to be there. He couldn't hope for an alibi."

"But I understand he actually fainted in your place."

Humberton laughed. "Oh, I mentioned that, did I? After all, what else could you expect of a high-strung man, after he had committed a triple murder? Bensen is a man of the highest intellectuality, you know. I could make out a very good case for a genuine faint on his part. By the way, his was not genuine!"

"The devil you say!"

"Of course, he knew me to be merely a necrologist—not a physician. But even with me, he should not have come out of it so completely all at once. Then, too, when he had called with the fixed determination to get me out there— that was very obvious—he should not have pretended to change his mind, as if the matter were of no consequence. His acting there was very poor. In fact, he alternately over-acted and under-acted. And you heard about the face he said he saw in the window?"

"Clyde told me."

"That was to account for his excited mental state. But people don't see faces at windows and then faint half an hour afterward—even in imitation faints."

"No." The coroner shook his head ponderously, and a street light they were passing revealed the movement. "You're entirely right there. Men of his type either faint at the time or not at all." He reflected a moment. "Why the bound bodies?"

"Another point against him. Almost as damning as the fact that he did not at once brand the fake image for what it was. How many people in this city, do you think, know of the Beltonus rite? Very, very few. Weekoff did. Perhaps he engineered the ceremony. But Bensen did know of it. And another thing—did you invite him to examine the bodies?"

"I hardly think so," the coroner replied, slowly.

"Clyde did. He refused, on the grounds that the examination of dead bodies—even of mummies—completely unnerved him. That was a defect of memory. He forgot that I was with him on one occasion when he unwrapped a mummy—showing no more emotion in the process than if it had been a side of beef. Don't you see?" Humberton wrapped his knuckles, for emphasis, against the back of the front seat. "Touch him where you will, he rings false—false!"

"All right, sir!" Ted Spang's strident rather high-pitched voice hailed his master from the driver's seat. "Another block and we'll be there. Going to drive up to the front door and ring the bell?"

EVIDENTLY TED surmised Humberton's answer, for he was drawing to the curb. The necrologist released the door catch and stepped out.

"Quite right, Ted," he returned. "We will walk the rest of the way. Perhaps I had better explain our tactics before we go closer."

"What I want to know is, why are we going at all?" Sollerby cut in. "As far as I'm concerned, this is a blind lead. I'm in on it because it looks like an adventure. But why am I in? Why are any of us in? Do you realize that as soon as we set foot in that museum we shall all be burglars in the eye of the law?"

"Not quite so bad as that, Sollerby. Not quite! I know the night watchman. I telephoned him this afternoon. It took some persuading, but he is willing to stretch a point in my favor and let us in. A reputation for honesty has some value."

"Front door?" the coroner inquired, quizzically; but Humberton, in the act of igniting a cigar, shook his head.

"Perhaps 'let us in' is not entirely accurate," he explained. "As a matter of fact, there is a small basement door at the rear, used chiefly by the fireman. That door will happen to be unlocked. If it came to a burglary charge—which it won't—the watchman would clear us."

The museum loomed ahead, two stories of stone, white in the darkness. The investigating party stopped talking. Only their footsteps sounded faintly on the cement pavement. Sollerby, the heaviest man among them, trod most lightly, while the diminutive private banker walked with a shuffle noisier than the tread of any two of the others. Even Isaacs, however, became comparatively quiet when they had rounded the corner of the museum and were following Humberton down an inclined runway to the basement level.

The necrologist seemed to know his way. He led them around a second corner, where the sub-grade path became level again, and so halfway across the rear of the building to a small door. The handle yielded readily. Humberton laid his half-smoked cigar carefully on the sill of a little window to the right of the door, and stepped inside.

"Furnace room," he whispered, out of the darkness. "One of Bensen's peculiarities is that he does not favor lights after closing hours. He says they are an aid to burglars— just the opposite of the usual view. His watchman carries an electric lantern, but keeps it off most of the time."

"Then we're likely to run into the watchman before we know it," Sollerby objected, also in a whisper.

"Hardly. Ted is remarkably good at seeing in the dark."

"What are we here for, anyway?" the coroner persisted.

"No time to tell you now. Come!"

He gave the others no opportunity for further whispering. Their attention was concentrated on following his lead, as he swiftly skirted the warm furnace and took a diagonal across the cement floor. In a few moments, his feet found the first step of a narrow stairway. He stopped.

"Ted!" he whispered, cautiously.

"Here, sir!"

"Keep beside me. I want the benefit of your eyes. You still wish to come, Sollerby?"

"I'm in this thing to a finish," the coroner declared.

WITHOUT FURTHER comment, Humberton climbed the stairs, accompanied by the useful Spang. Sollerby and the pawnbroker followed closely. A door at the top admitted to an even darker place than the basement. Humberton released the flash of an electric lantern. It revealed a large room, cluttered with boxes and packing cases.

"The receiving room—where they unpack the exhibits. Don't fall over the boxes."

He used the light again, for the benefit of the others. They threaded a zigzag path among the boxes to a door on the farther side. Humberton snapped off the lantern once more and pushed this door open.

"The great hall. It runs from front to rear, the length of the building. Careful, now. We are almost there."

They crossed the hall and stood in an enormous room—one of the exhibit rooms. Dim windows at the left let in enough light from the drab night sky to show in vague outline the rows of cases in which the exhibits reposed. Humberton placed his lips close to the coroner's ear to whisper again.

"Bensen is an expert in mental work. He could pull off the most intricate jobs without a jeweler's help."

"What of it? What's that got to do with this business?"

"Don't you see?"

"I'll be hanged if I do!"

Petulance raised the fat coroner's voice somewhat above a whisper. Humberton placed a cautioning hand on his arm.

"Never mind. These keys I have are numbered to correspond with the cases. Isaacs!"

"I am ready," the little Jew responded, coolly.

"Take the flashlight. When you find a case you wish to examine, let me know its number."

"The little circle of light, guided by Isaacs' hand, darted into the nearest case. A moment's pause, a shuffle of feet, and it was in the next one. Humberton followed closely. Sollerby, grumbling under his breath, turned suddenly upon the imperturbable Ted Spang.

"Do you know why we are doing this, Spang?" he demanded, in a penetrating whisper.

"No more than the man in the moon, sir."

"Humberton!"

The necrologist looked around; but at that moment Isaacs spoke. "Seventy-two," he said. "The number is on a metal disk on the side of the case."

"No time now, Sollerby." Humberton fumbled among the keys. "Watch Isaacs. Here is the key to seventy-two."

The side of the case swung open under the private banker's left hand. He reached in, withdrew a bit of delicate jewelry, and scrutinized it in the light of the electric lantern.

Apparently, a few minutes were enough. He laughed, quietly and rather grimly. "Imitation medieval, very skilfully done. Would you like to examine it, Mr. Humberton?"

"No. Put it back. Now do you see, Sollerby?"

The coroner's reply came in an exasperated growl. "Confound it, man, you don't have to speak in riddles! I see there's something wrong, if that's what you mean. How did you know he would find imitation jewelry in this museum?"

"I did not. I merely suspected. If an imitation angel, why not other imitations—things lower than the angels? Yes, Isaacs?"

The little Jew held a second small object in his hand. "Another!" he declared.

"Very well. Put it back. I think we will go to the upper floor. The most valuable exhibits are there."

"Is there only one night watchman?" Sollerby inquired; at which the necrologist laughed, softly.

"Good, conservative citizens serve on these museum boards," he returned. "They believe in economy. Perhaps they are right. Museum pieces are easy to identify and hard to sell."

THE CORONER followed quietly for a few minutes, as, under Humberton's direction but with Ted Spang's keen-eyed guidance, they skirted the somber cases toward a back stairway. Presently he put another question: "Did Bensen make the substitutions?"

"I think so."

"Could he sell the originals without causing suspicion?"

"Hardly. Not in any such quantities as seem to be involved here."

"Then why—"

The necrologist laughed again—rather too loudly for safety. "You're a doctor, Sollerby. Put two and two together. What kind of man plans profoundly, then makes the most ridiculous and elementary mistakes? What kind—"

"Begging pardon, sir," interrupted Ted Spang, in low-pitched but penetrating tones. "You're broadcasting kind of loud."

"Very true, Ted. I must be more careful. Ah, here we are at the top of the stairs. I see a light!"

They stood at the rear door of a large exhibition room—the Egyptian section. It was dark. Through its farther entrance, beyond the mummy cases and the stiff rows of votive offerings, flowed a narrow stream of yellow light from an unseen source.

"It comes from the left," the necrologist diagnosed. "No doubt from Bensen's private office. Ted, suppose you go on as quietly as possible, and see whether anyone is there."

"Right, sir."

The agile hearse-driver went very quietly, indeed; so much so that in a moment, though they could see his alert figure against the background of the lighted doorway, they could not hear his footsteps, at all. He paused, and peered cautiously around the door jamb. What he saw must have reassured him, for he vanished. Almost at once, he was back at the door. He beckoned.

The keen-visioned coroner started. "That fellow has seen something! Don't you catch his expression? Come on!"

He took the lead. Ted remained motionless at the door until they had joined him.

"What is it, Ted?" the necrologist demanded.

"Step this way and see for yourself, sir," the hearse-driver answered, coolly. "You won't wake no one!"

Humberton knew his assistant too well to waste words. The source of the light was plainly visible. It came from a little room just around the corner at the end of the upper hall. Through the half-opened door of that room, a roll-top desk, with its top pushed up, and the green glass shade of a lighted desk lamp upon it were to be seen. Sollerby was first in the room, with the tall necrologist just behind him. They saw the body of a man sprawled on his back between the desk and the wall.

Humberton ran forward. "Lyons!" he exclaimed. "The watchman!"

"The man who let us in?" Sollerby inquired. He was already kneeling beside the body.

The necrologist nodded, silently.

"Well! Not a bad idea to have the coroner along on this job, at that! Don't we need the police, too?"

Humberton nodded to the hearse-driver. "There's a telephone here on the desk, Ted. Call up Clyde, and be ready to let him in at the front door. Tell him it's another murder!"

"It's all of that," the coroner agreed. "Men don't shoot themselves through the forehead after tying their hands behind their backs. Feet tied together, too!" He looked up gravely at the necrologist from his position on hands and knees beside the body. "Do you know, Humberton, this thing is getting interesting?"

Horatio Humberton also dropped to his knees, carefully avoiding a sinister pool of blood on the rug. His long fingers deftly untied the cord about Lyons' ankles.

"Clyde won't mind my doing this," he exclaimed. "I rather think we need to work fast. How long has he been dead, Sollerby—an hour?"

"Not any longer. I'll have to see whether I can tell about these cords, offhand. The others were tied before death. I wonder if these were."

Humberton glanced at him with a smile—the smile of the specialist with whom the horror of tragedy counts for nothing as compared with the niceties of his calling.

"I can answer that question," he declared. "This man was shot before his feet were tied. The cord evidently fell into that pool of blood." He held up the dangling evidence. "There is blood inside the knot as well as outside!"

But the coroner's interest had become diverted from the cord. He leaned over the pathetic figure on the floor until his eyes were within a foot of the upturned neck. His breath came rapidly.

"Humberton!" he whispered. He looked up, to find the necrologist's eyes, through their thick glasses, focused on the marks he was examining. "I can't measure these marks right now. But they were made after death. I'm certain of that. And, I'd be willing to hold up my right hand and swear they are identical with the fingerprints on the other bodies. That damned angel has been getting into this, too!"

CHAPTER FIVE
THROUGH THE PASSAGE

DETECTIVE CLYDE stood in the doorway of the curator's little office, his face flushed somewhat more than usual from the exertion of stair climbing, and his eyes narrowed into an expression of considerable severity. Behind him, Ted Spang calmly lighted a cigarette.

"I get it!" the big detective declared, bitterly. "I get it sweet and pretty, Ho, just from looking in here. You've been law breaking again. Burglary this time. And you want me to square it because it's a short cut to justice. Well—I can square most of your stuff. Maybe I can even square burglary. But if this is murder, too, I can't square that!"

Humberton had seated himself in the open roll-top desk, the height of which from the floor suited his long legs nicely. He indicated the curator's chair to Clyde. Sollerby stood beside the body, still studying it gravely.

"Sit down, Clyde. I wonder whether you saw anyone else, out in the hall?"

"There was a bozo sitting on the top stair. I don't get—"

"You wouldn't. He is Mr. Solomon Isaacs, profoundly learned in precious stones and in all the intricacies of the jeweler's art, but not in the least bloodthirsty. He is sitting out there from choice. Mr. Isaacs, Clyde, has been very interesting, tonight. He has demonstrated that a number of the finest pieces in the Tate Museum are not so fine as the public imagine. Bluntly, they are fakes. The genuine pieces have been removed, and others substituted."

"The devil—"

Humberton cut short his friend's vigorous rejoinder. "I don't wish to seem hasty. But really, we have no time to lose. What I must know is—are you willing to come with me at once and take the responsibility of breaking into a private residence?"

"Without a search warrant?"

"We shall not be searching. We are going to arrest a murderer."

Clyde stood up, briskly. The prospect of immediate action had cleared his face as if by magic.

"I'm taking that kind of responsibility right along. Where do we go from here?"

"Just a minute." Humberton spoke rapidly, with a curiously grim intensity. "I can't let you come without a full understanding of the danger. You don't believe in the supernatural?"

The detective shook his head, with a half-grin.

"The little figure of the angel—The Angel of the Damned—was thought by its worshippers in the middle ages to have terrific powers. It could kill. It killed by throttling. And the marks it left on the necks of its victims were in exact scale to its own tiny fingers."

Sollerby interrupted—though not with words. He leaned over the body on the floor and silent exposed the throat to Clyde's gaze.

"Hell!" was the detective's earnest comment.

"The man we are going after is expert in this particular mystery. He knows how the angel kills. And he is bright enough to anticipate our visit and arrange a reception for us." The necrologist slid to his feet. "That's all. I wanted you to appreciate our problem. Shall we start?"

"Right now!" The detective rubbed his hands together like a ballplayer waiting for the throw. "Just you and me, Ho?"

"I'm in on it," the stout coroner put in.

Humberton nodded. "You may as well come, Sollerby. Any of us may need the services of a coroner before the night is over. As for you, Ted—"

"Here, sir!" the hearse-driver interjected, quietly.

"You will take Mr. Isaacs home. Unless I am mistaken, that is what he desires more than anything else. Then come back and park in front of Dr. Bensen's house."

Spang nodded understanding. "Got you, sir. His house is right beside the museum, ain't it? I'll be back so quick you'll think I knocked the little chap on the head and dumped him somewheres."

"I'm not so good at seeing in the dark, Clyde. Suppose you take the lead. Head for the back door. I think we are justified in forcing it."

"Not unless you're pretty sure he's the man, Ho."

"I am sure."

THEY WERE descending the broad front stairs of the museum. Ted Spang and the little private banker had gone ahead. Their footsteps were audible on the tiles of the lower floor. Quite in his element now that physical danger threatened, the big detective put a cheerful question: "How do you think he'll try to get us, Ho? With a gun?"

"Very likely."

"Be waiting behind the door, maybe. Or shooting through it. That's the kind of thing that makes this job interesting!"

The night had changed. As they let themselves out of the front entrance to the museum, a fine drizzle met their faces, driven by enough wind to give it penetration. Clyde descended the broad stone steps so rapidly that he slipped and came near finishing the descent head first. The tall necrologist took it more slowly. On his way down, he stopped several times to peer upward into the thick night.

"Expect something out of the sky?" Sollerby asked, walking beside him.

"In a way, yes. I was thinking of the moon. If it were out now, that might make a difference."

The coroner, about to put a puzzled question, suddenly started and nodded his understanding.

"I think I get you. Certainly I do! You mean a difference in what we may find—the supposed influence of the moon on insanity?"

"Exactly."

Clyde was waiting rather impatiently, at the foot of the steps. "Got a gun, Ho?" he inquired.

"No," was the necrologist's curt response.

"I never carry one," Sollerby volunteered.

"Then mine is the only rod in the party. You fellows lean pretty hard on your guardian angels, don't you? Better keep close to me."

A fence of old-fashioned iron pickets separated the two-story brick house next the museum from the property of the institution itself. Clyde asked no questions concerning the house. He led the way in silence through the street gate in the fence, and so around to the rear. The fact that the eccentric and learned curator had lived alone in this pretentious dwelling since the death of his wife, ten years before, was fairly well known. He took his meals out, and kept no servants. The public knew that, too. Newspapers had carried stories upon it. How successful he had been as his own maid-of-all-work was harder to determine. Inquisitive reporters had never penetrated farther than the small square reception hall.

The raiding party stopped when they had reached the rear. Clyde looked about him with professional acumen.

"Two doors," he ruminated aloud. "Steps leading up from the yard. Door at the top of the steps opening into the kitchen. Furnace-room door under the steps. In my house we always lock the upstairs cellar door at night. If Bensen does that, we'd have two locks to force. So what do you say to the kitchen, Ho?"

"Much the best," the necrologist agreed.

"You boys stay back in the yard. Or wait—doctor, are you handy with a gun?"

"I haven't shot a revolver for twenty years," the coroner replied.

"That's that! And I don't think Ho knows which end to point. I was going to ask you to cover me while I broke the lock, but we'll forget it. Stay here. If I don't come back, use your own judgment."

He climbed the flight of wooden steps, leading to the door. Entirely disregarding his instructions, Humberton followed. The coroner hesitated a moment, then, with a suppressed laugh, brought up the rear.

Thus it was that both of them were just behind him when Detective Clyde, as a preliminary to more forceful methods—and no doubt to learn where the bolt was placed—cautiously turned the knob.

The door was not locked.

SLOWLY, THE detective pushed it open. Protecting as much of his body as possible by the door jamb, he peered into the darkness. Then, with a sudden swift movement, he snapped on his flashlight, swept the luminous circle once around the kitchen, and turned it off again.

He turned to whisper to his companions, waiting until his face was close to theirs, and pitching his heavy voice so low that their ears were strained to catch the words.

"No one in there—no one that I can see. Ho, I'm asking you. I'm asking it as a favor. *Will* you stay out here while I go in?"

"No," the necrologist answered, curtly.

"Oh, all right." The big detective's voice was moody. "I didn't think you would. You wait here, Dr. Sollerby. We've got to have somebody to take charge of our bodies."

"Nothing doing," was the coroner's rejoinder.

"Come on, then, you darned fools!"

He stepped into the kitchen. They followed. Clyde had seen enough with the fleeting help of his flashlight, to know the directions. Though the darkness was nearly complete, he led the way confidently.

It was a broad, old-fashioned kitchen. They were about in the middle of it, dimly perceiving each other's figures in the blackness, when abruptly they found themselves looking into one another's faces. The lights had come on.

Clyde's mouth opened as if for speech. But he said nothing. His eyes were fixed on the outer door, which they had left ajar. He leapt for it—a little late. It swung shut sharply. He wrenched at the knob. He hesitated a moment, then retreated a few steps with the obvious intention of charging the door and forcing it.

"I wouldn't do that, Clyde," Humberton suggested, quietly. "Put in your time on this door to the left—the one that leads into the house."

"That's right." Clyde pivoted, crossed to the inner door, and glanced at it. "This ought to be easy. Wait till I see if it's locked."

His hand was almost on the knob—not quite on it—when the door opened. It was a thick, oaken door. Humberton looked up at its top, which his height enabled him to see better than the others, and nodded comprehension.

"Simple, but effective," he observed. "There is a lever at the top, which fits flush when the door is closed. Controlled by an electric button from the interior of the house. It strikes me, Clyde, that we are expected."

Clyde's reply was to produce a heavy revolver from his pocket.

"Come on!" he said.

The door had opened, not on another room, but on an extremely narrow dark hall. The light from the kitchen penetrated only a few yards. Beyond that point the passage evidently changed direction.

With something resembling a growl, the big detective plunged in. Humberton caught his arm.

"Easy, Clyde!" he cautioned. "You don't know where this leads. It's a trap."

"I don't care if it leads to hell, I'm going in," the detective retorted. "If you're afraid, stay in the kitchen."

Humberton released his arm, and followed. Just behind him, he could sense the coroner. They rounded the first twist in the passage. Then he could hear the stout medical officer's grunts and muffled imprecations, for the corridor had grown still narrower.

The necrologist whispered over his shoulder in the blackness. "Go back, Sollerby. You may get stuck."

"Go back, nothing!" The coroner was quietly laughing, with grim enjoyment of the situation. "You didn't see what I saw. You were around the corner by that time. Before I rounded it, the door behind us swung shut—I heard the lock click. We're in this, old boy, for better or worse, till death do us part. I only hope I shan't get stuck before the fireworks begin!"

THE PASSAGE twisted again, and began to slope gradually upward.

Suddenly, the detective chuckled. "Why don't I use my flash? Can you beat that for dumbness? Get it out of my right-hand coat pocket, will you, Ho? If I try, I'm liable to scrape my elbow against this damned wall."

Humberton, the only thin member of the party, still had plenty of room. He patted the detective's pockets—first the right, then the left.

"You laid it on a chair, when the lights came on and you charged the door," he said, mildly. "Did you pick it up again?"

"Would I pick it up?" the detective demanded, bitterly. "Did you ever know me to have brains? How about your flashlight, Ho? You generally carry one."

"No doubt Issacs handed it to Ted," the necrologist returned. "He forgot to pass it back to me."

"Cheerio!" Clyde quickened his pace, slightly. "We can sit around and laugh at this, boys—after we're killed and talking it over in heaven. Come on! Ouch! Damn!"

Humberton found himself jammed abruptly against his friend's broad back. The next moment, Sollerby had run into him.

"All right—back up. I just skinned my knee against the wall. Either this darned place twists again, or else—" The detective was silent a moment, while the others backed away and left him more room. "Yep, that's the answer. Blind alley! We're at the end. We can't go any way but back—and we can't go back."

"One minute." The necrologist's voice was low-pitched and calm. "Suppose you stand perfectly still, Clyde. Try not to breathe so hard, Sollerby. I should like to sound the walls."

He took the right-hand wall first. His long fingers traveled slowly upward, tapping every few inches.

"Find a thin place, and I'll bust through it so quick—"

"Be quiet!"

Humberton's hand crept rapidly up the left wall. Suddenly, it plunged, about shoulder-high, into space.

"What is it, Ho?" the detective whispered, excitedly.

"A side passage, up in the wall."

"Wide enough to walk through?"

"I can't tell. To crawl through, perhaps. It doesn't seem to be very high."

"Let me at it! Remember, I'm leading this party. Give me a boost."

The necrologist complied. Clyde was big, but athletic. He required little help. With the fat coroner, it was different.

"I'll go second," he suggested.

Humberton, tall and exceedingly thin, possessed a reserve fund of wiry strength. He assisted Sollerby's climb to the passage. The stout coroner stuck a moment, but a vigorous shove started him forward. Humberton himself, as soon as the others had progressed far enough to leave him room, easily wriggled in behind them.

The new passage sloped gradually upward. In the narrow hall they had just left, they had been unable to see one another. The darkness had been absolute. Here too, it pressed upon them, a palpable presence. Soon, however, there was a change in the air—a fragrant, freshening change.

Clyde's hoarse whisper floated back: "Darned if I don't smell pine woods! What's doing it?" Before either of his companions could reply, he spoke again. "Here's the end, Ho. No blind alley this time. Just a jumping-off place. That you behind me Sollerby? Let me grab your wrists. It's wider here—I can turn around. Ho, you hang on to Sollerby. I'm going to let myself down."

HUMBERTON'S LONG fingers closed on the coroner's ankles. In a moment, he heard a shuffle ahead in the thick darkness, and felt Sollerby's muscles tighten. The big detective was descending. His voice came to them in a cheery whisper: "O.K.! I've touched bottom. Must be a room of some kind. You fellows wait there."

But the coroner was obstinate. As Humberton released his ankles, his feet were drawn swiftly away. There was another shuffle, then a crash.

"All right!" he said, cheerfully. "No damage done. I landed hard, that was all!"

"You darned fool—"

Clyde's reproaches stopped, abruptly. The darkness about them was not quite the same. Some subtle change was taking place. An instant before, it had been impenetrable. Now, as Humberton lightly dropped to the floor beside the others, he could see them faintly. The odor of the pine woods was strong, but it was a hot and heavy fragrance, like the woods on a summer night, when there is no breeze and the clouds hang low.

"Ho!" The detective's deep voice quivered slightly. "What's that? What the devil is it?"

Humberton strained his near-sighted eyes. He was conscious of a faint rosy glow in the darkness. A suppressed exclamation from Sollerby told that he saw something more than that.

"It seems a little lighter, Clyde," the necrologist observed, calmly.

"A little lighter—hell!" The detective had drawn his revolver. "Can't you see it?"

The glow deepened. Behind them and just above was a grind of cogs, with a scraping sound. Humberton glanced up, over his shoulder. The light had become strong enough for him to see, gaping blackly in a wall of delicate iridescence, the opening of the passage through which they had come. As his gaze reached it, the diameter slowly narrowed. Unseen mechanism was forcing some sort of sliding panel across the passage from left to right. As the panel completed its journey, the entire wall reflected the shimmering radiance. There no longer was an opening.

CHAPTER SIX
THE ANGEL
OF THE DAMNED

HUMBERTON HAD watched the movement of the entrapping panel with a kind of fascination. A muffled exclamation from Clyde recalled him. He calmly turned about again. Then calmness forsook him for an instant.

"The angel!" His voice sounded strangely in his own ears. "The Angel of the Damned!"

A gigantic figure confronted them. It was the source of the ruddy light. It *was* the light. From its flaming eyes to the tips of its batlike, outstretched wings, so broad that they extended from wall to wall, it glowed with flickering, twisting fire. A heap of snakes from the Pit, burning unquenchably, molding their poisonous lengths together to form the figure of an angel, might have shone with some such glow. The eyes of a fallen spirit, damned forever, yet once built on a greater pattern than man, could have blazed thus hopelessly.

The necrologist took a step forward—an unwilling, involuntary step, drawn by the evil wonder of the angel's eyes. For that moment, his companions were forgotten. He thought himself alone with the figure. The majestic head of the angel inclined toward him, and he took another step. The focus of the light had changed—had come nearer. It dazzled him. He lowered his gaze instinctively—and saw the contorted face of Dr. Sigmund Bensen, with glaring eyeballs and protruding tongue, beneath the angel's feet. At that moment, too, he realized that the room was a death trap. The gigantic figure, with its spread wings, seemed to leave them no room to pass around it. Toppling forward, it would crush them to the floor like ants beneath a heedless foot.

The spell was broken. Humberton leapt lightly backward. The red light picked out with unnatural clearness every detail of the room—a room glowing with jewels, set into niches in the walls and even in the ceiling, and decking the shining angel. It showed him his two companions, backed against the wall. The coroner's shoulders were squared and his face rigid, with the expression of a man waiting for death. Clyde stood, one foot advanced, revolver in hand.

"Clyde! Sollerby! We must stop it! Bensen is committing suicide. The image is crushing the life out of him!"

"It's alive!" Clyde's voice was almost unrecognizable.

"No more alive than any other statue, man! It is falling forward. Help me push it back before it crushes us, too!"

The descending angel, now at half of a right angle, seemed to hesitate. Bensen's face was not to be seen. The necrologist flung himself against the glowing body. It was hard, smooth like glass, but only slightly warm. A second later, Clyde and the coroner joined him.

THE FIGURE had only appeared to stop, for that instant. In reality, it had been slowly, inexorably, moving downward.

"Hold it, Ho! For God's sake, hold it!" The detective's voice was normal again—the voice of a man struggling to the limit of his strength.

Sollerby's breath came in sobs.

There was another instant when they seemed to be holding. Then the heels of all three slipped backward along the polished floor.

Humberton suddenly flung himself clear. His eyes, desperate yet cool, took in the whole of the room still remaining visible: the glowing back wall, a small portion of the walls at the side, the majestic menacing head of the Angel, now almost directly above, between the outstretched wings. Suddenly, he perceived a vital, incredible fact.

"Throw yourselves on your faces!"

Clyde, catching at the note of hope in his voice, also leapt backward and asked, eagerly: "Where, Ho?"

"Here in the middle, with our faces to the wall. I think we have a chance."

"Let me try to crash the wall, first."

"By all means, try."

Three times, in rapid succession, the big detective hurled himself. He was gathering his forces for a fourth attempt, when the descending Angel grazed his head. With something like a sob, he reeled to the floor beside the others.

"All right, Ho," he gasped. "I guess we're done."

Humberton did not reply. He was on his back, where he could look up at the descending death. His eyes scanned it in every detail as it came closer. The others had flung themselves on their faces.

The burning orbs of the Angel were very near—so near that his myopic vision could detect the electric lighting behind them. They came nearer. They were a blur. There was a jar, a moan from the coroner, and they stopped.

"Got you pinned, Sollerby?" the necrologist asked, cheerfully. "I still have plenty of room. Try to bear it till I can wriggle under and find the controlling switch."

"Ain't we going to be killed, Ho?" Clyde demanded, incredulously.

"Not this time, Clyde." Humberton's laugh, a little high-pitched for him, was otherwise not noticeably nervous. "I fear Bensen overlooked a point. The wings of his angel project forward a trifle—just far enough, in fact, to make all the difference for us! I, at least, have room enough to crawl around it!"

IT WAS in the room back of the ruddy angel—a wide, barnlike apartment, in part a workshop, in part the studio of an artist or a sculptor—a shop or studio cluttered beyond reason. Horatio Humberton had propped himself upon a convenient sawhorse. His long legs reached the floor with ease. Part of a marble statue, which lay upon its side in a corner, served Detective Clyde for a seat. There was a sofa. Upon it the coroner sprawled, his face white and strained, the breath not yet coming easily in his stout body. He seemed more interested in a long bronze instrument he held in his right hand than in this physical discomfort. The instrument was a kind of tongs, with six powerful metallic fingers and a thumb.

Sollerby suddenly flung the bronze tongs from him. They bounded on the floor and came to rest not far from something covered by a sheet, which lay in the middle of the room.

"The confounded things frighten me!" the coroner said, explosively. "How many people have they killed? Three, to my present knowledge."

Humberton nodded. "To your *personal* knowledge," he corrected. "To read the full total you should have a view extending over perhaps seven centuries. This is a real antique, Sollerby. None of the stage properties which affected our nerves a while ago have any danger in themselves. These have."

He stooped and picked up the tongs.

"You don't mean they are dangerous without him?" the detective put in. He glanced toward the sheeted object on the floor.

The necrologist shook his head.

"No." He agreed. "Without him they are quite harmless, at least, unless someone else turns up to use them. Down through the centuries they have been the instruments of poor, distorted minds like his. Perhaps no other such mind will ever direct them. We can hope so, Clyde. After all, they are out of place in the twentieth century, when men no longer worship Beltonus in the forest."

The detective lit his pipe. "What I want to know—" he began; then stopped and puffed twice, with an air of bewildered determination. "Well, I'll be darned if I can tell you what I do want to know, Ho. But I'm all mixed up on this thing. I see why you suspected Bensen, all right You explained that before we came here. And I can savvy why you hit on this house for his hideout. When a fellow has lived alone for years, in a big joint like the one we're sitting in, and nobody is ever allowed inside, that's naturally the first place to look for any funny business. But why all the hoop-lah stuff? Why the dark passage, and the phony doors, and this damned angel that had me scared out of a month's growth? And why the murders? Was the man crazy?"

"Do you doubt it?" the coroner demanded, languidly.

The big detective scratched his head, meditatively. "Well, maybe not," he admitted. "No, I guess he was bughouse, all right. Think he was always that way, doc?"

The coroner emitted a long yawn, which ended in a groan. "My ribs won't feel natural for a month," he complained. "I'm a doctor, not a clairvoyant, Clyde. I don't know whether Bensen was always crazy. Perhaps he suffered a head injury at birth."

CLYDE SHOT a suspicious glance at the reclining Sollerby; but the latter went on, languidly: "Natal brain lesions are curious things. They've been known to change the characters of men who have lived blameless lives for years. Perhaps that was Bensen's trouble, I don't know." He yawned again, long and profoundly. "He started by being interested in the Beltonus cult, I suppose. Studied it intensively. At last it got him. Eh, Humberton?"

"These devil-worship cults have a trick of getting people," the necrologist agreed. "I've known of such cases—at least, I have read of them. If there is a devil, I admire him immensely. He always knows enough to attack a man's strength rather than his weakness."

Clyde shook his head. "I don't get that, Ho."

"Bensen's strength was his versatility. He could do a number of things supremely well." The necrologist held up a long hand, and ticked his points off on his fingers. "First, he was an authority on archaeology. He knew these medieval cults inside and out. He even knew that the Beltonus priests throttled their sacrifices with these tongs—which was something I had never realized, though Servetus hints at it. He was a master goldsmith and jeweler. He was a sculptor—I never even guessed that, but it is very apparent, now. And he must have been a good deal of an electrical expert. He made that marvelous figure of the giant angel, with its lighting effects. That was his masterpiece, I think—the masterpiece of his strength. And that was where the devil started with him."

Sollerby grunted acquiescence, from his place on the couch. "When a man builds an idol, the next step is to worship it," he suggested.

"Precisely. Look up the incident of the Golden Calf, Clyde. I think we can say that he made the angel, and lighted it. Then, as his mind became twisted, all the rest followed: the pine incense, to produce the atmosphere of the woods in which Beltonus was worshipped, the lever motion for tilting the figure downward to kill—that was an idea from a Babylonish temple, I fancy—and finally the theft of valuable articles from the museum. He used these as offerings to his idol, and made imitations to take their places. The last was the imitation angel, itself."

"That's one thing I wanted to ask you," Clyde put in, excitedly. "Where do you suppose the real angel is?"

"Oh, yes!" The necrologist smiled, rather mischievously. "I am near-sighted, yet not entirely lacking in observation." He slid his hand into a trousers pocket. "While you and Sollerby were trying to resuscitate poor Bensen, I found the angel. It stood squarely in front of the giant image—a final offering! Take charge of it, Clyde. To your eyes, no doubt, it looks exactly like the spurious angel, but Isaacs could tell the difference, I assure you!"

The detective accepted the tiny, glistening figure, looked at it with interest for a moment, and callously dropped it into a coat pocket.

"O.K.," he said. "We'll hold it with the other one, for evidence. Probably the poor devils he killed borrowed or stole the fake image to try out some Beltonus stuff with at the house. That's how it happened to be there. My guess is they were on to some of Bensen's stealing, too, and were dumb enough to tell him. That cooked their goose. Think so, Ho?"

Humberton nodded. "No doubt he offered to initiate them into the Beltonus mysteries. When two of them were tied, the rest was easy. He made the marks on their necks with this tongs—for my benefit, I imagine—returned the tongs to these house, and came to my study with his story. It was partly cunning and partly transparent."

"I follow you there, all right. Think he tumbled to the fact that the watchman had left the door open for us?"

"I fear he suspected something, and forced the watchman to confess. He very evidently was waiting for us."

"That's what comes of dealing with a bughouse guy," the detective declared, emphatically. "Those batty bozos know too much. Take the way this guy killed himself. Would anyone with his brains ticking right have figured out how to get his neck beneath that darned Angel's feet, so it would choke him to death when it started forward? Not only that, but he counted on getting us, too—and, believe me, he'd have done it, but, for those wings sticking out a little in front. Why did he ever overlook that, Ho?"

"Because he was insane," the necrologist replied.

Clyde shook his head, doubtfully. "That's too much for me." He glanced toward the recumbent coroner, who now slept peacefully, with even rise and fall of breath. "Let's go. I've sent for a man to guard this place, till your fellows can stop around with the dead wagon. Shall I wake Sollerby? He's likely to be so stiff we'll have to carry him."

"Clyde—" Horatio Humberton smiled—a whimsical, reminiscent smile. "Were you ever a Desert Hoot Owl?"

In the act of stooping to tickle the coroner's nose, the big detective stopped, and straightened up. The look in his face was compounded chiefly of incredulity.

"A *what?*" he demanded.

"Ah, youth! Youth!" The necrologist spoke with a note of gentle sadness. "It was all of twenty-five years ago. I was a Hoot Owl, Clyde. In fact, I rose to be Thrice Opprobrious Screecher of the Order. I had charge of the initiations. Time passes, one's memory grows dim, but it came back to me—even to the opening in the wall, that led to the final passage. Some of the mechanical and electrical arrangements are new—the room where Bensen and his angel, for instance, was where our neophytes crossed the Burning Sands—but—"

"This house—" the detective shouted.

Humberton nodded. "The Order went into bankruptcy; its club house had to be sold. Bensen bought it. I have often wondered what he did with the secret passages. No doubt in his wife's time they were kept blocked off. She was a sane, sensible woman. Well—Sollerby is sleeping very soundly. I fear ordinary measures would not awaken him. Suppose we try this."

The tongs were still in his hand. He extended them, and, with infinite care, used their fingerlike claws to grasp the coroner's uplifted throat. Instantly, he withdrew them again; which was as well, for Sollerby, with a hoarse cry, reached the floor in a bound.

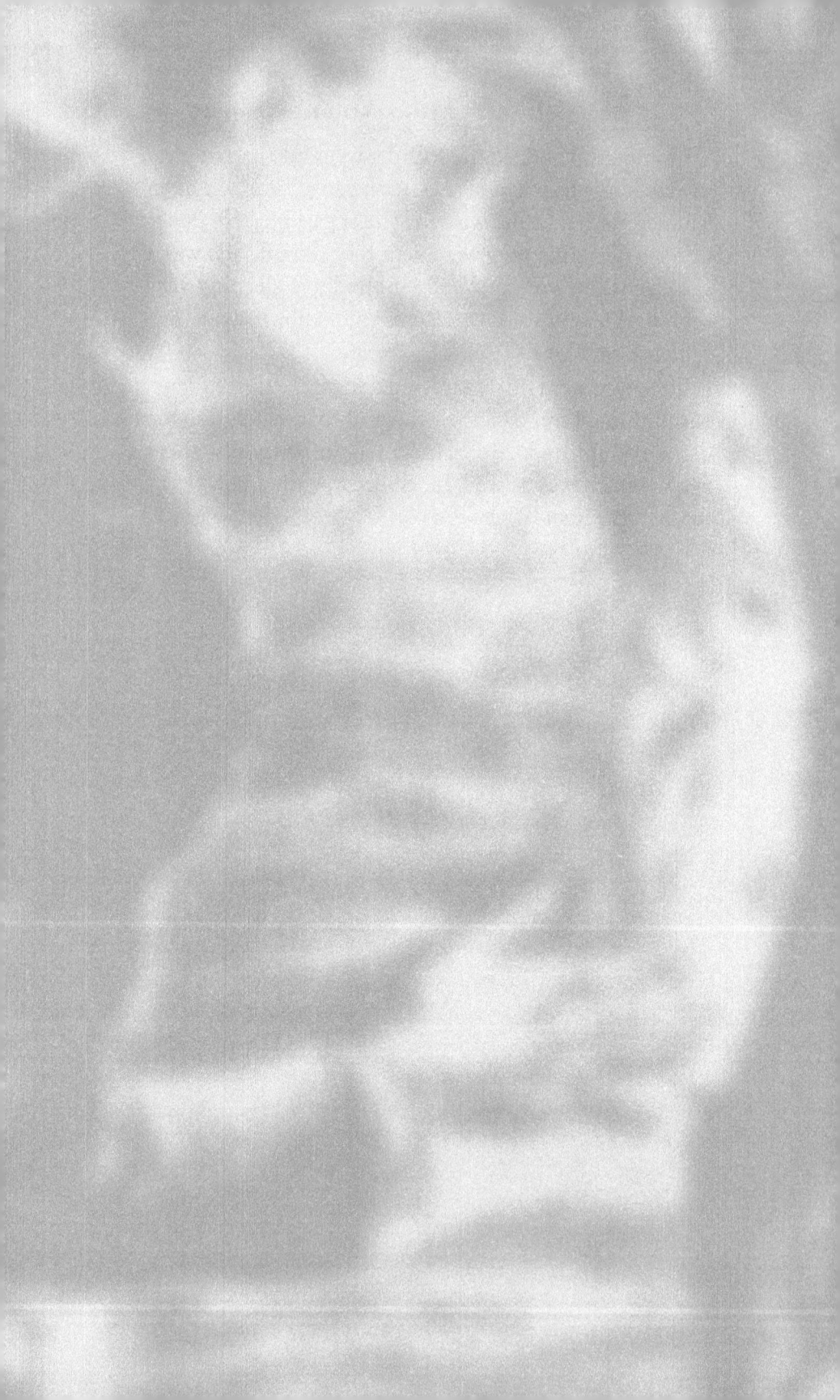

EYES OF THE DEAD

"THE LITTLE BIRD IS GONE FROM THE NEST!" THAT WAS THE CRAZY PHRASE THE HALF-WITTED BLAKE GIRL KEPT MUTTERING TO THE PRICELESS PAINTING ON THE WALL. WHAT COULD HER WORDS MEAN? WHY SHOULD THAT SIMPLE STATEMENT MARK HER FOR MURDER—TURN THE RANCE MANSION INTO A FLAMING HORROR TRAP?

CHAPTER ONE
THE SINGULAR MR. SMITH

T **ED SPANG,** senior hearse driver and general assistant in the funeral parlors of Mr. Horatio Humberton, waited jauntily just within his employer's book-cluttered office, and behind him, his harsh outlines softened by the green shade of the lamp on Humberton's table, a huge giant of a man stood and also waited, with surly impatience.

Spang's employer was sitting at the table. For quite five minutes he did not look up. His high forehead, surmounted by a chrysanthemum-like bloom of yellow hair, was wrinkled in contemplation of a curiously misshapen skull, which he slowly revolved on the table for examination. Suddenly, he smiled. His thick spectacles lifted, and he saw Ted.

"A suggestive specimen, Ted," he remarked, briskly. "The people at the museum were kind enough to lend it to me. It was dug up near Verdun, in some very old strata. The more I study these prehistoric crania, the more convinced I am that crime is a throw-back, the reversion to an ancient type, for which the criminal is hardly responsible."

Spang accepted the statement without argument. "Now, this Smith, Mr. Humberton—" he began, confidently.

"What Smith?" Humberton's tone was sharp. He sensed an interruption.

"This man we've had working around the parlors. You remember, you let me hire him for a while when I fell downstairs a week ago and sprained my arm? He's been fixing the roof this afternoon, and now—"

The huge man in the shadows cut in. His deep voice quavered with an unpleasant quality, midway between a snarl and a whine. "And now I'm quitting, guvnor," he said. "Quitting cold on your blasted job, and I'd thank ye to give me my money."

"Give it to him." Humberton cut the words off short, and returned to the examination of the skull.

Spang grinned, and scratched his red head. "I could have paid him off without worrying you," he explained, easily. "But you're interested in queer things, Mr. Humberton. I thought maybe you'd like to pop a question or two at him. He says he keeps seeing a dead woman."

TED SPANG'S judgment of what appealed to his employer was accurate. The tall necrologist placed his prehistoric specimen carefully on the table, pushed back his chair, and stood up. That gave him a better view of the man Spang had brought in. He saw a big, heavy-featured face with pendulous lower lip and eyes which were red and bleary. It was the face of a drunkard.

"He's a good carpenter," the driver put in.

Humberton nodded, and stepped around the table to confront the man.

"We can't make it," the necrologist gasped.

"Now, what did you see?" he demanded.

"A dead woman, guvnor, looking at me from the back of the big house on the next street."

"How could a dead woman look at you?"

Smith pushed back a dirty cloth cap, which he had not bothered to remove, and scratched his head. "This one did."

Through his thick glasses, Humberton studied the massive, dull-witted face. Nothing was to be gained from impatience. The man was defiant and in haste to be gone. Given his money, he would not have waited for questioning.

"Where were you when you saw this?" the necrologist pursued.

"On your roof."

"And the dead woman was on another roof?"

The giant shook his head with a surly growl. "Gimme my money!" he demanded. "I've told ye where she was. In the big house on the next street."

"The rear attic window of the old Rance house on Clifton Avenue," Spang volunteered. "You can see it from the roof. Smith says the dead woman wasn't there all the time. She came and went. Sometimes when he went up he wouldn't see her at all. Then again she'd follow him, when I had him working around the yard."

"I didn't say she followed," the giant snarled. "I said I could see her. She was still in that house."

"You can't see the Rance house from the yard," Spang objected.

"I don't care. I saw her. Look here, guvnor—"The heavy eyebrows lowered threateningly. "I ain't always done odd jobs of carpenter work. I was head man in a quarry, once. Played with dynamite the way you're playing with that crazy skull. I ain't no man to fool with. If you know what's good for you, you'll give me my money—and you won't argue!"

Humberton smiled at his red-haired assistant.

"Give it to him, Ted. Who knows? He might blow us up if we keep him waiting. I fear, though, he is troubled with delusions produced by alcoholism. Did you go up on the roof yourself and look at the window he refers to?"

"I did, sir. Couldn't see a thing."

"No doubt because there was nothing to see. By the way, Smith, how did you know the woman was dead?"

The carpenter had just received his money from Spang. He glanced at it, slipped it into a pocket in his greasy trousers, and looked up again with a sneering grin. "Can't you tell a dead woman when you see one, guvnor?" he inquired.

HUMBERTON RETURNED to his table, and the examination of the skull. The office door slammed—the door to the long, narrow hall of the establishment, on the rubber matting of which the heavy, shuffling footsteps of the man Smith were audible as they receded toward the street.

"Sorry to keep on bothering you, Mr. Humberton—"

"I thought you were gone, Ted." Humberton looked up, with no trace of his former impatience. The singular case of Smith, carpenter, quarry man, and seer of dead women, had been worth the interruption. "Do you wish to see me about something else?"

"There's another queer bird out there." Spang's already ample mouth widened in a grin. "He's waiting in the reception room. Poor devil, he's one of the lamest birds I ever saw. Takes about six motions to every step. He says he wants to talk to you about a funeral."

Humberton sighed. After all, he was a funeral director by profession. Engagements of this sort could not be declined. His hobby of crime detection, aided and indulged by his friend, Detective Clyde of the Cleveland Police, absorbed him to such an extent that he was prone to forget his legitimate calling. Funerals thrust it back upon him.

"Show him in, Ted," he said.

There was quite an appreciable wait. Humberton had time to use a pair of calipers on the skull, to note down several dimensions, and to forget all about the impending interruption. When Spang's brisk tread became audible in the hall, followed by a curiously dragging sound, the necrologist therefore looked up with freshened annoyance.

"Mr. Pokemoff," announced Spang, holding the door wide so that a tall but pitifully bent young man, leaning on a cane, could enter.

The young man smiled, easily. "The name is Vladimir Pobedoff," he corrected, in a surprisingly pleasant, low-pitched voice. "Our Russian names are difficult. I am speaking to Mr. Horatio Humberton?"

Humberton nodded. His visitor's unusual countenance interested him. It was not a handsome face, but there was high intelligence in the broad dark forehead and black eyes. Possibilities of humor flickered in the subtle turn of the mouth, beneath a small, precisely trimmed mustache. But the expression at this moment was very grave.

Spang left the office. The lame man took the chair Humberton indicated. Resting both hands—long, slender hands—on the head of his cane, he looked keenly across them at the necrologist.

"Mr. Humberton," he said, slowly, "I come to you to arrange for a funeral. Am I correct in assuming that you still discharge such duties personally?"

Humberton nodded again.

"That is well. My friend would be greatly disappointed if you should refuse."

"Who is your friend?" the necrologist demanded.

"Mr. Bartholomew Rance."

HUMBERTON'S INTEREST, which had been entirely in his visitor and not at all in his visitor's mission, suddenly quickened a little. If this was a coincidence, it was an odd one. Perhaps the man Smith actually had seen a dead woman in the Rance mansion.

"Do you mean Bartholomew Rance, the art collector?" he asked.

"The art collector," Pobedoff confirmed. "He has also been a noted explorer, I believe. His house is directly back of yours, on Clifton Avenue."

Humberton recalled that Rance was reputed to live alone. "Who is dead—one of the servants?" he inquired.

The lame man shook his head. "Mr. Rance is my friend. It grieves me greatly to tell you this. You are asked to conduct his funeral."

The necrologist leaned both elbows on his desk and scrutinized his visitor's calm, grave face. He was thoroughly interested now. "When did Rance die?"

"Ah—that I cannot tell you. Half an hour ago he was alive and well. He assured me of that, over the telephone. Quite well, in body and in mind, he put it—but bored of this life and curious about the life to come. You see? He intended to kill himself. He wished you to conduct his funeral. So he called me, his friend. Wait one moment, and you will hear the shot,' he said. But I did not wait."

Slowly Horatio Humberton rose to his feet. His mouth was set in a thin, accusing line. His voice was deliberate and cold. "You are a lame man," he said. "No doubt you could not personally prevent this suicide. But you have a telephone. I am waiting to hear how you used it."

"I used it to call the police." A faint smile curled on Pobedoff's grave mouth. "Surely I would not neglect so obvious a duty. Even though I am but a tobacconist now, there were days—old days, in Russia—when I was considered intelligent. I have come to you with the tardiness of a lame man, and have spoken calmly, because all I could do has been done. When one has done that, he can take his time."

Humberton sat down again and slid a telephone directory from the table drawer. He had just begun to search in it when an idea struck him. "Do you know Rance's telephone number?"

Pobedoff shook his head. "I seldom had occasion to call him up. I became acquainted with him because he dropped in to buy cigars. Later he would come in the evening, after closing hours."

"Did he ever talk of suicide?"

The lame man gazed dreamily, speculatively into the shadowy corners of the office. "How does one talk of suicide?" he said, softly. "If you mean the physical act—the gun to the temple—he did not talk of that. But I have heard him say that he had seen all of the world that interested him. At last, he said, even art lost its capacity to charm. Would there be art in the next world—glorified art, relieved of our narrow sense limitations? He often wondered as to that, Mr. Humberton."

Humberton had found the number he wanted—that of the Rance house. He called it. A familiar voice answered—a voice which even tragedy could not rob of its naturally cheerful timber.

"Clyde!"The necrologist's own voice expressed his satisfaction. "I understand Bartholomew Rance intended to commit suicide. Were you in time to prevent him?"

"Can you come over, Ho?" the voice at the other end countered.

To no one else among his circle of friends was the dignified necrologist known as "Ho" but coming from Clyde's lips the familiar term implied not the least lack of respect. Humberton expected it. Any other name—from Clyde, and Clyde only—would have been hardly short of unfriendly.

"I'll come if you want me," Humberton replied.

"I want you, all right."The detective's short laugh had an edge of excitement to it. "Something has broken here that will make every front page in the country. Come right over, if you can. You'll find the door open."

"Then it is suicide?" Humberton inquired.

"Suicide?" Clyde laughed, again. "Not on your life! It's murder!"

CHAPTER TWO
THE THIRD BULLET

SOMEWHERE IN the back of his mind Horatio Humberton cherished a conviction that the well-rounded man should be interested in everything. His career had been modeled on this theory. He had taken up criminology as a hobby and it had developed into a passion. Without having made a study of architecture, he had a smattering of that, too; enough to know that the old Rance mansion, before which his sedan drew up, was late Georgian, and to appreciate some of its minor structural features.

His sedan was driven by Spang. On the way they had dropped Vladimir Pobedoff at his little cigar store, which was less than a square from the Rance place. As the necrologist stepped rather gingerly to the curb, the front door of the house opened, and Detective Clyde's large figure appeared on the top step. Three other figures appeared from the darkness outside with a smooth promptitude which threatened an attack on the police, but he brushed them gruffly aside and came down the steps two at a time, his substantial shadow dancing before him. In spite of the blackness of the street, he evidently recognized the sedan and its occupants.

"I forgot to ask you, Ho," he cried, when he had reached the sidewalk; "how did you know about this affair?"

The tall necrologist favored him with an unhurried smile, which was lost on the darkness. With equal deliberation, he stood and looked up at the house. The second story windows were alight, the remainder dark.

"The answer to that is very simple," he returned, at length. "I was informed by the same man who telephoned you. Tell me something—isn't this the place from which a servant girl disappeared some months ago?"

"Have a heart, Mr. Clyde!" interrupted one of the three men who were following as Humberton and Clyde went up the steps.

"Listen, you fellows!" Clyde stood on the top step again, and addressed them curtly. "Up to now, you know just as much about this thing as I do. When something else breaks, I may let you know—if I can without gumming up the investigation. You're not coming into the house yet—get that?"

"Care to make a statement, Mr. Humberton?" The youngest of the three started forward, hopefully.

The necrologist shook his head and followed his friend into the hall. "You seem rather short with the newspapers, Clyde," he observed, dryly.

"Why wouldn't be short with them? Haven't they been riding me for a fare thee well?" Clyde's tone was bitter. "Gang murders have hit this town, just as they have every other big city in the country. Only here the police are the goats. And the papers have elected me chief goat. If it keeps on, they'll have the citizens helping me out of town on a rail. I'm glad this one isn't a gang murder!" He stopped, abruptly. "You asked about the servant girl, Ho. This is the place, all right. She disappeared from here. You weren't in on that case. I hardly thought you'd recall anything about it."

HUMBERTON STOPPED just within the entrance hall, nodded to the policeman on duty, and looked past him to the broad staircase directly in front of them. He sized up two paintings, one on each side wall, and turned to Clyde. "As I remember, Rance was writing a book," he remarked. "Something about Assyrian art."

Clyde grunted assent. "And he had an odd little trick of giving the servants a few days holiday when he wanted to concentrate. Remember that, Ho? This girl—her name was Minnie Blake—went on one of those vacations and never came back. We couldn't get a trace of her—not a smell. Odd, too. She wasn't very bright—not much more than half-witted. Such people are generally easy to trace. Rance was pretty well cut up about it. Offered a reward. No good. It's astonishing how many disappear each year in a city the size of this. Come upstairs, Ho."

He started up, but Humberton laid a detaining hand on his arm. "One minute. I wish to get my thoughts straight. There was another odd circumstance about the girl's disappearance. I noticed it in one of the news accounts at the time, but paid no particular attention to it. It was something about a bird."

"About a bird?" Clyde's ruddy face was blank. "I don't seem to recall that, Ho. Suppose we go up to the library now, and when Lurdle, the butler, happens around, I'll ask him. He ought to remember. He's been here for years. And of course he knew the girl."

The scene in the library—one of the lighted rooms in the front of the house—was of a kind very familiar to Humberton. The body of a man lay on his back on the floor. He had a high, narrow forehead, a large nose which seemed incongruously assertive in death, a gray Van Dyke beard. A very diminutive man, so small as to be almost a dwarf, knelt beside the body, making an examination with quick, nervous movements of his pudgy hands. As they entered, this man rose to his feet.

"Very good, Clyde," he said sharply. "Cause of death, shooting. Wound is at base of the brain. There are two bullet wounds in the body, also, but neither of them would have been fatal. In my opinion, those two were made after death. Have the body taken to the morgue, where I will extract the bullets and tag them to show from which wounds they emanate. Good evening, Clyde. Good evening, Mr. Humberton."

Coroner McNamara walked out, radiating importance as he went; and almost colliding, just outside the door, with Ted Spang, who was coming in. The driver's small eyes were twinkling.

"Well?" demanded his employer.

"I was just thinking that these little men haven't got any more dignity than the rest of us, after all. They just have to spread it thicker to get it all on. The bull downstairs said you were looking for Lurdle, the butler."

"I shall want him presently."

"Well, he came around the corner of the house to talk to me in the machine. He's in the butler's pantry now."

"Bring him to me in a quarter of an hour, Ted."

AS THE driver departed, Humberton looked inquiringly at a revolver which lay near the body.

"That's just where it was when we came in, Ho," Clyde volunteered. "I lifted it with a handkerchief, looked into the cylinder, and put it back. I did that because what I saw in the cylinder made me feel, right then, that I'd like you in on this. If you had been two minutes later telephoning me, I'd have called you. You heard what the coroner said. He's a pompous little duffer, but thorough. This man Rance had three bullets in his body—three."

Humberton nodded, absently. He was looking about the room—which really was entitled to be called a picture gallery rather than a library. There was one section of an inner wall, hidden from floor to ceiling with comfortably filled book shelves, but the remaining wall space, though most of it was likewise covered, owed its concealment to row after row of paintings in oil and water color. Clyde hesitated a moment, then seeing that his friend's attention was still concentrated on art, sprang his bomb.

"Three bullet holes in the body, Ho," he said, impressively. "But only two discharged shells in the gun! Get that? If there's any other gun in this room, I haven't found it, after a careful search. I'm asking you—where did the third bullet hole come from?"

Humberton's retort was curious. He stepped up to a small landscape, hung at about the height of his head on the wall by the hall door, and examined it carefully.

"A Murphy," was his verdict. "A sterling artist whose work will grow more valuable with age. Suppose you stand where I did a moment ago, Clyde. The light there falls just right. What do you see?"

"It isn't—" The detective pushed his cap back and ran fingers through his dark hair, as he came closer. "It isn't a bullet hole in the canvas, is it, Ho?"

"I believe it is." Humberton crooked his head critically to one side. "It has been very neatly repaired, and but for the accident of light reflection from where I stood, it would not have been apparent at all. I wonder—" He grasped the frame firmly with both hands and after a little manipulation took the picture down. "No, the hole in the wall is still there. Would you call it a new hole, Clyde?"

From a side coat pocket Clyde produced a flashlight. "Lucky thing this hole is in the paneling—we can tell more about it," he remarked. "The wood is thin. The bullet went right through it into the plaster. See that brown dust, Ho? That didn't settle in an hour or two. I don't believe that bullet was fired this month or last or the month before."

"Suppose you dig it out and add it to the collection McNamara gives you," Humberton suggested. "I am going to talk with Lurdle."

Ted Spang was a highly satisfactory assistant. He had a way of obeying orders with imagination and speed. Humberton's remark was sufficient now to bring him in with a very large and very fat man behind him—a man whose pendulous cheeks fell almost comically at sight of the pathetic figure on the floor.

"James Lurdle, the butler," was Spang's introduction.

The butler achieved a complicated movement, made up of a bow and a dive into the coat-tail pocket of his dress coat, from which he exhumed a handkerchief. He dabbed each eye separately and blew his nose, then held the handkerchief ready for further need.

"Suppose you take me through the house," Humberton suggested.

"Very good, sir," was the reply, in a deep and liquid bass. "Will you begin with the top or the bottom, sir?"

"With the attic."

"If you're through with the body, Ho, I'll call up and have it taken away," Clyde put in. "McNamara might as well be taking out the bullets, then we can go right ahead with getting them examined, to see which came from this gun. I'll tell the boys to step on it. We ought to hear the dope before we leave here."

CHAPTER THREE
THE TITIAN DOGE

CLYDE WAS a fast worker. Humberton followed the butler's deliberate lead through the picture-hung upper hall to a narrow attic staircase, but they had no more than reached the top of this before the big detective was after them, two stairs at a time.

"Taking the grand tour with you, if you don't mind, Ho," he announced, cheerfully. "I haven't been through the place yet, myself. Ted is in charge of the body."

The necrologist received this information with a non-committal grunt. "Lurdle, are you the only servant?" he asked the solemn and puffing butler.

"Oh, no, sir." Lurdle mopped his forehead, then, with an evident after-thought, dabbed his eyes again. "There's a little Russian girl, Sonia Hansky. She took the place of the girl that disappeared, sir."

"I haven't seen her around here," Clyde interjected.

"You wouldn't till day after tomorrow, sir. This afternoon, Mr. Rance gave us a little vacation. He did that occasionally, sir. When he reached certain points in the book he was working on, he preferred to be entirely alone in the house."

"Then how did you happen back?" Clyde demanded. "You know, Ho, he walked in on us just after we got here."

"In a way, sir, that was chance." Lurdle elevated his eyebrows and turned an earnest gaze upon the inquiring detective. "In another way, it was not. Of late months—perhaps I should say for nearly a year—the master has been acting rather peculiarly. Nothing important, sir—little things. I have been worried. I really feared for what he might do when all alone in the house. So I have made a practice of walking past occasionally when I was supposed to be absent, and keeping an eye on the place. Of course, when I glanced in and saw a policeman in the hall—"

"What were some of the little things you noticed?" Clyde demanded. Humberton, meanwhile, walked about from one attic room to another, all of them dimly but partially lighted by the beams from an ancient chandelier hung midway of a broad, uncarpeted hall. He kept within earshot, nevertheless, and after each excursion into a room stood a moment at the threshold with his eyes fixed thoughtfully on Lurdle.

"They were so very little, sir," the fat butler was explaining, "that folks who didn't know the master as I did wouldn't hardly have noticed them. Take the way he used to stop and look behind him." The butler shook his head, sadly.

"He used to be the kind of man, sir, that didn't care for god nor devil. Yet I've seen him again and again, these last few months, stop short and glance behind him—for all the world as if something was following him up, treading on his heels. He'd be walking down the hall. All of a sudden, that's what he'd do."

"In the daylight?" Humberton queried, from the doorway of the third room he had explored.

THE BUTLER scratched his closely cropped gray head. "Mostly at night, sir. Sometimes in daylight, but it was on dull, dark days, when the house was in a kind of twilight, as you might say, sir."

"What other little things?" Clyde inquired.

"Well, he'd groan and talk to himself, sir. I don't like a man to do that. It gives you the creeps. He never used to do it. And he'd got a lot sharper lately—almost bad-tempered, though I say it with proper respect. Little things again, sir. Just the other day, I was going down cellar to bring up a bottle of wine for his dinner—we have an excellent cellar, sir, all pre-war stuff—and he said to me, 'Where are you going, Lurdle?' When I told him, he flew at me like—like a tiger, sir. 'I'll have you understand that I am not a drunkard,' he said. 'I resent your taking it for granted that I require liquor. Hereafter, you will go into the wine cellar only on my orders.'"

"Was he a heavy drinker?" the detective asked.

"Not at all, sir. For weeks at a time he would take nothing. I have brought the same bottle up a dozen times and returned it to the cellar, without having had to draw the cork."

"Any other little thing?"

"Nothing that occurs to me at present, sir," was the staid reply.

"Then if you've seen all you want to, Ho, suppose we go down a story. There ought to be more to look at on the lower floors."

"First, come into this room at the rear," requested the necrologist. "Bring your flashlight—and bring Lurdle."

"Now, Lurdle," he went on when they were assembled in the bare, narrow room. "I wish you to look through this window. You will see a house with a mansard roof, facing on the next street."

The butler bent his tall figure, obediently. "Your own establishment, if I am not mistaken, sir," he suggested.

Humberton nodded. "Is there any other window from which you can see it?" he inquired.

"I believe not, sir. This is the only window on the north side of the third floor. The second-story windows would not be high enough."

"Lurdle, so far as you know, has any dead body been in this room recently?"

The fat butler's start was real. His pendulous cheeks sagged. For a moment his jaw seemed to drop. "A dead body, sir?" he repeated. "No, indeed, sir!"

"Very well. That is all I wish to ask."

They descended to the second floor accompanied by the puzzled butler, and here Humberton became an art connoisseur, passing rapidly from picture to picture hung along the hallway, and applying to Lurdle for confirmation of his views.

"Where is the Titian, Lurdle," he inquired; "the one Sir Michael Denton commented on last year?"

The fat butler's expression became cherubic. "I am glad to hear you inquire about that, sir," he said, cordially. "So many gentlemen don't know art. And this is an art treasure. Mr. Rance always used to say so, sir. We keep it in a room by itself, with electric lights which were installed especially for it. It's the next room to the library. This way, sir."

In his eagerness he almost hurried to the room, opened the door with a benevolent sweep of his arm, and stood back expectantly. Humberton, however, first glanced into the library. The body of Rance was gone. Spang sat reading in a Turkish rocker. His chief turned without speaking, and followed by Clyde, stepped into the next room.

"The 'Portrait of Doge Gilberto,' sir," intoned the butler.

"How much is it worth?" Clyde demanded, looking without emotion at the painting of a white-bearded old man perusing a scroll in the shade of a tree. The butler replied in a reverent whisper: "At least a hundred and fifty thousand dollars, sir! I know, because a gentleman from Australia was here less than a month after Sir Michael. He offered that amount, but Mr. Rance refused to sell."

"Is it insured?"

"Yes, indeed, sir."

LURDLE HAD turned on the electric lights above the painting. They brought out the luminous depth of the shadows and made the seamed yet benignant face of the old man startlingly lifelike. Even the straw-and-twig structure of a bird's nest, tucked into an angle of the limbs near the top of the tree, stood out distinctly on the side nearest the trunk, though on the other it blended with the soft Italian background.

The detective shook his head with a sigh. "A hundred and fifty thousand berries—and he refused it! And only two servants in the house! What a pipe for a high-class crook! Of course, you and I know, Ho, that paintings like this aren't stolen once in a generation—they're too hard to dispose of without detection—but think of the opportunity if a man was willing to take a chance!"

"The sight of that bird's nest reminds me," Humberton put in. "What was the name of the girl who disappeared?"

"Minnie Blake, sir," the butler volunteered.

"Something about a bird was connected with that case. I'm sure of it!"

The butler bowed. "Your recollection is entirely correct, sir. It was not a real bird, however. You may recall that Minnie Blake was weak-minded—poor girl! Well, she seemed to get it into her head one day that there had been a bird in that nest in the picture—that painted nest, sir— and that it had flown away. I might tell you that she was particularly fond of the Titian. Odd, is it not, sir, that a girl of low mentality should show such good taste? I have known her to spend an hour before it, just gazing. But after this odd notion struck her, she used to go about the house crying to herself and saying, over and over, 'The little bird is gone from the nest! The little bird is gone from the nest!' It was most annoying, sir. It got on Mr. Rance's nerves terribly, though he was too kind-hearted to give her the sack."

Humberton nodded, with satisfaction. "That's it. I recall perfectly now. The point was brought out in one of the newspapers at the time of her disappearance. I suppose you never learned what she meant, Lurdle?"

"I don't believe she meant anything, sir. That was the master's view. As he said to me, 'There's the picture and there's the nest. If any birds are in it they are not visible. So how can one of them have flown away?' And anyway, as he used to say, painted birds don't fly. It was just her poor mind, sir."

"When did she get this notion?" the necrologist pursued. "Was it before Sir Michael passed on the picture?"

"After that, I think, sir."

"Before the Australian made his offer?"

Lurdle's fat chin creased into two double chins in his effort to recollect. "After that, too, sir, I believe—but not very long after."

"Oh, well." Humberton shrugged his shoulders. "Unless you have further business on this floor, Clyde, we may as well go downstairs. I am particularly anxious to look at the wine cellar."

Clyde was an easy man for Humberton to work with. On investigations of this sort he always yielded to his friend's eccentric and sometimes sketchy methods, even though he might return later to make a more thorough examination on his own account.

"The cellar, Lurdle," he directed.

"Very good, sir. The steps go down from here."

CLYDE HAD unlimbered his flashlight, but he soon put it back. It was not needed. Lurdle touched a switch when they reached the extensive cellar, and it blazed with light. Humberton stood on the lowest step, blocking the way for the genial detective, and regarded this phenomenon with interest.

"Why so much light, Lurdle?"

"Mr. Rance's wishes, sir. He installed this system within the past year. I remember he told me that a cellar ought to be the most brightly illuminated part of the house, because everything else was built upon it."

Clyde snorted. "What in hell did he mean by that?" he demanded.

"I haven't the least idea, sir. As I have said, the master was just a little odd lately. One didn't like to ask him to explain himself, sir."

Humberton's interest in the cellar, now that he was there, seemed perfunctory. He walked about the extensive cement floor, glanced at the furnace, and at a neatly piled supply of wood beyond it, favored the stationary washtubs with a slightly closer examination, and at length pulled vigorously at a locked door at the nearer end.

"I forgot to mention, sir," the butler put in, hastily; "only last week, Mr. Rance made me give him the key to the wine cellar. To tell the truth, sir, I felt rather hurt."

"Then you have no key?"

"No, sir."

"I can fix that in a hurry, Ho," Clyde suggested. "Probably the key is on Rance, but this'll be quicker."

He picked up the heavy furnace shaker, eyed the lock for a moment, and struck it one well-placed, shattering blow.

"There are no lights in the wine cellar, sir," volunteered the butler. "We used to have two in there, but Mr. Rance transferred them to the main part of the cellar when he had this other change made. He said wine kept better in the dark."

"That's all right." Clyde tugged at the door, and the split lock parted. "What have we got flashlights for, eh, Ho? Well, I'll be—"

The necrologist pushed in behind him. Clyde's first inquiring sweep of the light had caught the most significant feature of the fragrant basement room.

"He's been digging in here!" was the detective's amazed comment.

"Let me have the light." Humberton directed it first at the long narrow excavation, with a pile of yellow soil beyond it, at one side of the wine cellar; then at the rows of bottles looking down at them from shelves which climbed higher than their heads; then at the dark dirt floor. Finally, he walked up to the hole in the ground and shot the brilliant beam into it. "A grave," was his verdict; "an open, unoccupied grave. You can bandage up your wounded feelings, Lurdle. This is why he took the key from you."

The butler's deep voice broke in a heavy sob. "Then he must have killed himself, sir. He was digging his own grave!"

The tall necrologist smiled. "You think so? Well—everyone to his own theories! Tomorrow I shall try to find the little painted bird!"

CHAPTER FOUR
THE LITTLE BIRD IS GONE

DETECTIVE CLYDE pushed his cap back from his forehead, and his normally humane face assumed an almost vindictive expression. He stood across Humberton's office table from his friend, who remained seated, busily writing on a telegraph blank.

"I suppose you've seen the morning papers, Ho?" he inquired.

The necrologist shook his head.

"Well, it seems this is another gang murder—another one the police are going to muff. The Clarion suggests that if I don't get on the job pretty soon I mustn't be surprised if respectable citizens take matters into their own hands. But what amuses me is this—" Clyde grinned without relaxing his tone of indignation, "I've picked up Pobedoff so quietly that not one of them has tumbled yet to his arrest. That's one on them. You haven't put them wise, I suppose?"

"I have declined to talk to reporters."

"That's that! Now let me tell you something. I don't pretend to be infallible. I've made enough mistakes myself, and seen enough of them made, to be as modest as anyone. But when I come across a man with a Russian name, who looks and talks like a college professor, yet keeps a cigar store—"

"You feel that he must be a murderer." Humberton pulled the telephone toward himself over the smooth surface of his work table, and murmured a number into the transmitter.

"Well, not exactly that." Clyde grinned again. He could not remain ill-tempered for long at a time. "You haven't heard the half of it yet, Ho. Suppose I tell you that two of the bullets in Rance's body came from that gun which we found on the floor beside him, and that Pobedoff's finger prints are on the gun?"

"And the crime—has be confessed to that?" The necrologist finished his message, read it over slowly, and enclosed the blank in an envelope.

"He will. Take that as a prophecy, if you like, and remember it when I report to you a few hours from now. He's weakening fast. We're going to get this whole thing from him. By the way, Ho, did he tell you anything about his business relations with Rance?"

"Only that he sold him cigars."

"He told me that, too. I saw Lurdle early this morning, and learned that Rance smoked nothing but cigarettes. Just a little slip, which Master Pobedoff will have difficulty in explaining! Now I'm off again. Found your little bird yet?"

"I am cabling to Australia about the little bird," Humberton returned. "The name of the Australian who visited Rance some time ago is Patrick Trigal, and he lives in Melbourne. Newspapers are excellent institutions, Clyde. The Plain Dealer dug this information up for me, and promised to keep my asking for it a secret, for the present. By the way, can I get into the Rance house?"

"There's a policeman in charge. He'll let you in. I am detaining Lurdle at headquarters as a material witness. When the maid shows up we'll make a house guest of her, too."

Humberton nodded. "No doubt I shall drop in there this afternoon. My morning will be taken up with visits to art stores, and possibly to the public library. I expect to get track of my little bird in that way, and then I must visit the Rance house again."

"Righto! See you later, Ho." Clyde left, shutting the courtyard door briskly behind him, but immediately looked in again, with a grin. "If you don't find it in the art stores or library, why not try a bird store?" he suggested.

HUMBERTON DID not trouble to reply. He had relapsed into meditation from which Clyde's second shutting of the door failed to rouse him. He merely glanced up when the messenger boy entered, some minutes later, and pushed the envelope toward him mechanically.

"To be sent by your fastest way and reply rushed to me," he directed. "If no one is here, get in touch with Detective Clyde, and he will find me."

For ten minutes longer he remained motionless with closed eyes. Then his finger slid down the telephone dial again.

"Clyde? Has your man confessed?"

"Not quite, Ho, but—"

"Where was the pool of blood in Rance's study?"

"By his head. You don't think—"

"I saw none from the body wounds. Did you?"

The detective's voice was hesitant. "No-o-o—" he began.

"I advise you to have a talk with the coroner. And when you have had it—"

"Yes?" Clyde's tone was thoughtful and distinctly respectful.

"Try the effect of asking Pobedoff why he fired two bullets into a man who was already dead."

Humberton replaced the receiver, put on his hat and walked down the hall of the funeral parlors. He found Spang eating a belated breakfast in a spare room at the rear, which was used for a kitchen.

"Any more visits from reporters, Ted?" he inquired.

The senior hearse driver juggled half a fried egg into his mouth, by dexterous manipulation of a table knife, and looked up with a grin. "The reception room is alive with them. Are you going out, sir?"

"I am likely to be out all morning—on a walking tour. Tell the reporters I have nothing to give them, as yet."

But his mission took more than the morning. By the middle of the afternoon he had exhausted the pubic library's resources and had worked through the principal art stores to their more obscure competitors, without finding what he sought. It was nearly closing time when, from a grimy little uptown shop, he telephoned Clyde.

The big detective's voice was exuberant. "See the papers, Ho?" he demanded.

Humberton returned a rather curt negative.

"Then you're missing a real thrill. Pobedoff has confessed! Not only that, but it is a gang killing, after all. For once, the papers took a wild shot and hit the bull's eye. Rance was put on the spot."

"You have the gun that killed him—the one which fired a bullet into his brain?"

"Pobedoff threw it into the river. He told me where, and I'm having the river dragged. You remember that bullet which went through the picture into the wall? Well, he had a run-in with Rance once before. Rance took a pot-shot at him and missed. Pobedoff got Rance's gun away from him then, so he had two guns when he actually put the old man on the spot. He became excited and dropped one of them. They always slip somewhere, Ho—darned if they don't! Going to call it off now, I suppose?"

"I have not yet found the little bird," the necrologist returned, enigmatically. "Unless I do find it soon I shall be obliged to leave for New York tonight. What reason does Pobedoff give for firing two bullets into a dead man?"

A shade of hesitation was noticeable in Clyde's reply. "To tell you the truth—I forgot that point when I questioned Pobedoff," he admitted.

The old man—a dried husk of an old man with an ear trumpet—who ran the little shop, was hovering at the necrologist's elbow, waiting for the telephoning to be done.

"It was Titian you said you were interested in, sir? I have some portfolios here. Quite old. Portfolios of old masters have their vogue, like everything else. These are sadly out of the vogue, I fear—you are not likely to find them at all in the bigger shops. Still, it might be worth your while—"

The light was poor—a single dangling carbon bulb in the dark back room of the little shop. Humberton was about to bring the portfolios to the light of the street window when he discovered that there no longer was anything of the sort. Evening of a cloudy day was at hand. He returned to the ineffectual bulb and began a search through the pictures.

There were three portfolios. The fifth picture in the second one was that of Doge Gilberto.

SOME HOURS later—having supped meanwhile—Humberton and his versatile hearse driver drew up in the big sedan before the Rance place.

The avenue on which the old mansion fronted was dark, except for occasional street lights. It was a thick evening, however; a light mist already had begun to drift in from the winding Cuyahoga, and stronger lights than those would have had little authority. Humberton walked up the steps, Ted Spang just behind him. He expected to find a policeman in charge. Yet the sudden appearance of the latter, who seemed to separate himself from the darkness at the top of the steps, took the necrologist slightly by surprise.

"Beg your pardon, sir. Didn't know you till you near ran into me. I'm Kennedy. You want to go in, I suppose?"

"Why have you no lights in the house, Kennedy?"

The policeman's hoarse voice dropped to a confidential growl. "There's someone about, sir."

Kennedy had unlocked the front door and pushed it open. Humberton stopped at the threshold. "What do you mean?" he demanded.

"I've seen him twice. Better come inside where we won't be spied on. He's trying to get into the house. You know, sir, there's a sort of walk on both sides of the place, and a little yard behind it. I saw him once in that yard. The second time he was here in front just as I come around the side, and that time I heard his footsteps but I can't rightly say I saw him. You see, there's more light in back than here, because of the way one of the lamps on the next street shines into the yard. That's all, sir, but I'm keeping a mighty close watch."

"Did you challenge him?" the necrologist inquired.

"I did not, sir. I thought maybe, I might have a chance to get him by the heels a little later on."

"Quite right. If you catch him I should like to be notified. You can find me through Clyde, if I am gone from here."

"Very good, sir."

"Ted and I will carry on our investigations by flashlight, so the house will still be dark."

Humberton had Ted's flashlight in his right hand, the print of "Doge Gilberto" in his left. He led the way up the broad staircase.

"The room next to the one where the body was found, Ted," his chief announced. He noticed suddenly that the driver had stopped halfway up the stairs. "You are not nervous?"

Spang came on. "Just fancied I heard something moving, sir. Rats, likely enough. You never know what you'll hear in an old house like this."

Humberton was about to grunt an impatient reply to this reflection, as he continued down the hall, when he too stopped abruptly. "I must telephone Clyde," he said. "Suppose you hold the light, Ted, while I do so."

THE PHONE was in the library—in which Rance's body had been found. Clyde was a glutton for long hours. His friend expected to find him at headquarters, and so he was.

"Heard the latest, Ho? The papers have a new song now. Since Pobedoff confessed himself a gangster, they're beginning to ride the courts. You know the racket—'An Outraged Citizenry Demand Justice, Not Mercy.' It's O.K. with me. I can stand to see them ride somebody else for a change."

"Has the girl come back?" Humberton interrupted.

"The crazy girl?"

"The servant who was given leave of absence and who is due back today, according to Lurdle."

Clyde laughed. "Beg pardon, Ho. I'd forgotten her for the minute. But we've been on the lookout. She hasn't come to the house and we have no track of her yet. I suppose she reads the papers."

The necrologist hung up, thoughtfully took the flashlight from Spang again, and walked slowly to the room next the library, where the Titian reigned supreme. He pulled the chains which controlled the picture's special illumination. The figure of the old man reading beneath the tree, with the Italian landscape in the distance, was flooded with light. Elsewhere, the room remained in darkness.

"Pull down the blind, Ted. We must not interfere with Kennedy's trap. He may stumble on to something."

With little regard for the sanctity of antiques, Humberton mounted an upholstered chair and held his microscope close to the painting. He unrolled the print he had bought, and examined that, too, with the aid of the powerful electric bulbs above the Titian.

"Your eyes are good, Ted. Look without the aid of this glass at the spot I indicate on the painting—the nest in the tree."

"I see is very clearly, sir."

"Now take the microscope and examine the same place on the print."

Spang obeyed. He referred again to the painting, then held the lens once more above the print. Presently he looked up, with a grin.

"Now that's an odd thing. As sure as I live there's a bird in the nest on the print. You can see her wing. But if that nest in the painting on the wall ain't empty, I'll eat it. What do you make of it, Mr. Humberton?"

"The print is old. It was taken from the original painting," his employer returned.

Spang stared a moment, and his lips slowly puckered into a long-drawn whistle. "Are you telling me that the painting on the wall is a fake?" he inquired.

" 'The little bird is gone from the nest!'" Humberton quoted, enigmatically. "Gone because a superb imitation, precise in every detail except for that one curious slip, was substituted for the original! The half-witted girl knew the painting perfectly because she loved it. She noticed the change in the nest—but never understood the reason. I begin to think we are nearing the end of the case, Ted, though perhaps I am mistaken. After all, it is not much more than a hunch. I shall take a minute to instruct Policeman Kennedy—who seems intelligent—to let his visitor effect an entrance and not to arrest him too soon; then we will go to see Pobedoff, in his cell."

CHAPTER FIVE
LYNCH LAW

THEY HAD reached the main hall again when upstairs the telephone began ringing. Humberton halted within a few steps of the street door.

"Get it, Ted," he said, tersely.

Spang was up the stairs, two at a time. The circle of his flashlight zigzagged before him. In a moment his rather high-pitched voice floated down. "Western Union for you, Mr. Humberton."

As the necrologist hastened upward, helped by Spang's light from above, he offered a brief but caustic commentary on second-floor telephones not equipped with ground-floor extensions. Once actually at the receiver, however, and listening to the gradually unfolded message, his vexation gave way to amazed delight.

"Ted!" he cried, excitedly, hanging up. "The newspapers! They have done what I couldn't possibly have done! I have just listened to a day letter from a man in Chicago. He saw the news account of Rance's death. He wires to say that he was on the point of closing a deal with Rance for 'Doge Gilberto.'"

Spang whistled. "The fake painting, sir?"

"I was expecting a cable from Australia. But I did not expect this telegram. If the Australian cable contains what I believe—"

The telephone interrupted.

"I'll take it, Ted." In the yellow circle of the flashlight, Spang saw his master smiling broadly. "If this is the cable, it will be a coincidence. Yet not so much so. There has been time—"

He picked up the receiver. Spang kept the light on him and waited breathlessly. Again he saw an unwonted smile broaden on his chief's face. At length Humberton leaned back in his chair at the telephone table, as the receiver clicked on its hook, and indulged in a silent laugh.

"It was from Australia." Humberton's laugh became audible. To the driver, accustomed to his employer's almost invariable reserve, there was something uncanny about it. "Mr. Patrick Trigal, of Melbourne, bought the Titian for a hundred and fifty thousand dollars. He has it now in his private gallery. A confidential condition of the sale was that he should keep the purchase secret for ten years."

"Why should he do that?" Spang inquired, out of the dark.

"No doubt he is a genuine collector. There are such, Ted. There are men to whom the joy of possession is everything. I think I understand Mr. Trigal. And I understand Rance's reason for the request. Ten years is a long time. Australia is on the other side of the world. If he could sell his excellent copy of the 'Doge' as an original he could make double money, and his chances of escaping any ultimate penalty would be quite good."

"But it's a fake. The Chicago man—"

"No doubt he was relying on Sir Michael Denton's word—which applied to the original painting. The purchaser would be quite unlikely to observe for himself—that 'the little bird had flown from the nest.'" Rance had an excellent reason for getting the half-witted girl out of the way. What she was saying as she went about the house was dangerous to him. She stood between him and a fortune. You see that?"

"Yes, but—"

"There was an old bullet in the wall. It might have been fired about the time she disappeared. Rance was killed by a bullet from the same gun. Pobedoff says he shot Rance and threw the gun into the river, but if so why did he pump two bullets, from another gun, into Rance's body some time after Rance had died? You are following?"

"Y-e-s, sir," the driver maintained, manfully.

"You saw the grave down cellar—the open grave. Is it very deep?"

Before there could be a reply to this last question, a confused noise came from the street. Spang rushed to the window. "Mr. Humberton! Quick!"

TWO CARS had drawn up to the curb. Both were filled with men. A man in the tonneau of the front car stood up. It was an open touring type, with the top down. As he rose, someone else opened the door, and a light was switched on; not a strong light, but strong enough to show the pale countenance of a man with a rope around his neck, who was being forced to his feet.

A deep, powerful voice, hoarse with excitement, carried clearly even through the closed window behind which Humberton and Spang watched.

"Have a look! We can't hang you here. Some fool would come along and cut you down. Have a look at the place where you did it! Then you're going for a ride, you dirty gangster, the way you've taken plenty of others."

"Come on, Ted!"

"It's Pobedoff. They've got him out of jail to lynch him!"

Humberton bumped into the telephone table and upset both table and phone. The echoes of the crash followed him into the hall. Going down the stairs, the driver passed him. Yet they were almost neck and neck when Spang wrenched open the broad front door.

A revolver barked outside. One of the men in the rear car brought his flashlight beam across the face of Policeman Kennedy, rushing forward across the sidewalk, his gun still smoking. Humberton and Ted Spang were on the top step when they saw this. They had not reached the bottom one before Kennedy was garroted from behind, and forced, kicking and swearing, into the second machine. With a snort and a vomit of pungent exhaust smoke it lurched forward to follow the first car, already roaring up the street.

"We must follow them, Ted!"

Spang seemed to open the door and slide behind the wheel all in one move. His chief tripped, getting in at his side. Ted's hand gripped his collar and almost lifted him in, with the car in motion.

"They mustn't lose us!" Humberton gasped.

"They won't, sir."

The two cars ahead were driven not merely with wild speed but with skill. At the first crossing they crashed a red light. The opposing traffic was heavy, yet they both got through. The second won clear only by jumping the curb and rounding a telephone pole.

"Shall I crash the light, too?" Spang shouted.

"Yes," his employer returned, grimly.

But the light changed at the critical moment.

They gained a little in the next block when both cars slowed suddenly, with screaming brakes, to avoid a machine which came composedly out of an alley. Spang had time to swerve without cutting speed. At the next street—a quieter thoroughfare without traffic lights—the cars turned right. A siren shrilled, somewhere in the distance.

"Police cars," the necrologist diagnosed.

"Running by on another street," Spang agreed. "Now if they should look this way when they cross—"

But the two cars jack-knifed to the left after one short block. Spang gave the wheel a mighty wrench and followed.

"They're clever boys," he muttered. "They gave the police the slip that time. We've got new tires, but they won't stand too many twists like that. I wonder—"

He was interrupted by a sharp report from the second of the two cars ahead. Humberton instinctively ducked. But his driver chuckled. When the car involved plunged violently to the right and smashed to the curb as they passed, he laughed aloud.

"That's what I was wondering, whether their tires were good. We've got just one to trail now. That's the car they forced the policeman into."

HUMBERTON LOOKED around, with his arm on the back of the seat. The occupants of the wrecked car were piling out. He was turning frontward again, when something touched him lightly on the arm. He glanced back with a jerk. It was a human hand.

"Please! Pardon, please!"

Not ten times in as many years had the tall necrologist lost his poise. He lost it now, for an instant. His startled cry so astounded Spang that the car lurched, ominously. Then Humberton recovered himself.

"Don't slow down!" he directed, sharply. "Our business is to be with that car when it stops. There is a woman in our back seat."

The machine lurched again.

"Keep the car straight and give it all the gas it will take. I will attend to this matter. No doubt she crawled in and hid when we were parked in front of the Rance house." He turned again, and addressed the dim figure in the darkness of the tonneau. "What do you mean by this? Who are you?"

"Sonia Pobedoff," was the faltering response.

"Pobedoff's wife!" The words thundered even above the roar of the speeding car.

"Yes." Her voice was high-pitched yet tuneful. It carried without the necessity for being loud. "I am—maid—Mr. Rance," it explained.

Humberton glanced at the tail-light of the machine ahead. If it was no nearer, neither had it widened the distance between them.

"Give it everything, Ted," he directed.

"Her tail's on the floor board now."

Then Humberton turned his attention again to the tonneau. Conversation was difficult. Yet there was something in the agonized crouch of the figure behind in the darkness which impelled him to learn more of her.

"Where have you been?" he demanded.

"In the house. I came back. I have a key."

"How did you get into this car?"

"I jumped in—when you started. I ran out of the house after you. Please— please—"

"What?" The entreaty in her voice grated on his nerves. He shot the word at her harshly.

"You must save him. Please! See, I am kneeling to you! I love him!"

"Do you hear that, Ted?"

The driver replied with a grunt. They were making a sharp right turn, and all his attention was required at the wheel. At once they were off the city streets. A rough macadam merged into a rougher dirt road. The machine ahead bumped on, but seemed to be slowing.

"They are stopping. Oh, they are going to kill him! They must not! He did not do it! I tell you, he did not!"

The other machine, pulled suddenly into the ditch, stopped with a grind of brakes, and its occupants leaped out. They were dragging their prisoner with them. Several flashlights in the party illuminated their way toward a wooded ravine at the farther side of a field.

Spang came to a noiseless stop, a few feet behind the other car.

"Soft pedal it, sister," he advised, gruffly, toward the back seat. "They're thinking we're shook off. If they don't know we're tailing them, maybe we'll have a chance to save your boy friend's life."

"I will be quiet." The words came with a sob, but in a voice that was barely audible. She dropped lightly to the footpath, just behind the necrologist. Usually, he walked with dignified deliberation, but now he started across the field at a rapid, jerky pace rather too fast for the others. Spang flashed his light just often enough to show them the ground.

"They've reached the trees. Got a gun, Mr. Humberton?"

"I have not. One gun would be useless, anyway."

"And we haven't even got that. Come on, sir! Let's run for it. They're throwing the rope over a limb!"

"Shout!" his chief commanded, tersely.

CHAPTER SIX
FIRE!

THEY RAISED a stentorian halloo. It echoed from some night-enshrouded height and came back almost as loudly as its original. In the circle of light from their lanterns, the group turned sharply; all except one who was tying the hands of the man with a rope about his neck. A tall member of the party spat out a hurried order. Instantly, everyone slipped on a mask. Some of the masks were mere bits of cloth. Most were black dominos. The tall man had donned a red domino. It might have been a Hallowe'en revel. He stepped forward—not excitedly, but with a quiet air of determination.

"Sorry, friends, but you'll have to stay where you are. Don't try to go back till we say the word. We are doing a little clean-up job." He motioned to his companions. "All right, boys. Get it over with!"

"Just a minute." Humberton had continued to walk forward. He spoke slowly—almost casually. The man in the red domino laughed. "Oh, hello, Mr. Humberton. Hope you don't know me with this mask on. We'd rather not be known. You see, we've stolen this fine bird from the police, and we intend to make an example of him for the benefit of other gangsters. If the officers of the law can't clean this town up, we will."

"By hanging an innocent man?"

"Innocent?" Three men had begun to pull on the rope. It was tightening. The girl, just behind Humberton, was sobbing quietly, but she had not spoken. Rather, she was listening desperately to the exchange between him and the man in the red domino. Red Domino laughed again. "Just a minute, boys. I guess the police won't be on us right away. Now, Pobedoff—you've confessed already, do it again. Tell Mr. Humberton—did you kill Rance?"

"No, no! He did not! I tell you he did not. I know who did!"

It was the girl. She had run forward. Her arms were around the prisoner. "You must not hang him without hearing what I have to say!" she cried.

Humberton spoke—still very quietly. "Isn't that fair?" He looked about the masked circle. "I don't know what she wants to tell. I haven't heard her story—yet. But I should like to hear it. What if Pobedoff has confessed? Perhaps he did it to save this girl."

The girl involuntarily stepped back from the lame prisoner. "Vladimir! You think I did it?"

For the first time the tobacconist spoke. "Silence, Sonia!" he commanded, sternly. "I am the guilty one."

"But, no! You were not there! You—"

THE NECROLOGIST laid his hand on her shoulder. In the converging circle of the electric lanterns, he now shared the stage with the two of them. The masked company in the shadows were frozen into sudden immobility. The men at the rope had relaxed their grip. Only Spang shifted his position a little, to a spot where he could operate to better advantage if his chief gave the word for an attack. But his chief did not. Instead, he smiled about him at the lynching party.

"I'm sure we wish to hear this girl's story, gentlemen," he said confidently. "Of course we must hear it before, rather than after the painful ordeal you have in mind. Mr. Rance gave you a little vacation yesterday, did he not, Sonia?"

She nodded. The matter-of-fact question evidently steadied her. "I was to finish the lunch dishes, then go," she said. "Go—and not come back till this afternoon. I went to a movie." She smiled at the prisoner, who was watching her with compressed lips and tense eyes. "Poor Vladimir, he would be busy all day, so I had to go alone!"

"Vladimir and Rance were close friends?" asked Humberton.

"Friends? They did not know each other. They never knew each other."

The necrologist nodded. "I suspected that. And after the movie—"

"It was dark. I had supper—all by myself, at a little restaurant. I was going to Vladimir's then, but I had forgotten my vanity case. It was in my room. I should not have gone back." She shook her head, so vigorously that the dark hair fell over her low, straight forehead and had to be tossed upward out of her eyes. "Never should I have gone back. Mr. Rance did not permit that, when he gave us vacations. But I had my key. If I went in quietly, and right out again, would that be wrong? How should I know they would be fighting in the library?"

She stopped, with her hand to her throat.

"Careful!" Humberton noted with satisfaction that the masked circle had drawn in closer. "We want to know exactly what you saw."

"I did not see. How should I see with the door shut? But Mr. Rance was talking, and a great, a terrible voice was shouting back at him. I can not tell you what Mr. Rance said. I do not remember. But the other man was swearing at him, and saying, 'You want to kill me? You want to kill me? Well, I'll kill you!'"

"You are sure?" In his eagerness, Humberton shot the question at her in what was almost a whisper. "You are sure that is what was said? And it was not Rance speaking—it was the other man?"

"It was the other man. And I shall not forget what he said." She shuddered. Her dark eyes had lost their fear of the menacing faces around her. They were filled instead with the memory of a past terror. "I wanted to run in and save Mr. Rance. But what could I do? I am not strong enough to fight a man who could shout like that. Then I remember that Vladimir has a gun in the drawer under his counter. I ran to him. Oh, how I ran! He was alone. I think he asked me why I wanted the gun. I said, 'Mr. Rance!' I ran back again. Poor Vladimir, I knew he could not run."

"Wait!" The prisoner's pale face was blazing with emotion. "I asked you whom you were going to shoot!"

"How should I know what you said? I knew I must run back, to give the gun to Mr. Rance. The front door was open—wide open. I ran up the stairs. The library door was open—it was shut when I heard the man with the terrible voice. I went in." She stopped again. Her breath came in short, sharp gasps. "He was lying on the floor. He was dead!"

"And then?" Humberton prompted.

"I ran out of the house. I was crazy. I think I must have run about the streets. But at last I went to the house of my aunt. I was afraid. I did not even want to see Vladimir."

THE LAME man's hands could not have been securely tied. He freed them suddenly, and, grasping the girl by the shoulders, turned her so that she faced him. His dark, cleanly chiseled features were working convulsively.

"Sonia! My little Sonia!" His thought was for her alone. At this moment the blaze of lantern light in which he stood, the pressing darkness without the circle, the variously masked lynching party, did not exist for him. "Sonia!" he said again, hoarsely. "You did not kill him? After all, you did not kill him?"

She met his imploring gaze wonderingly. "Why of course not, Vladimir!"

"I should have known it! But after what you said, I thought—I thought—" His face relaxed into a smile; but still it was a scene between the two of them only, with the rest of the world non-existent. "Listen to me, little Sonia. Then you will see how cunning I have been. And what a fool! I could not keep up with you. You are lithe and graceful and fleet, like a gazelle. I followed on these twisted legs of mine. As soon as they would take me there, I was in Rance's library—the only lighted room in the house. I found him there. My gun was beside him. You dropped it, I suppose?"

She nodded, mutely.

"I picked it up. He was dead. Because I thought you had killed him, I put two more bullets into his body—so that I should take the blame. I left my fingerprints on the gun. You see, Sonia?"

"Vladimir!"

"Do you know why I chose Mr. Humberton, Sonia? Or do you even know that I went to him? It was because he is an undertaker and also a detective. I could not confess at once. That would excite suspicion. The police would discover that I was shielding someone. But if I went to him to arrange a funeral for my friend Rance who was about to commit suicide—you see. Sonia—that would start everything—the investigation—the discovery of my gun—

my finger prints. Then afterward I said I was a gangster, to make it surer. Then—"

Suddenly, Humberton spoke. His voice overbore Pobedoff's, with quiet authority. "Am I to understand that you do not know who killed Rance?"

"I do not!" the lame man said, calmly.

"And you, Sonia?"

"But, no."

The tall necrologist whirled abruptly upon the red-masked leader of the lynchers. "You have heard this man's story—and this girl's. I can add to what they said my profound conviction that they are telling the truth. Are you satisfied that you have made a mistake?"

"We are!" the man in the red domino declared, heartily. There was a general nodding of heads.

"What you have done is serious. You are all amenable to the law. You will maintain, I suppose, that you are good citizens, and that you have taken this way to stamp out lawlessness. Well—consider where the way you took led you. I shall expect you to drop these two within a short distance of police headquarters. That is the least you can do. After that, your getaway is your own affair. You, Pobedoff, will tell whoever is on duty that I have gone back to the Rance house to search for the killer, and that I should like official help. Come, Ted! We have lost too much time, already!"

AS SPANG whirled the car around, with reckless disregard for the elementary principles of safety on a dirt road with a deep ditch at one side, his chief issued a terse command. "We must develop real speed this time, Ted!"

"O.K., sir!" His turning maneuver complete, Spang stamped on the brakes with a tooth-loosening jolt, shifted gears in the same split second, and threw his weight on the accelerator. The rear wheels skidded clear of the ground. They gripped the uneven road surface, and the big machine leapt forward with a roar. The hearse driver permitted himself a joyous chuckle. "Do we crash all lights, Mr. Humberton?" he inquired respectfully.

"Yes."

"Then hold tight. This isn't going to be a funeral procession."

The necrologist leaned forward tensely. The speed at which they were traveling affected him not at all. His thoughts were racing ahead to the solution of the odd problem of the Rance killing.

"You remember what Kennedy said, Ted—about the prowler around the Rance house?" he asked.

Spang's answer was exactly what it would have been had he occupied one of this wonted spots in the morgue, instead of the driver's seat in a seventy-mile-an-hour car. "Was that the same one I heard in the house do you think?" he countered, thoughtfully.

"I think not. No doubt it was Sonia, the maid, whom you heard. But remember Kennedy is gone now. The prowler may try to, carry out his plans—whatever they are."

The car lurched into higher speed. Humberton involuntarily gripped the seat for a moment. Spang leaned across his steering wheel, peered alertly to right and left at the intersections, once or twice glanced at his impassive companion.

"This is the street," he said, surprisingly soon; then— "Hey, Mr. Humberton—what's that? There's a—"

But the keen edge of another sense had made up for the necrologist's near sightedness. He leaned forward in his seat, sniffing the air, and interrupted his assistant's exclamation with a curt— "The house is on fire! Faster, Ted!"

There was still another cross street. Ted crashed the red light squarely. The big car veered sharply to the right, slowed down, bringing Ted's chief off the seat and abruptly to his knees, and stopped within an inch of the curb.

"That's as near as we'd better go, sir. The fire department will need the ringside seats."

It was quite near enough—not more than two lots away. The sullen old house stood lurid and transfigured. Fire spouted out of its front windows. Humberton raced forward, hesitated an instant, and plunged around the side. "Find a way in, Ted!" he shouted. "We must save him. We can't wait for the firemen—they'd be too late!"

The hearse driver's sense of obedience was too well disciplined to permit a question at that moment. He followed, out of the glare, into the comparative darkness at the side. His roving eye caught the dull black of an open window.

"Here we are!" he announced, briskly. "The fire's in front. This'll be a furnace before the firemen get here, but we ought to have a minute to spare. You stay here, sir. Tell me where to look for him and I'll get him—whoever he is."

CHAPTER SEVEN
MURDER WILL SPEAK

HUMBERTON PLACED his hands deliberately on the window sill. Great height has its advantages. He raised himself easily on the sill, and squirmed over it into the room. But youth and agility have their points, too. He had hardly found his feet when the active Ted Spang was behind him. Ted had gathered himself like a cat, and vaulted over the sill. Since he was not permitted to take all the danger upon himself he was at least sharing it.

"The cellar, Ted!"

"This way, sir." The smoke was suffocating, but Spang put his head down and ran infallibly in the right direction. Talents which might have made him a distinguished burglar had been sacrificed when he took up hearse driving. The tall necrologist followed, thankful for his expert guidance.

The cellar door was off the kitchen. Reaching it and finding it shut, Ted seized the knob, but Humberton's large hand was laid on his shoulder.

"One minute, Ted," he gasped. He braced his foot against the door, and very slowly opened it an inch. There was no pressure, so he pulled it wide.

With the opening of the door, the dull roar of the flames had deepened, yet the air seemed a little clearer. There was a flickering glow from the wide cellar, but no fire to be seen. Spang descended swiftly and very cautiously.

"No fire down here," he diagnosed quietly, at the foot of the steps. "Wait a minute, though—it's breaking through at the front end. See there—right above the wood pile? That's where the flicker and smoke come from. Once it reaches that dry wood—*pouff!*"

"The wine cellar," his chief said, briefly. "That's where our man is."

"Right you are, sir—I see a light in it."

"I see nothing," the necrologist whispered.

"Bend down a little. Stand where I'm standing. The door's shut, and it fits good and tight. See?"

Humberton did as directed. At first his near-sighted eyes still perceived nothing but darkness in that direction.

Then he became aware of a slender strand of light, threaded into the darkness.

"Want me to open the door?" Spang demanded, eagerly. "We'll have to work fast. After that fire reaches the wood pile and starts shooting across, we're trapped!"

But Humberton declined to be hurried. "The man in there is not afraid of death," he replied. "I think he wants to die. He will defend his right to do so. Open the door very gradually. See whether he is armed."

"Keep right behind me, then," the driver whispered. "You'd better be where you can see just as quick as I do." He listened, his head cocked to one side. "There's a queer noise there, and it ain't the noise of the fire. Hear it?"

Humberton did not reply. Spang crept forward alertly. He reached the door—his chief just behind him—fumbled a moment, and slowly pushed. The thread of light broadened. The door swung inward, and they were able to look into the wine cellar.

THE INEXPLICABLE sound they had heard became clear. It was a queer, muffled sobbing—the sobbing of a man. He knelt beside the open grave at the farther end of the fragrant room, and an electric lantern, so placed that it shone into the excavation, emphasized at once the deep furrows and ignoble puffiness of his face.

They need not have been cautious about rousing him. His thought was only for what lay in the grave; except when he straightened a moment, groped dully in the shadows beyond his huge torso, and tilted his head back while he pulled at a bottle he found there.

Humberton stepped into the wine cellar. "Smith!" he said, sternly.

The man by the grave slowly turned his head, with something of the wavering irresolution of a gigantic measuring worm. He remained posed uncertainly upon his knees, one hand behind him, until he found the bottle again. He did not lift it to his mouth, but its presence seemed to reassure him, as he struggled to his feet.

"No!" he said, thickly. "Not Smith! Blake!"

"Blake?" The crackle of flames from the front of the cellar became a little louder, but, for the moment, Humberton had forgotten them. He walked over to the man by the open grave and looked into his face. "You called yourself 'Smith' when you worked for me. The girl who disappeared from this house was named 'Minnie Blake.'"

The big shoulders heaved. Though the man was half drunk, there was something profoundly tragic in his attitude which lent him dignity. He pointed with his right hand, still keeping the left behind him.

"Look down there. She was my sister. Buried her in lime he did, and I guess that's what preserved her. She was a good girl. She had better things coming to her than to die at the hand of a dirty hound like him. Look for yourself!"

Humberton glanced into the open grave; merely glanced, and averted his face.

"Chief!" Spang was urging tensely, just behind him. "Get him out of here! Get him out, quick! The fire's almost on us!"

The sodden man heard. No one would have credited him with keenness of ear—with keenness of any kind—but he heard. His left hand came slowly from behind him. It held no gun. He seemed to be struggling to say something, but a strident voice cut in from the main cellar: "Hey, you folks! Want to get burned to death? Out with you! Out!"

It was Detective Clyde. His red face appeared in the doorway of the wine cellar, just behind Ted Spang.

The man Blake looked at him deliberately, and smiled: "Wait a minute, mister!" he said.

His bleared eyes had cleared for the moment, purged by profound emotion. His left hand, in front of him now, held one end of a copper wire, which glistened for a few brief inches in the light then wriggled into the shadows behind the lantern.

Clyde's deep voice muttered something inarticulate. It sounded like an exclamation of horror. Blake answered, as if it had been spoken words.

"Think you're going away?" he demanded, heavily. "You're staying with me." His right forefinger stabbed toward each of them, in turn. "You—and you—and you!"

Clyde's red face had turned white. "Drop that wire!" he snarled.

BLAKE'S HAND slowly lifted, palm outward. It held a small, boxlike contrivance, attached to the end of the wire. The hand twisted a little, and a round, white push button became visible.

"Drop it, you fool!" Clyde screamed the command. All he accomplished was to bring another smile to the sodden face.

"You must know what it is, mister! Maybe you used to work in a quarry, too? Maybe you was in charge of the blasts, like I was?" He laughed, discordantly. "Maybe you can figure what's at the other end of this wire—eh? Dynamite!" His voice rose to a scream. "You hear that? Dynamite! Think you're going to get out of here? Think because I killed that dog it pays for her death? She was worth a lot more than him. She was worth more'n all of us. We're all going to pay for it—here, by her grave!"

Clyde's reply was magnificently foolish. He leapt for the mocking, tragic giant. But Humberton's long arm shot across his body like a bar, and sternly pushed him back. The voice of the flames had jumped an octave higher. It had become a ravenous snarl, rather than a roar. As the tall necrologist began to speak, soothingly, a hot wave from the cellar caught him by the throat, and he faltered. But he went on, slowly, evenly, as if talking to a child.

"Don't press the button for a minute, Blake. Detective Clyde thinks Rance didn't kill your sister. We don't want anyone to think that, do we? You and I know he did it. Do you know what Clyde says?"

As he spoke, he was inching forward, without lifting his feet from the clay floor. But Blake's eyes blinked with the cunning of madness. He laughed at the necrologist, and retreated a good twelve inches.

"Playing for time, ain't you? Trying to bluff me! It won't do you no good. See that little button? Watch me press it! Watch, now! Wa—"

A high, soaring laugh interrupted. Ted Spang, his voice ripping through the roar of the flames behind him, screamed ecstatically: "I've cut the wire! I've cut the wire! Look! Look!"

For an instant—only for an instant—Blake's eyes shifted, to where the driver's gesticulating finger pointed. In that instant, Spang's hand flicked past him, with the short, quick chop of a basket-ball player. The little box in which the fatal button was set spun from Blake's grasp. It had hardly reached the earthen floor when Clyde, leaping across the open grave, smashed his blackjack down upon the giant's head.

"Great work, Spang!" he shouted. "Grab his feet, Humberton. I'll take his head. You lead the way, Spang!"

"We can't make it," the necrologist gasped.

"We've got to make it! If Spang could cut that wire—"

"I didn't cut it. I was bluffing. Come on! We're going—out!"

"Don't stand there like that, Humberton!" The big detective was almost weeping with excitement. "Don't you understand? We've got to get out! Before the fire reaches the dynamite!"

But Humberton stubbornly shook his head. "We can't," he repeated.

Before either of them could stop him, he ran back toward the interior of the wine room. He blinked a moment at the copper wire, dully reflecting the glare of the flames. Then, with a curious chuckle of satisfaction, he followed the wire half a dozen steps into the shadow, and returned staggering under the weight of a box.

Suddenly, Clyde understood. He jumped into the grave. Humberton handed him the box. In a moment, the detective was out again, and the three of them were pushing the pile of earth over the brink until it covered the dynamite a foot deep.

They had forgotten the unconscious Blake. Now they were recalled by a stentorian laugh. He was on his feet, facing them. A wall of flame, blocking the entrance to the main cellar, reflected from his eyes. He turned and looked at it without blinking, then, with a hoarse shout, deliberately ran into the heart of the fire.

"After him!" yelled Clyde. "Crawl along the floor, where the air is. It's our only chance!"

Humberton sank to his knees, in an effort to obey. He was aware that Ted Spang, looking as if framed in fire, had caught his hand. Then he pitched forward.

HORATIO HUMBERTON had come very close to requiring the services of his own funeral parlors; but he lay instead between the clean sheets of a bed in one of the sunny wards of St. Luke's Hospital. The ward really amounted to a commodious private room, which he was sharing with Detective Clyde, who filled another bed at his right, and—resting easily at his left—with that dauntless spirit, Hearse Driver Ted Spang.

Nothing much was the matter with Humberton. His luck had held magnificently. The firemen had dragged him out suffering merely from shock. In the language of the attending physician, he was being held "for observation." Ted Spang, unfortunately, had broken an arm, besides receiving minor burns. He could account for the burns, but not for the break—yet there it was. As for Clyde, he was burned somewhat more severely, thought not dangerously, and in the part of his body where a large man might expect to be burned if crawling on hands and knees on the floor, with the fire above him.

It was the afternoon of the day following the fire. The detective had decided that his friend in the middle bed had been silent long enough. Humberton was awake, as he could see, and beyond doubt there was much the necrologist could say which would be of interest. So why should not Humberton talk?

"It was a grand way to die, at that," ventured Clyde, by way of opening the subject. "I suppose it's pretty clear that he set fire to the house and planted the dynamite, isn't it, Ho? That way, he'd go up in a funeral pyre, along with his sister's body. Would you say I was dumb, Ho, if I asked you why Rance killed her?"

Humberton turned his head and smiled at Ted Spang, who was listening, bright-eyed and attentive, to this catechism.

"I trust that I should not be so discourteous Clyde," he replied, gravely. "He killed her because she knew too much—about the little bird that was 'gone from the nest.' He had to silence her in one way or another—and what other way was there to silence a half-witted girl?"

"That's it, sir!" Ted Spang, eager and enormously interested by the turn of the discussion, broke into it. "I can see that he must have killed her, all right. But what I can't see is how this drunken bum, this brother of hers who used 'Smith' for an alias, got wise." His voice sank. "Do you remember how he said there was a dead woman looking out of the Rance house? He must have known it even then!"

" 'Known' is too definite a word, Ted. Suppose we say 'suspected.' Did you ever read 'Hamlet?' "

Ted Spang shook his head.

"I've heard of it," Clyde contributed.

"You might look it up some time." He was speaking to both of them now. "It contains a curious statement, to the effect that 'murder, though it have no tongue, will speak with most miraculous organ.' That seems to me to cover the present case very accurately. This 'drunken bum,' as you call him, Ted, became more and more suspicious. At length, he actually began to have hallucinations—at least, so I surmise. From that point, it was only a step to his vengeance. He chose a spectacular finish for himself—and us—but since we escaped I think we can afford to be charitable and credit that to his dramatic instinct." He glanced at the big detective, who lay awkwardly on his stomach. "Life, Clyde," he observed to the latter, "is a queer business."

"I've often thought so," was Clyde's rejoinder.

"An artist whose name I do not know, and who probably lived many years since, was careless," the necrologist went on. "He left the wing of a dove out of his copy of a famous painting. Because of that—solely because of that slight omission—a fraud is prevented, and two human beings are dead with violence."

"At that, it might have been worse," Ted Spang observed, philosophically.

And his chief, thinking back to a circle of masked figures near a country road, and a man in their midst with a rope around his neck, silently nodded where he lay.

THE WEREWOLF HORRORS

OUT OF THE NIGHT IT CAME—
THE BANSHEE WAIL OF THE
WEREWOLF. THREE GENERATIONS
OF CLAVERINGS HAD HARKENED
TO IT, HARKENED AND DIED AS
THEY TRACED THAT HORRID
HOWL. AND NOW A FOURTH WAS
DUE TO FOLLOW—DUE TO DROP
MANGLED BENEATH THE THRUST
OF PHANTOM FANGS.

CHAPTER ONE
DOORWAY TO DANGER

AT THE top of the path Horatio Humberton stopped. Ted Spang, two steps behind him, was carrying their joint traveling bag. It was dark—very dark. But the tall funeral director realized his hearse driver's nearness by other signs than sight. For one thing, the night was still, and Humberton could hear his breathing. It was a sound not to be confused with the long low whisper of the lake far below them. For another thing, Ted spoke.

"Where do we go from here, sir?" he inquired.

"You have your flashlight?" was his chief's counter question.

"In my pocket."

Humberton looked about him thoughtfully; at the gray union of restless water and sky behind them and the impenetrable blackness in front. "This must be the place," he said. "So far as I can tell we are at the very top of the mound." He tapped about cautiously with one foot. "The ground seems to fall away in every direction. Now, if I can find three white birches growing together in a triangle—"

"Wait till I flash the light about, sir."

"No!" Humberton bit off the word savagely; then went on, his face close to the driver's. "I don't know whether there is really any danger, Ted. Clavering, the man who

"Ted—his throat is torn out!"

wrote me, may have gone insane in this wilderness. His letter rather points to that. But I am going to do exactly what he directs. He says I am to use a light for one purpose only."

"Very well, sir," returned Ted, undisturbed. "You're to use it for a signal of some sort, I suppose?"

"I am to stand between two of the three white birches, with the third one at my back and between me and the lake, and then I am to point the light downward into the valley while I count ten."

Ted was scurrying about, causing a busy rustle of dead leaves, like a hound picking up a scent. His voice came cheerfully from a few feet away. "Sounds good, sir. The way this is starting off maybe we'll see some action. Here's your birches. One of them is on the side by the lake, so I guess you stand between the other two. I can just make out a path going down the side of the hill. It looks to be at right angles to the one we came up."

Humberton joined his eager assistant. He was studying the faintly luminous dial of his wrist watch. "It lacks ten minutes of eleven, Ted. If the train had been a little later, we could hardly have got here in time. I am to flash the signal at exactly eleven o'clock. Clavering will be watching. If we spot an answering light, we are to descend this path. He says it leads straight to his front door."

"You mean there's a house down there?" Ted asked.

"A large house. It is Clavering's ancestral mansion. I never saw a darker place than that valley, Ted. Can you distinguish a house down there? I can't."

The hearse driver was silent for a moment. Humberton sensed that he was straining his eyes into the blackness below them. But he grunted a negative. "Not a thing, sir. I can't even tell it is a valley.

"Can you see the path at your feet?"

"Fairly well. I can lead the way easy enough when we go down, if that's what you mean. Once we get the signal, I'll take you right to it. Good thing we travel light."

"We may not get it." Humberton still held the watch close to his face. It's dim glow glinted against his thick spectacles. "We are to wait for ten minutes after flashing our own signal, and if nothing appears are to make our way back to the road, thence to the village inn. It will be a walk of about a mile, Clavering writes."

"Then we come back in the daytime?"

"No. We wait till this time tomorrow night."

Ted chuckled. "Gets better and better, don't it, sir?" he commented. "Clavering must be crazy, all right. What time is it now?"

"Half a minute before eleven. Hand me the flashlight, Ted. Now—one thing more. He writes that if we hear the howl of a wolf after he shows his light, we are not to waste a second. We are to run for our lives to his front door."

Ted whistled. Apparently it was the only appropriate reply he could think of for the moment. Before he had time for any other, his chief pushed him silently aside, stepped between the two birches, and switched on the light.

It shot a narrow, dancing beam down the descending path. The exceeding straightness of the path became plain. Birches to right and left must have been felled to make a broad way from the summit of the mound to the house. The end of the beam mushroomed against something vague and huge. Humberton permitted his hand to shift upward for an instant, and the beam revealed a massive front door, flanked with slitlike windows on each side, with other sealed and brooding windows of a second and even a third story above them, and still higher a brick chimney against the sky.

He counted slowly to ten, then slid his thumb along the switch. Darkness closed in once more.

"Look sharp, Ted. Your eyes are better than mine," he cautioned.

"Nothing yet, sir." Spang was crouched alertly, peering down the slope. "Ah-h-h!" he exclaimed, suddenly. "No, it's too small. Must be a firefly. It isn't, either; it's bigger. It's a light. Our signal, sir!"

"Come!" his chief directed.

But the driver did not move. He whispered: "Listen!"

Then Humberton caught the sound, too. Far away and melodious, rising and falling in the forest-scented air. It stopped a moment; began again—nearer.

Ted Spang laughed a little grimly. "Guess it means 'Scram!'" he said. "That's a wolf, or I never heard one. It's apt to be closer than it sounds. They generally are. Let me have your hand, sir, and I'll lead the way down this path so fast you'll think you're falling!"

BEFORE HUMBERTON could reply, his wrist was snatched in Ted's firm grasp, and he found himself plunging downward with giant strides. Ted had not snapped on the light again. He seemed led through the darkness by instinct. Their descent was so swift that the dim shapes of the birches, shouldering up closely to the broad path, were little guidance. Instead, they were charged with danger. Once or twice even Ted's skill failed to keep the tall necrologist from grazing a tree as he hurtled past it. The dead leaves, too, were perilous. Ted slipped on them, but they could not slow him up.

The howl of the wolf came again. It seemed behind them, just above.

"Faster." Ted panted.

Suddenly, they left the trees. The descent became more gradual. They were on a broad lawn, with the house, black and enormous, just beyond.

The howl changed to an eager whine.

"Open the door." Ted shouted, frantically.

Humberton wrenched his wrist free. He could run faster now by himself.

A thin vertical streak of light appeared in front of them. It widened. The light trickled down a flight of broad stone steps. Ted spat curt advice back to his chief. He was still in the lead, though by inches. "Jump the steps, sir! It's almost on us!"

They leaped together. The door yielded to their impact and opened further. They plunged through it. Someone on the inside slammed it shut. It closed with a reverberating roar.

"Phew!" Ted's cheerful, rather sharp-featured face, now visible in the light of a swinging lamp, revealed his agitation. "That was quite a workout, sir. Lucky I didn't drop the bag. I'd like to know who opened the door and slammed it after us like that." He gazed curiously about the large, square room in which they found themselves. "I don't see anybody here, but that door didn't swing by itself."

His employer was too busy to answer at once. He was actively examining the room. They seemed alone in it. But were they?

The strong outer door was reinforced with a wooden bar that had dropped into position when it shut. There were two other doors—one at each side of the room. Humberton examined them and found them locked. A log flickered in the fireplace just opposite where they had entered. Above the fireplace and on both sides of it were long shelves of books. The necrologist shuffled about, peering into the book-cases. Ted Spang, too, made an inspection of his own.

"The front door is operated mechanically from some other place," Humberton said, at length. "No doubt you have noticed the levers, Ted. As to the other doors, they seem bolted. The books are highly significant, too. I fancy we shall do well to make ourselves comfortable and await our host."

Ted flung himself into an easy chair before the fire, and lighted a cigarette. "Got any idea what was chasing us?" he inquired, casually.

"Not as yet. Unless—" Humberton had continued his walk about the room, but now he sat down facing his driver. "I was going to say—unless the books furnish a key to it. But that is hardly possible. You've been very considerate not to question me about this trip, Ted."

Ted Spang shrugged his shoulders. "I figured you'd tell me when you got ready, sir," he returned.

"Quite true. I am ready now." He fumbled in the inside pocket of his dusty black coat. "You are aware, Ted, that business has been poor with us these last few months?"

"Lousy," agreed Ted.

"Precisely. The other day I received a letter—the most remarkable letter ever addressed to me. I have it here, Ted. It begins abruptly. It says: 'I am expecting to be killed at some time in the week beginning October 16th. Can you and one trusted friend leave for this place on the 15th, and spend a week with me, or at least remain until my demise? I am enclosing New York draft for $1,000.00 as a retainer fee. Should I be alive and unharmed on October 24th, you will receive $4,000.00 more. Speak to no one of this, not even to your friend—except for absolutely necessary instructions to him—until you are in my home.'" Humberton glanced up over his spectacles. "That is why I have been so close-mouthed, Ted. When a client begins his communication with a draft for $1,000.00, any reasonable request he makes should be complied with. I shall not read the rest of the letter to you. It consists merely of detailed instructions as to the manner of our arrival. You already know what that manner was. The letter is signed 'Roger Clavering'."

"Ever hear of him before?" Spang inquired.

"Never."

"He may be as mad as a hatter."

"Very likely." Humberton lighted one of his long, black cigars.

"You're sure the New York draft was good, sir?" Ted persisted.

"I cashed it."

"Oh, well." Ted grinned, and settled back comfortably in his chair. "He can be plenty loony for a thousand berries!"

Humberton smiled. The adventure on which they were embarked might be wild and incredible, but he knew that this buoyant assistant of his would stay with it to the finish. Ted—

A bolt rattled, the door at the western end of the room opened, and a voice said: "Good evening, gentlemen!"

CHAPTER TWO
WEREWOLF

THOUGH HORATIO Humberton earned the principal part of his living by the direction of funerals, another science, the study of crime, was much nearer his heart. When it came to embalming a murdered man, he could do a good job; but he would be far more enthusiastic in the task of finding the murderer. He enjoyed studying people—deducing their strengths and weaknesses, and more particularly their criminal tendencies.

And so he had sized up Roger Clavering even before he saw him; sized him up as a coward. The letter pointed to that. It seemed to have been written by one who had given way completely to his fears. Were they imaginary fears? Humberton was not sure. But as to the writer's cowardice he had little doubt.

And now their host stepped into the room. Physically, he was a little man, with a rather large head, the gray hair carefully brushed back from a broad brow. His eyes were deep set. He was dressed with almost foppish care. These things the necrologist was able to observe in the scant interval before he grasped his host's outstretched hand. Then he felt his own by no means feeble palm caught in a powerful grip, and the other turned so that the light of the swinging oil lamp flooded his face and made it visible in all its details.

It was not the face of a coward. It was the face of a resolute man.

He shook Ted Spang's hand, too, and threw himself into a chair with a quick, nervous movement. He lighted a cigarette and proffered one to Ted Spang. The necrologist already was smoking his own black cigar.

"You have been wondering, Mr. Humberton, whether I am crazy," he began abruptly. "Well—you have had a good look at me now. How about it? Am I?"

Humberton thought of the letter, the strange journey and the incredible arrival, the thousand dollars. His eyes twinkled behind the thick glasses. "I suppose we are all crazy in one way or another," he said. "You seem no more so than I am. Probably you are less so."

"Fair enough." The little man smiled, dryly. "Yet I might point out that there is something quite material about my madness—something which would have caught you had you been a little slower of foot, or I a trifle less alert to let you in. But the sooner we get down to an explanation, the better. Suppose I begin by asking you to examine the windows in this room. That will be a good way to break the ice."

Humberton smiled. "I did that before you came in," he said, "The windows have heavy steel shutters. I notice they are new, and you have thick window shades, too, extending several inches on each side of the sash. You saw that, Ted?"

The driver nodded.

"That explains, of course, why the house seemed absolutely dark from outside. Are all your windows muffled the same way, Mr. Clavering?"

"All," their host confirmed. "And the front door—"

"I observed the levers," the necrologist put in.

"Ah! I must remember that I am dealing with a detective. There are reasons, Mr. Humberton, why it is wise to be able to open and shut that door without being too near it. Tonight, for instance, if your pursuer had followed you into this room, I should have preferred to be absent."

Ted Spang involuntarily shivered at these words, but the little man went on blandly. "Possibly you noticed my books, too?" he suggested.

"I did!" Humberton made the answer so emphatic that their host laughed.

"Another evidence of my madness? And perhaps you consider the kind of fortress I live in still another. Yet don't forget—don't forget, gentlemen—that there is something in the woods which is better kept outside. Much better, I assure you! The house was built in Eighteen-hundred, by my great-grandfather, but I am responsible for the fortifications. Good old man! He died in his chair before this very fireplace. He was the last of my progenitors to reach old age—and the last to die indoors."

HE STOPPED, abruptly. Humberton stared at him with some surprise, but the hearse driver, whose senses were exceptionally acute, started to his feet. Then the sound came. It had been so soft at first—like an added sharpness in the whisper of the wind—that only their host and Ted Spang had grasped its significance. Now there was no mistaking it—a long, vibrant scream.

Their host sprang up. His lips were compressed, and his face had turned pale. "Remain here, gentlemen," he said. He walked rapidly to the door by which he had entered. There he turned again. "If you leave this room, I can't be answerable for your lives. I shall be back."

He was gone. The bolt rasped on the farther side of the door.

Ted sat down, heavily. Even his habitual calm had deserted him for a moment. "What was it, sir?" he whispered.

Grim-mouthed, Humberton looked about him slowly, endeavoring with his near-sighted eyes to take in every foot of wall and ceiling. "Would you say it was the sound we heard in the woods, Ted?" he asked, at length.

"No, sir."

"Have you ever heard anything like it before?"

The driver shook his head.

"I am not sure, Ted," his chief continued thoughtfully, "but I think that I have heard a scream like that at some time in the past. It is human—but not normally human. There is nothing to do but wait for the explanation."

Their waiting was not for long. The door by which their host had left them reopened, and the little man stepped quietly into the room, carrying a small book in his hand. He was very pale. But there was no change in the smooth, brisk tones of his voice.

"Did you hear anything after that first noise?" he asked, looking from one to the other; and, upon receiving a negative answer: "Sometimes this is the only room where it can be heard. I don't like it to continue long. It's devilish hard on the nerves of people not accustomed to it. I suppose you'd swear it was made by a human throat?"

"Ted and I were discussing that," Humberton returned. "We were not sure."

"As a matter of fact, it isn't. It is a noise made by the wind in the room just above this—the room from which I flashed my signal to you and opened the front door. The house is old, you see. There are long, drafty halls. When the wind is in a certain quarter, and three of the upstairs doors are open in line, it produces that eery noise. I rushed upstairs to shut the doors, and you see the noise has stopped."

"And the danger you mentioned?" Humberton inquired dryly.

The little man stared a moment. "Oh, you mean what I told you—to remain in this room?" He laughed. "That had nothing to do with the noise. The danger is outside. I didn't want you to go out there. Now, you are both tired, no doubt, so I shall get down to business. There are a few things you need to be told tonight—just a few. Then we can all go to bed."

HE THREW himself into an armchair, and flicked his cigarette ash into the grate. "Ever have any insanity in your family, Mr. Humberton?" he inquired, abruptly.

"I am happy to say not."

"You should be happy. Unless you have had it, you don't know what horror is. I know—yet I never saw our insane member. Think of it! Here is a man who died—if he did

die—in Eighteen Fifty-seven—seventy-five years ago—
and his shadow has hung over me all my life. You can read
about it at your convenience." He held up the little book
he had brought back with him. "The whole miserable, wild
tale is here, in my grandfather's diary."

"And you are telling it to us now?" Humberton suggested,
as he paused.

"Only enough so you will understand—in case anything
happens tonight. Things do happen around here," he added,
with a curt laugh. "My great-grandfather had two sons,
you know—Denis and Sard. Denis was my own grandfather. Sard went mad. Let me see—" he closed his eyes—
"that was in Eighteen Fifty-one—his first seizure, I mean.
He was confined in this house for six years. He blamed
Denis for it. He escaped again and again. They brought
him back. And each time he gnashed his teeth and swore
to kill his brother, Denis. Yet it was a choice between this
place and a madhouse, Mr. Humberton. You wouldn't feel
there was really any blame there, would you?"

"I should hardly say so," the necrologist returned, judi-
cially.

"No one would—no one in his senses. Then there came
the night of August Thirteenth, Eighteen Fifty-seven—
when my great-grandfather had been dead seven years.
Sard lacked just a week of being fifty years old. That night
they did not bring him back. You follow me? These dates
are important."

"Eighteen Fifty-seven, and he was a week short of fifty
years old," Humberton responded.

"That's it. You will see in a moment why I'm so particular. Now, on the night he disappeared, Sard was locked in
an upstairs room—on the third floor. He broke out, crept
down the stairs, and surprised his brother sitting before

this fireplace. As I understand it, Denis was about where I am now. My back is toward the east door, as you see. Sard pushed that door open, tiptoed across the floor, throttled Denis from behind. My grandfather never had a chance."

"He was killed?" the necrologist suggested.

"That's one of the odd things about it—he was not. It would appear that Sard never intended to kill him. For when Denis came to himself, he found the front door swinging wide and a note in his brother's writing addressed to him and pinned to his coat. Now, this is what the note said. I have had it by heart ever since boyhood. It is an important family tradition, you see. It read: 'I have gone to the wolves. Within a week of your fiftieth birthday, you too will go to them. And so it shall be for your descendants, till there are no more.'"

"That note is in this book?"

"A copy of it, in my grandfather's handwriting. The original didn't come down to me. The next morning, they found Sard's body on the lawn, near the edge of the woods. His throat had been torn out by a wolf."

"Let me ask you something," Humberton put in, as their host paused. "Does the record show that your grandfather attached much importance to the warning in the note?"

"I can't say that it does. In fact, you will notice all through the family history in this little book of ours, that the feelings of the writers are largely kept to themselves. I seem to have come of a courageous race. God knows, I wish more of their courage had descended to me! They wrote down what happened—wrote it down coldly and accurately— and left the comment to their readers. The next record I need to tell you about is in my father's hand—he was a young man of twenty at the time—and that is just as terse and precise as the other entries. Let me read it to you. I can't possibly put it into less words that he used." He leafed through the little book, holding it to the light of the log fire. "Here it is. It is dated January Twenty-seventh, Eighteen Sixty-two. He says: 'Found my dear; father's body last night in the woods, his throat terribly slashed apparently by a wolf. He lacked five days of being fifty.'"

HE SHUT the book again, threw his cigarette stub into the fire, and leaned forward in his chair, silently staring into the blaze.

"I fear that I'm a poor bough on the family tree," the little man went on. "I haven't the courage of my grandfather and my father, and I don't keep up the written family record as they did. Oh, I've made a few notes, at odd times, but the most important event of all has to come out of my memory. I never brought myself to write it down. I didn't forget it, however—no danger of that. Even a ten-year-old, as I was at the time, couldn't forget it."

He relaxed in his chair and looked dreamily at his small audience: Ted, darting uneasy glances about the room, Ted's chief with his cold eyes fixed on the narrator.

"Things seem to change very little from generation to generation in this old house. Here I am tonight, a bachelor, cared for by my capable housekeeper, Mrs. Tommaso and her daughter, Nina. I can go back forty years, and there is another housekeeper, Mrs. Mapes. There was a butler, too—Jory. Mrs. Tommaso sends to the village when she needs any masculine help about the place, so nowadays we have no butler. But the house has altered very little. Here we sit in the same room with the same old furniture, and the same oil lamp. I can almost imagine that it is the night of July Third, Eighteen Ninety-two and that Mrs. Mapes is running through the house screaming that a wolf has howled on the lawn and that father has rushed out like a madman. I was sitting in this chair, by the way. I wonder whether it is the same chair grandfather sat in when Sard came down the stairs and snatched at his throat. It has a high back, you see. I should have been in bed hours before, but I was slouched down here reading and no one noticed me. After a boy's mother is gone, what he does isn't of so much importance.

"Well, here I sat, and in came Mrs. Mapes, wild-eyed. Jory must have been in one of the west rooms. He rushed in before she'd got as far as my chair. I remember he stood a moment staring at her. Then the meaning of what she said got into his brain. He grabbed up the poker—a poker, to fight a wolf—and ran out the front door. I was just behind him. He noticed me then and tried to turn me back. But of course it was no use. Well—" He shrugged his shoulders, listlessly. "You can guess what we found, Mr. Humberton. He lay on the lawn. He was on his back—my father, who had never harmed anyone. It was the same death. Four days more, and he would have been fifty years old."

He rose, rather more stooped than he had been, and gazing moodily at the floor. "The coroner returned a verdict, by the way, of death by wolves. That was exactly the same verdict as in the case of my grandfather and my great-uncle."

The others had risen, too. Humberton gazed thoughtfully about the room, as if to get the feel of the warm, comfortable place, with its fragrant smell of old book bindings, tinged with acrid wood smoke, and the rich shadows of the massive furniture. The shadows shifted with slow, stately movements, in sympathy with the hardly perceptible swing of the hanging oil lamp.

"That's the story?" the necrologist asked.

"That is the story."

"Your books are interesting. I hope to look into them while I am here. It is quite the best collection of werewolf lore I ever saw."

"I have made a special study of the subject, lately."

Humberton nodded. "And now, Mr. Clavering," he said, "just why did you send for me?"

The little man smiled at him. "That's so," he returned. "I didn't make that clear, did I? A week from tomorrow I am to be fifty years old. That answers your question, I am sure. I have told you the story tonight because I want you to be in immediate possession of it, but I think we can go to bed in security. This strange, mad thing—whatever it is—seems to have followed certain invariable rules. It strikes within the period of a week—never before or afterward. It does its work after midnight but before dawn. I feel perfectly safe tonight. I even doubt whether any real danger threatened you this evening, though of course it was best to assume that it did. You and Mr. Spang have adjoining rooms in the east wing. Mrs. Tommaso made the beds before she retired. I myself sleep in the west wing. No doubt you are both sleepy, so I shan't keep you up any longer unless you have some question to ask?"

The necrologist shook his head. "My questions can wait till morning," he said.

"Then let me ask you one. I shall sleep the better for knowing your opinion on this point. I have told you briefly the stories of my grandfather, my great-uncle, and my father. You know how they died. In each case that death occurred in the week before they would have been fifty years old. Could that fact have been mere coincidence?"

For a long moment Humberton returned his host's stare of eager inquiry. Then he replied, curtly: "No!"

CHAPTER THREE
"WE HAVEN'T
BEGUN YET!"

THE HALLWAYS were broad but dark. Following the lead of his host, who carried a small oil lamp, Humberton had directed his gaze at each black corner after they had reached the top of the stairs, and had made mental notes of directions. It was a vast house, long and sprawling. He had been comfortably conscious of Ted's crisp footsteps behind him, and of the fact that Ted probably would retain his bearings perfectly. He looked now about the broad room which was to be his, and again felt comfort in his driver's nearness, separated from him only by a connecting door.

There was a quiet knock and Ted stepped into the room. He gazed about him with a chuckle, and grinned cheerfully at his employer. "We've been in some hot spots, sir, but I'm betting on this one to beat them all," he observed. "It's a fine house, though, no mistaking that. Look at this furniture. Even though the light is terrible, you can see it's the real thing. That four-poster bed you're going to sleep in could hold an elephant just as easy, and there's the mate to it in my room. And, speaking of the light, have you happened to take a squint out the window?"

The necrologist shook his head.

"Well, there's a moon, sir—now we don't need it, and are all set to pound our ears for the rest of the night." He yawned, heartily. "If you don't want me for anything else, sir, I'm going to turn in quick."

His coat and vest were off and he was removing his shoes while he spoke. Horatio Humberton, however, was still fully clad. He looked thoughtfully at his assistant. "I gather that you are sleepy, Ted?" he suggested.

"Sleepy?" Ted hesitated catching a glint in his chief's eye. "Aren't we done, sir? Is there something else on tonight?" he demanded, abruptly.

"We haven't begun yet," the necrologist said, grimly. "Why do you think we are being put to bed this way, by a man who declares that he fears for his life? If there is no danger tonight, what did we hear in the woods? What chased us to this house?"

It seemed that a few words could have a miraculous effect on Ted Spang. He stared for a moment—then, with a laugh, he began putting on his shoes again. "Did you ask me whether I'm sleepy, sir?" he inquired, innocently. "Why, I couldn't go to sleep if you paid me! I don't know when I've felt less like it. What I want to do is run out and romp around on the lawn with one of those what-you-call-ems. When do we start?"

"Sit down, Ted," his master returned. "Suppose we sit on the side of the bed. We can talk then without raising our voices. We need to talk. Unless all my instincts are wrong, we've never been in a more ticklish position. Usually I can see at least a glimmer of light in anything; but I can't in this. It's the most outlandish, inexplicable thing I've ever known."

"Maybe it's just a real wolf, after all," the driver suggested.

"A real wolf? Oh, yes—possibly. I'm not thinking of the wolf. I am thinking of Clavering. Why is it worth a thousand dollars to him to have me here?"

Ted's bewilderment was plain. He scrutinized his employer's face, but nothing he saw there helped him in the least. "Maybe I'm dumb, sir," he said, "but I should say that if he's a rich man and thinks he's likely to be killed in the next week, a thousand isn't any too much to put up for a little life insurance."

HUMBERTON DID not reply. Instead, he walked to the window and looked out at the broad expanse of lawn, and the trees bounding it, now shimmering in limpid moonlight. To the right the tapering end of the mound could be seen, with the lake rippling beyond it. He sighed, and resumed his seat beside the wondering hearse driver.

"Ted," he said, "I have seen you when you were dressed for a social affair. It seems to me that you use excellent taste in your clothes. That is hardly in my line. I come to you, therefore, as to somewhat of an expert. What did you think of Clavering's clothing?"

"Couldn't have been finer," the driver replied, promptly. "Looked like Fifth Avenue to me. Take his tie, now. I rather go in for ties. That one Clavering had on was an exclusive pattern, if I know anything about it. I'll bet it set him back ten to fifteen dollars if it cost a cent. And the rest of his togs were right up to it."

Humberton nodded. "I am glad to hear you confirm my amateur impressions," he commended. "There were some other little points, too. Did you notice that his hands were very nicely manicured?"

"I did, sir. When he was reading that diary the light showed them up."

"And still another thing. I observed this, but I can't even begin to see any reason in it. I refer to his shoes. You haven't, by any chance, a comment to make on his shoes?"

"They were good. I doubt whether you could buy much better."

"True. They were in keeping with the rest of his clothing. The particular thing I have in mind is that when he came back, after going out when he heard that odd cry, he had changed to another pair."

"Good Lord, sir!" Ted's eyes were rounded with astonishment. "What, in the name of common sense—"

"I have no idea of the reason—no idea, whatever, Ted. The second pair of shoes had ornamental perforations across the toe caps, the first pair did not. Anyway, the matter of the shoes may be a mere side issue. But I am wondering, too, why a man who is up-to-the-minute in his clothing and his personal grooming, and who very evidently is wealthy, should not install electric lights in his home? Certainly, he is not a stupid man. He must know that he could buy a home lighting plant for a few hundred dollars."

"That does seem queer," Ted agreed, thoughtfully.

"We come here," the necrologist went on, "in response to a wildly fantastic letter. It would not be a letter to take seriously for a minute save for the substantial fee enclosed with it. From its general tenor, and from the weak, uncertain handwriting, I expect to find an infirm man, half mad with terror. Do we find that kind of man, Ted?"

"Not so far as I could see," the driver declared.

"On the contrary, we find a man with a strong face and a quick, incisive manner; a man of courage, I believe. If he is afraid, to the point of offering five thousand dollars to save his life, undoubtedly the danger that threatens him— whatever it may be—is not imaginary."

Ted nodded.

"While we are with him, we hear an outlandish noise. I don't know what made that noise, Ted, but we can both testify that he was there in the room with us when it came.

It was not the wind. It came from a human throat. Now, tell me something. You will recall that he went out of the room when we heard the noise, and that he was gone for a few minutes. That was when he changed his shoes. Did you notice his face when he returned?"

"I thought it seemed kind of white."

"Was he terror-stricken?"

"Not any more than before, I should say, sir."

"That's my point, Ted. He was pale, but not particularly unstrung. I think he was pale with anger."

THE DRIVER'S cheerful face revealed his lively curiosity at this suggestion. "That's certainly interesting, sir," he said. "And why was he angry, do you think?"

"I don't know." Humberton rested his elbows on his knees and shook his head dolefully. "Not only that, Ted, but at this moment I haven't even a theory. I sit here tangled in a maze of contradictions, with no clue that seems to lead through them. In such a situation, the safest course is to assume the worst, which is that there is danger tonight, in spite of what Clavering said to the contrary."

"That's O.K. with me, sir," Ted declared. "What do we do?"

"I'm coming to that. You are armed, I suppose?"

"I've got my forty-five."

"I am not, of course. A gun in my hands would be dangerous to everything but the target. Now, Ted, we have one definite fact to go on with respect to the peril here. We believe that something followed us to the front door of the house."

"You bet we do!" Ted agreed, positively.

"That means that the danger is outside, in the grounds. The family history, however trustworthy it may or may not be, points to that, too. None of the victims were killed in the house. Perhaps by tomorrow we can clarify our reasoning, by questioning Clavering and examining the old records, but if we are to protect him tonight I believe we had better go out."

Ted stood up and rubbed his hands together, after the fashion of one about to plunge into an icy pool and relishing the prospect. "I knew this was going to be good, sir!" he exclaimed. "Now, maybe I can give you a little surprise. I take it you don't want to look up Clavering and ask him to let us out if you can help it. What I mean is, this is going to be private. We sneak out, and for all he knows we're safe in our little beds. That's the ticket, sir?"

"Yes, if we can possibly arrange it so," his chief concurred. "What is your plan, Ted?"

"I kept my eyes open when he was bringing us along the hall. You noticed what a lot of dark corners there are, and little passages that don't seem to lead anywhere? Well, I spotted one that had stairs going down. That lamp he had wasn't much good, but he tilted it or something just as we passed there. Maybe I'm mistaken—I don't think I am. And if I'm right, I can find those stairs again in the dark. They seem to lead out at the back of the house. Suppose I step into the hall now and have a look? What do you say, sir?"

Humberton laughed, quietly. He was always receiving fresh proofs that this young man, who followed the prosaic occupation of hearse driver, had the instincts of a born adventurer. "By all means, Ted!" he said.

TED UNLOCKED the door of the bedroom with no noise, and was gone. Humberton walked to the window again. He looked out at the moonlit lawn, and wished that he had been looking when the change had come from opaque darkness to this. It must have been a matter of only a few minutes. The moon had been behind the woods, then it had risen above them. That was all. Now it was even possible to see the straight, broad path by which they had descended from the top of the mound.

"Well, what do you think I found?"

Humberton turned, with a suppressed exclamation. He had not heard Ted come in.

"The stairs are there, all right," Ted proceeded to report. "There's a door leading to the outside. There's a bolt on the door—they seem to be strong for bolts around here. But—get set for a shock, sir—the door was open!"

"You mean unbolted?"

"I mean open and swinging."

Humberton bad stepped toward the bed, unconsciously, as he first heard Ted's voice. Now be sat down upon it, rather suddenly. "Open and swinging!" he repeated.

"Just that, sir. What do you think it means?"

"It means—" He stood, as abruptly as he had sat down, and clapped his shapeless felt hat firmly upon his head. "It means, Ted, that something is already happening. Come!"

It was Ted who had presence of mind to blow out the lamps in both rooms. He did it with speed, and also locked the door of Humberton's room behind him after they were in the hall. Then he took his chief's hand and led him swiftly through the dark passage. The near-sighted necrologist had learned to rely on Ted's eyes as fully as Ted did on his employer's reasoning powers.

They turned right into a somewhat lighter hallway. It was made so by reflected moonlight on the ceiling. A breeze met them, freighted with the fresh, cool breath of the woods. The reason for the light became clear. The wide-open door at the foot of the stairs was a luminous rectangle, looking out upon an expanse of waving, moon-transfigured grass. They were at the back of the house, but the moon-light, coming from the east, flooded front and rear alike. Farther to their right the shadow of the building sliced off the lawn like a knife. Beyond that were trees. The house had been built in the center of a great cleared space in the forest, with the mound, higher even than the chimneys, between its front and the lake; as if the builder, forced by some compulsion to be near the water, nevertheless feared to look out upon it, so hid his dwelling behind the mound.

"Shall we work round to the front, sir?" Ted inquired, in a whisper.

"I think so. Keep near the house."

"What's your plan—just to wait?"

"What else can we do?" Humberton retorted.

"Not a thing, sir." Ted was calm and cheerful as if they had been discussing some commonplace in the austere privacy of the funeral parlors. "Unless—" He stopped, drew in his breath sharply, and grasped his chief's arm. They had reached the corner, from which the front lawn was visible. "Look there, sir! By the edge of the woods!"

CHAPTER FOUR

THE BODY ON
THE GROUND

SOMETHING WAS running by the edge of the woods. The overhang of the trees cut off the brilliant moonlight, and the runner kept in the shadow. All that was visible was a white figure, silent and fleet.

"It's heading for the path we came down!" the driver surmised.

"We must follow," Humberton said, shortly.

Ted Spang needed no pressing. He was off in a straight line across the moonlit lawn, with his chief, whose legs though much longer lacked the speed of youth, trailing behind. Not very far behind. Ted was a bare fifty yards in the rear of the fleeting figure when it turned into the path and began climbing upward, and Humberton was close on his heels.

"It's a girl, sir!" Ted panted.

"Catch her!" his chief urged.

Saying that was easier than doing it. The white-clad girl climbed almost as rapidly as she had sped on the level ground. Both men slipped again and again on fallen leaves, but she seemed to skim along with the grace of a swallow. Going uphill, Ted had an advantage over his tall employer. Long legs afford too much leverage for easy climbing. The driver forged ahead.

His quarry, however, still held her lead. She reached the top. It was the spot in the center of the three birches where Humberton had flashed his signal. Here the moon broke through between the trees to create a little plot of clear, pale light. She paused. The lake breeze whipped her draperies about her. For an instant she looked back at them.

Ted shouted to her frantically: "Stop where you are! That's a cliff!"

It might have been a summons to doom. For she whirled suddenly, and without a trace of hesitation jumped off.

The kindly driver's shout of warning changed to something like a sob. He had reached the top a second too late.

"She's done it, sir!" he lamented. "She's—" Then he looked over the edge. "There's a path! I can see her flying down it! Come on, sir!"

Humberton saw him disappear, as the girl had done. And when the necrologist was himself at the top, a moment afterward, his eyes could dimly discern two figures descending what looked at first sight to be sheer cliff. They were appearing in patches of moonlight and vanishing again, only to come into view farther down. The girl still kept her lead. The lake had turned rougher; its smooth whisper earlier in the evening was changed to a pulsating roar, but the scuffle of their swift descent was still audible. Ted glanced up in one of the luminous patches and apparently saw his chief's face looking down, for he let out an unintelligible shout.

Horatio Humberton groaned. He had little doubt of his ability to make that wild descent, but he knew how he would feel later if he did. Still, there seemed no help for it. The beginning of the path was there, in the moonlit space at his feet. He started down.

It was steep. Almost at once his feet slid from beneath him on a mat of dead leaves, and he had done a dozen fast yards before his left shoulder snagged against a tree. With his legs under him again, he blundered into a sudden dip which necessitated a short series of giant strides. He was net usually a profane man, but his exclamations, while righting himself against another tree which had particularly rough bark, probably were heard by Ted. Then the descent eased a little, and he managed it with fair credit. At the very bottom, however, a large pool of dead leaves masked a deep hollow. Ted shouted a warning, but too late. His chief ended the downward journey with a giant somersault, and landed squarely on his back on the glistening beach.

"Hurt, sir? Any bones broken?" the driver inquired, anxiously.

THE NECROLOGIST sat up. "Nothing serious has happened to me, thank you, Ted," he replied, with cold dignity. "But I fear it will be some days before I can take any pleasure in sitting down. Where is she?"

"Right out there, sir."

Ted helped him to his feet, and he looked in the direction indicated.

"A rowboat!"

"Yes, sir. She was in it and off before I had a chance to reach her. I never saw anything slicker."

"But where can she be going?"

"Out into the lake, so far as I can see," the driver answered. "She can't be just running away from us, either. She was running before she ever saw us." He stopped, abruptly. "Good Lord, sir! Do you hear it?"

The long, melodious howl was somewhere above them—somewhere on the further side of the mound. It rose and fell like a wild solo above the chorus of the waves.

Ted patted his pocket with satisfaction. "Anyway, I didn't drop my gun," he said. "You can call the thing that makes that noise any fancy name you want to, sir, but it sounds like an ordinary wolf to me. And if it's a wolf, one of the pills from this little forty-five will stop it. Look there!" he pointed down the beach. "There's a regular wall of rocks and dirt running right out into the lake. Someone did a lot of work to make this a private beach. That's why the girl climbed up on the mound and came down the way she did, instead of going around. Let's hope this wolf or what-you-call-it has to do that, too, if he's after us. We'll have a good chance to pot him when he reaches the bottom of the path."

But Humberton was not listening. He was more interested in the view over the lake. His eyes, none too good for distant vision, still could make out the figure of the girl rowing farther and farther out. But was she doing so now? "I believe she has stopped, Ted," he said.

"She's safe enough from us out there," the driver returned, caustically. "Look how her boat rocks! I don't know whether I'd like to be rowing in those waves or not. Wait a minute." He shaded his eyes with his hand. "She's coming back!"

There was no doubt of it. She was rowing straight toward shore. Soon she waved to them.

Ted laughed suddenly. "I know the answer, sir! She's heard the wolf, too. She's coming back to take us out there before he gets us. Maybe she was running away from him all the time, and didn't even know we were after her till she saw us on the beach in the moonlight."

The weird, lilting howl came again, and Humberton glanced anxiously over his shoulder. It was nearer, he thought. Ted noted his uneasiness, and chuckled, reassuringly. "It's just coming down the wind, sir. I know what wolves sound like. If the girl's going to pick us up, we'll be out in the lake before that fellow even gets his toes wet. I only wish he'd try swimming after us!"

The boat was near shore. Its occupant steadied it with a short, expert stroke. Then it shot forward like an arrow, almost to their feet. The girl stood up and beckoned to them, frantically.

Humberton hesitated a moment. "Where do you wish to take us?" he demanded.

She did not answer. Her gestures merely became more urgent. She stamped her foot on the rowing seat.

HORATIO HUMBERTON, peering at her through his thick glasses, observed that her lips were parted as if she were screaming to them, though no intelligible sound came forth. Her face, beautiful in the moonlight, with dark eyes and flying, wind-tossed hair, was alive with excitement. She jumped from the boat and tried to drag him to it. "She is deaf-and-dumb, Ted," he said. "We must take her on faith. We must go."

"Very good, sir. Both of you jump in and I'll shove off," the driver concurred, with no sign of astonishment.

She sensed their agreement instantly, leapt in, and extended a small, firm hand, to steady the tall necrologist. He made a gesture to take the oars, but when she waved him sharply aside did not press the point.

"I believe she intends to row, Ted," he said, as the driver, having given the boat a shove, landed lightly in the prow.

"She might as well," Ted returned. "She certainly knows how, and I'd hate to try and figure out where she wants us to head for. Is it just a boat ride, do you think, sir, or are we going somewhere?"

Humberton sat in the stern. He was studying the girl as she bent to the oars. "We are going somewhere, Ted," he concluded. "Something is wrong, and we are being taken to help. It can't be merely the wolf. We are safe from that danger—all of us."

"How do you know there's anything else?"

"Her face, Ted. She is still frantic with apprehension."

"Maybe she thinks the wolf will get Clavering while we're away."

But Humberton shook his head. "If Clavering remains in his house, he should be safe," he declared. "This girl is not fleeing from something—she is going to it. She is an expert with the oars, and she is putting every ounce of her strength into them."

"And I see where she's going!" Ted announced, triumphantly. He had been glancing over his shoulder at intervals. Now he was staring fixedly in the direction the boat was going.

"I see nothing but water," Humberton said, straining his own eyes.

"Look over to the right. Look hard, sir," Ted urged.

They were both shouting, so that their voices would carry to each other the length of the boat, above the roar of wind and water. But the girl evidently heard nothing. Her face was set, her mouth grim. Clearly, Humberton's opinion as to her infirmity was correct. Not once did she even glance over her shoulder. She seemed to know her direction by instinct. But the necrologist still shook his head.

"I see some very large waves ahead, Ted—nothing else," he insisted.

"What you see isn't waves, sir," Ted returned, in tones powerful enough to carry in a hurricane. "Not unless trees and bushes grow out of them. What you see's an island. I didn't know there was one in this part of the lake. I'm sure of it!"

Horatio Humberton was an open-minded man, but he had to be convinced. He stared earnestly over the moonlit waters. Had his glasses not been wet with foam he might have stared to better purpose. Then, suddenly, he saw. "I believe you are correct, Ted," he admitted.

"Of course I am," the driver retorted. "She's heading into a sort of little cove this minute. It's rough, but I wouldn't be afraid to swim from here."

THE LAKE became calmer. They were in the lee of the island. The boat leapt forward, as the oars, taking even hold, drove it under the girl's skillful hands. Her face lightened a little, and she smiled. Then she looked sidewise at the island, and the worried, haunted expression returned, as if at thought of what she expected to find there. With a final flirt of the oars she beached her boat, and instantly she was out of it and beckoning them to follow.

"Here's where she puts us wise to that's bothering her," Ted surmised aloud. He gave the boat a mighty pull up the narrow beach. "Lead on, sister!" he shouted.

She seemed to understand. Just to the right of where they had landed bushes grew almost to the water's edge. She ran toward them, and as her figure left the brilliant moonlight, appeared to vanish.

Ted, immediately behind her, stopped, bewildered. "Where is she?" he demanded.

Then she was before him again. She held the bushes aside.

"All right, sir. Come on," Ted called back to the plodding necrologist. "There's a little track here, but she certainly had me buffaloed for a minute. I guess we can follow now."

"Use your flashlight," his chief counseled.

Ted laughed. "Call me anything you want to," he said. "I took it out of my pocket back at the house, when I expected to turn in. Then I forgot to put it back. But I won't let her get away from me."

That might have been easier to promise than to perform had she not taken care to see that he followed. As it was,

Humberton was in constant difficulties. Not so well justified in trusting his eyes as was the nimble driver, he tried
to supplement them by hearing and sense of touch. The
latter was occupied chiefly when he bruised himself against
some tree which Ted had avoided. But his ears served to
keep him generally straight, because he could hear Ted's
running stream of comment when a sudden spurt had put
both the driver and his guide out of sight for a moment.

"Hold hard, sir! Where's she going?" Humberton heard
his driver exclaim, suddenly. Then, evidently to the girl,
"No, you don't. Wait here till the chief comes up. Looks
like a cave to me," he called back. "She's got me by the hand.
She's trying to drag me in."

By that time Humberton was behind them. "Very well,
Ted, let her drag you in," he directed; whereupon Ted
Spang, with a short laugh, disappeared into the dark open-
ing which yawned before them.

His employer followed gingerly. If it had been dark
among the trees and bushes, it was black here. Except at
the very entrance, no moonlight could filter in. But they
were not going far. After only a few yards, Ted cried out:
"It's a man, sir. Lying on the ground. Dead, I think."

The deaf-and-dumb girl was making a queer little
whimper. Humberton felt his way forward and knelt beside
the prostrate man. "We must get him out of here, Ted," he
said.

"I think that's what she wants us to do, sir. She's been
taking my hands and trying to tell me by signs. You grab
his feet. I'll carry the shoulders. Now—easy, sir."

There were no obstructions on the cave floor. They got
the man out with little difficulty.

Ted was sniffing busily. "What is that smell, sir?" he
demanded. "Seems to me I've smelt it before."

"Chloroform," his chief replied. "Well lay him prone here on the ground. Wait till I free his tongue." He inserted a long forefinger in the man's mouth. "Now, I'll start artificial respiration. He may not be dead. You can relieve me in a few minutes. I'm tired."

Ted stood in silence until his turn came, then eagerly took his employer's place and carried on the rhythmic movements. They were in a little patch of moonlight, dimmed by scudding clouds. The girl was at the edge of it. Her slim figure quivered with emotion. When the two men changed places she ran forward and looked down earnestly, only to retreat again in disappointment.

At last, when Humberton's hands again manipulated the unconscious figure, she gave a little, inarticulate cry of triumph. "She is right, Ted," the necrologist declared. "He has begun to breathe. It's only a matter of time, now." He bent to his task. Soon he looked up again. "I think we may venture to carry him to the boat."

They turned him on his back.

"I thought I knew that tie!" the driver exclaimed. "It's Clavering!"

CHAPTER FIVE
THE SHADOW
BY THE STEPS

WHEN THEY had reached the shore with their unconscious burden, the necrologist was wet with perspiration. His muscles ached more than ever.

"Think the four of us can ride back in the boat, sir?" Ted inquired.

"We must, Ted," Humberton said, shortly.

"I can stay behind, and the girl can make another trip for me."

But Humberton shook his head. "We may need all our strength on the mainland. Our adventure is not over. For one thing, we don't know how Clavering can possibly have been brought to this island, drugged and unconscious, in so short a time. We have no idea who brought him. It can hardly have been this girl. Then there is the wolf. Until we know where he is, we shall be very wise to keep our forces together."

Once more, the deaf-and-dumb girl seemed to sense what they were arguing. She motioned peremptorily to the boat. Ted Spang, with a wealth of gesture, did his best to present his objections. Ted was a confirmed landsman. But the girl shook her head impatiently, and began dragging Clavering toward the boat.

"I guess that settles it, sir," Ted conceded, resignedly. "She's the sailor in this outfit. All right, sir, let's get him in."

Again Ted sat in the prow and his chief in the stern. By virtue of proved skill, the girl took the oars. Clavering was stretched in the bottom of the boat.

"Rougher and rougher!" Ted groaned, after they were clear of the island, and the waves were striking them fairly. "Look how low we are in the water. Let one big wave hit us square, and Clavering will drown right where he is!"

The necrologist did not reply. He was by no means a seaman himself, but he had the faculty of detachment. The boat tossed dangerously. Her lips compressed, her lithe body bent to the oars, the deaf-and-dumb girl was hard pressed to keep the tiny craft from slipping broadside-on. But there was nothing Humberton could do to help so he sat back as comfortably as possible, and began to marshal his facts.

They had talked with Clavering less than an hour before, at the house. That was one fact. Now they had found him on the island, unconscious and all but dead. That was another. Had the girl taken him there? If so, why should she seem so desperately anxious to bring him back? Undoubtedly she knew the solution of the mystery, but she could not speak. Probably she knew the cause of the strange howling, too.

When this second thought came to the necrologist's orderly mind, they were exposed to the full force of the wind. The boat was pitching, end by end. The girl was fighting desperately. When the moonlight caught her face, she looked haggard and hopeless. But Humberton was serenely fitting his theories together.

"Ted," he shouted, above the roar of the waves, "are you sure that was a wolf we heard on the mainland?"

Ted's mind, occupied with more pressing matters, did not catch the question. It had to be repeated. Then he replied, bitterly: "It was a wolf, all right. But we don't have to worry, sir. We'll never have a chance to hear it any more!"

Evidently no help was available from Ted; although on land, as Ted's chief reflected with amusement, no degree of danger could have rattled the young man. Perhaps then, the girl might help. Though the moonlight was not quite so clear as it had been, she might be able to read his lips, and let him know whether they had a real wolf to deal with. But that lead failed, too. He looked at her closely, saw that she was nearly spent, and instead of trying to question her offered to take the oars. She shook her head.

SO HIS thoughts snapped back, with some relief, to the problem. After all, the mere question of whether or not they should all live to reach shore had no bearing upon that. What other curious facts had he to weigh and consider? Clavering's shoes, of course! Why had their host exchanged a pair of shoes with plain toe caps for a pair with perforated caps?

Humberton's eyes strayed to the unconscious man's feet. And he received a shock which affected him far more profoundly than even the biggest of the waves had done.

The shoes Clavering was wearing now were of soft kid. They had no toe caps whatever!

When, a few minutes afterward, the deaf-and-dumb girl, with a deft sweep, shot them far up the beach, then crumpled face forward on her oars, Humberton lifted her out as mechanically as he would have picked up a bag of flour. His mind was still vexed with the insignificant, but unreasonable and outrageous, mystery of the shoes.

He might almost have forgotten their passenger in his absorption. But Ted was on land again; and Ted was once more his usual, practical self. "All right, sir, you take one end of him, I'll grab the other," he said, briskly. "The girl did her part, now it's up to us."

Humberton climbed into the boat and lifted the feet of the still unconscious Clavering. The deaf-and-dumb girl wriggled to her feet and began making violent gestures toward the steep path up the mound. Her meaning was perfectly clear; so much so that the necrologist groaned. His lake trip had made him stiff, and muscle-bound.

"We are going to find this very difficult, Ted," he said, gloomily.

"We're lucky if we don't find it impossible," the driver agreed, blithely. "You wouldn't be in favor of waiting here for him to come round?"

"I'm afraid not. We must get him where he can be examined."

"Very good, sir. Ally-oop!"

To the base of the hill it proved, as Humberton had described it, a difficult task. That was owing to his stiffness. The nearly impossible part began at the base of the hill and extended upward.

Ted took the lead, climbing backward with marvelous certainty of footing. He grasped Clavering under the arm pits. Humberton rested the unconscious man's legs across his own shoulders, and climbed doggedly. Part of the time he was lying prone against the side of the hill. The driver kept up a running fire of encouragement, which was occasionally interrupted as his foot slipped and he grasped at some tree or root.

"You're doing fine, sir! Pike's Peak or bust! Easy, now. Ouch!"

That was halfway up. Ted's foot and both his chief's feet slipped at the same moment. It was a bare spot, almost vertical, with not even a tuft of grass for a handhold. With a despairing cry, Humberton started to slide.

Suddenly, he was braced from beneath. Ted and their limp burden fell atop him. He slid downward a little, but again his feet were held. This time they remained rigid.

Then Ted's voice came cheerfully from above him. "It's all right, sir. She caught us. I've got hold of a root now. She's been trailing us all the way up. We'd have had a nasty spill!"

HUMBERTON LOOKED down and saw the deaf-and-dumb girl. She was solidly braced against a tree. Reaching up at arm's length, she had caught his feet as he slipped.

He was desperately tired, his muscles ached intolerably, but for the rest of the climb he felt safe.

He was even able to smile when Ted announced, suddenly: "Here we are, sir! I'm at the top. You'll be up in three steps."

A moment later, the driver's muscular hand grasped his arm, and again he felt a boost from below. He was up.

"Want to rest a minute, sir, before we start down with him?"

"I—I must, Ted," the necrologist gasped.

He threw himself flat on the ground. It was the place, in the center of the three birches, from which he had flashed the signal. He felt, rather than saw, that the girl had reached the top, too. She and Ted were standing beside him. A little moonlight filtered through the frees and dappled their figures, but the moon was now well beyond the woods. Its brightness was over for the night.

"Wonder where the wolf is," Ted said, casually.

The girl might have heard him. Perhaps she had read his lips. Perhaps it was mere chance. She held up her hand imperatively for silence.

The long-drawn howl floated in on the breeze. It sounded far away—so far that Ted had begun some cheerful comment, when the deaf-and-dumb girl's actions stopped him.

She gave a queer little cry of terror, tugged at the necrologist, who was now sitting on the ground, and pulled him to his feet. Then with another cry, like the first and yet subtly different, she threw herself to her knees beside the man they had brought in the boat.

"Nina!" he whispered. It was barely audible.

"He's coming to!" the driver shouted, joyfully.

The far-off wolfish sound came again, high and clear above the moan of the wind. This time it was like a summons to the man on the ground. His voice rose to a feeble shriek.

"The Werewolf!" he cried. The shriek disintegrated into a gurgling sob of weakness and horror. Then it found words once more: "Take me—take me to—"

Ted grasped Clavering's feet. The deaf-and-dumb girl had already seized his shoulders.

"Come on, sir, if you can," he said. "If you're too done up to help lift, let her do it. We'd better start before they both go crazy. Funny how she seems to sense that darned wolf's call, even though she can't hear! I guess it's vibration or something."

Whether from excitement or from the brief rest, Humberton felt his strength returning. He took the prostrate man's shoulders. The girl yielded to him. She was trembling violently.

The girl went first. With her guidance, Ted fairly ran down the broad path. His tall chief would have preferred a more conservative rate, but he had no choice. The man they carried seemed to listen rigidly for the wolf's cry. It came when they were halfway down. He greeted it with a feeble wail of terror.

Ted retorted with a growl. "Never fear, sir—let the fool thing come on. I've got a dose for it, here in my hip pocket!"

The helpless man answered something.

"What does he say, sir?" Ted inquired.

"He says bullets can not kill this wolf," Humberton replied.

"I never saw the wolf they couldn't," Ted returned, undaunted, without lessening his speed. "If he catches us, he'll have to prove it to me, that's all."

"Hurray, sir, we're out of the woods!" he exulted, a moment later. "We're not two hundred yards from the door."

"Side door," Humberton reminded him.

"Surest thing you know!" Ted agreed. "Funny how the moon falls on this part of the lawn," he went on cheerfully. "It's way beyond the back woods now, but—" And the words died on Ted's lips.

They were just at the corner of the house, the girl leading when high and piercing, just in front of them, a rising crescendo of horror ended with a sob that trailed away on the breeze.

Humberton recognized it for what it was. "The deaf-and-dumb girl!" he said, in a voice that trembled in spite of him, so inhuman had the sound been. "She sees something by the front door. My eyes can't make it out. She is pointing."

BUT EVEN as he said it, she was no longer pointing. She was tugging at them madly to hurry their steps. Her breath came and went in staccato cries nearly as weird as her first wail of terror. Until she got them around the corner of the mansion her eyes still seemed fixed on something in the shadows by the great front door.

They dashed for the side door, which was open as they had left it. When she had slammed it behind them, the girl's cries gave way to a frightened whimper.

"We'll take him up to my bed, Ted," the necrologist directed.

"O.K., sir. She's running on ahead. I hope it's to light a lamp."

It was. They had hardly reached the top of the stairs when she was there with the lamp from Humberton's bedroom.

"There, sir, just lie and rest. Don't try to talk," Ted advised, as they laid their burden down in the bedroom. The man they had been carrying did not reply. He seemed dazed. Ted gave him a cheerful grin and turned to his employer.

"If you don't mind, sir, I'm going to grab my flashlight and find out what it was this girl saw down below. We can leave her with him all right for a while. Here she comes with some water in a basin."

Humberton watched the girl a moment. She set the basin on a chair beside the bed and began to bathe Clavering's forehead. Her terror of a few minutes before seemed forgotten in a great wave of tenderness apparent in every action.

"She's fallen hard for him, poor kid!" Ted exclaimed, returning from his own room with the flashlight. "I'm going down, sir."

"I with you, Ted," the necrologist declared.

Ted grinned. They were leaving the room without the deaf-and-dumb girl's appearing to be aware of it, so absorbed was she in her task.

"Did you see anything, Ted, when the girl shrieked?" Humberton asked.

They had reached the top of the side stairs. Spang was using his flashlight to guide them through the hall. He halted a moment. "I've been wanting to talk to you about it, sir," he whispered. "You know when she yelled? Wasn't that the same sound we heard in the house, while Clavering was sitting with us?"

"I believe so," his chief averred.

"That's what it seemed like to me. Well, when that yell came, sir, and I saw her pointing, I looked toward the steps. I looked hard. It was pretty dark there, so I can't be sure just what I saw. But there was something, sure enough, in the shadows."

Humberton was silent for a moment. Then he asked: "You have your gun, Ted?"

"In my pocket. When we jump out of that door, it will be in my hand. Shall we go?"

Ted, in advance, opened the door cautiously and glanced about him before stepping outside. He did not turn on the flashlight. When they reached the corner of the house, however, he first made sure that his chief was beside him, then pointed the light toward the great stone steps and suddenly switched on the brilliant beam.

"See it, sir?" he demanded, excitedly.

"I see something. It is very indistinct," Humberton returned.

Ted was advancing, slowly and cautiously, the flashlight in his left hand, the revolver in his right His employer, close beside him, strained his myopic eyes to make out the nature of the huddled form on the steps. Suddenly Humberton, near enough to be sure of what he saw, ran ahead of his aide, and stooped swiftly.

"It's a man," he announced. "He is dead, I think. Flash your light here." He recoiled, suddenly, in horror. "Ted—his throat is torn out."

The driver was bending over the body. "Mr. Humberton," he said, thickly. "Look, sir! Don't you see? Am I crazy? Tell me, am I crazy? It's Clavering!"

But before the necrologist could reply, the great front doors opened. A woman appeared. The light in the room behind her cast her shadow grotesquely down the steps.

She was the biggest woman either of them had ever seen. She was a giantess.

"Carry him in," she said, in a stern, deep voice. "It is the judgment of God!"

CHAPTER SIX
MISTRESS OF
THE WOLVES

THEY LAID the body on the floor. Horatio Humberton looked at it for a long moment. Then he snatched an ornamental table cover—the nearest thing to hand—and laid it over the upper part of the dead man. After that, he glanced up at the tall woman. As he did so, he saw the deaf-and-dumb girl peer in at the doorway, now open, through which they had been led to bed. Her dark eyes stared at them with some strange emotion in their depths. It was not fear. It was not horror. Could it be triumph? Then she was gone, leaving the door still open.

All the while, the giantess had been standing, with folded arms, gazing down at the body. She gazed while the dreadful wound was bare to view in the light of the swing-ing lamp, and also after it was covered, but there was no change in her expression. Her face was quite impassive, as if the capacity for feeling had been sucked out of it. Suddenly, she spoke: "You are the detectives?"

"Yes, madam," Humberton answered.

"I must tell you what you need to know. It is only right. I must tell you tonight By dawn I shall be dead. That girl—" She nodded toward the hall door, and it flashed through the necrologist's mind that her dull, fishlike eyes must be keener than they appeared. The girl had been there only for an instant, yet those eyes had seen her. "What did he say about her?"

"If you are the housekeeper, he told us that you and your daughter were the only people in the house with him," Humberton replied, in even, matter-of-fact tones.

"I am the housekeeper. But she is not my daughter. She is an orphan. Her father and her mother were killed together. They fell from the trapeze in the big top. When I left the circus, I took her with me. Tell me this—did she show you the secret of the island? Did she take you there?"

Humberton nodded. If this strange giantess resented what the girl had done, he felt that her resentment could do no harm now. But she revealed no emotion of any kind.

"I thought so. After she screamed, I tied her and gagged her. She escaped. I knew she had gone to the island. She must have felt that Stephen would take him there. She loves him—the deaf-and-dumb girl loves the rich fool!" She glanced again at the silent form on the floor. "You thought you left him upstairs just now, didn't you?"

When he did not reply, a shade of feeling crossed her face. She raised her powerful voice. "You think this is Roger Clavering? You think that, don't you? Answer me!"

HUMBERTON PERMITTED himself a sidelong look at Ted. The driver was leaning easily against the library table, not far from the outside door. He was obviously bewildered; but, just as obviously, he was alert. This woman, stolid as she seemed, was holding herself together by some mighty effort. It showed in an occasional twitching of her thick lips. Her hands were clenched—they had been clenched from the first. She had better be encouraged to tell her story while she could and as she wished.

So, without changing his own position—across the body from her—he shook his head, and said, gently: "This is the man who received us tonight, in this house. There is another man upstairs. We have put him to bed. He is recovering, I hope. For a time, I mistook him for this man, but the lamplight showed me my mistake. I believe the man upstairs is Roger Clavering."

"You are right," she confirmed, heavily. "This man—" she nodded toward the body—"is his second cousin, Stephen— his only relative. He would have inherited the estate. There he lies. Do you believe in the judgment of God, you detective?"

"I have seen it, often," Humberton answered, quietly.

"You are seeing it tonight. I came here a year ago, with that poor girl I called my daughter. I came as housekeeper. You would have seen God's judgment many a night when I paced the floor, and sleep stayed away from me, because I was betraying a kind man who trusted me. But did I repent? No! I wormed myself into his secrets. I learned everything he knew and feared about the family legend. I turned it all over to Stephen. Then he came here a month ago. He knew the time was ripe. And where Roger Clavering had been merely afraid, Stephen made him crazy with terror. Roger sent for you. But do you think it was his plan? It was Stephen's. He wanted you for a witness. They look alike. If you had found Roger's body with the throat torn out there on the lawn, you detective, and had not seen Stephen again, what would you have thought?" She leaned forward, and for the first time her dull eyes gleamed. "You would have thought it was the same man who had received you. Wouldn't you, detective?"

Humberton looked her in the eyes. There was no reason for being less than frank. "If I had not seen both men alive,

I fear I should have thought that very thing," he admitted. Then he hesitated. "Yet, I don't know. There were his clothes—"

"They wouldn't have helped you, detective!"

"I think they would," he said, good-humoredly.

"But they were dressed alike," she protested. "Stephen made a great point of the fashions. All through his visit he laughed at Roger's things. He lent Roger an outfit just like his, so that Roger should not look outlandish while you were here. You would not have found out that way. Stephen was too clever for you there!"

"The shoes!" Humberton said, simply; and she laughed. It was a grim, deep-throated laugh, with no humor in it.

"Then you noticed that? You are brighter than I thought. Roger's feet are tender. He has had his shoes made to order and sent to him by mail for years. Stephen overlooked that point till too late. I told him to wear the same kind of shoes as Roger, even if he had to get a pair of Roger's old ones. He said you wouldn't see the difference. Well—you did, it seems!"

"Shoes were his weak point, first and last, weren't they?" the necrologist suggested, courteously. He felt the time had come to draw her out a little.

"What do you mean?" she demanded.

And with the certainty that he was about to arrive at something important, Humberton went on, in the same casual tone: "When we were talking to your friend, Stephen, there was a scream. He left the room to investigate. While he was away he changed his shoes."

THAT WAS as far as he got. The veins swelled on the big woman's forehead. She was rapidly losing her air of unconcern.

"A scream!" she exclaimed, scornfully. "I suppose you know what it was. The little fool! She is dumb enough at most times. But when she is thoroughly frightened she screams like a banshee. She came into the room where she thought Roger was. He wasn't there. Stephen had taken him to the island to get him out of the way till we were ready. He was so slow doing that that I had to show the signal light for him when you came. And I had to operate the front door and let you in. Even then you waited for him, didn't you? Well—she didn't find Roger. So she screamed. And Stephen came running in to shut her up. He didn't know I had got to her first. He tried to strike her, but he strikes too hard. It would never have done to kill her, too. So I threw my arms around him. There was the chloroform bottle on the shelf—the chloroform we used on Roger. We knocked it off. Now you know about the shoes, detective. He couldn't come back to you in shoes that smelt of chloroform!"

She was going on to say something further when she was interrupted—by the howl of the wolf, just outside on the lawn.

She listened until the long, bell-like note died away into silence. Then she smiled.

"Hear him!" she said, fondly. "One of my children! The only child I ever had. Long and lean and swift, with quick snapping jaws, and sharp teeth! He can tear the life away between one breath and the next! Do you wonder why I speak this way, detective? I was born in the circus. I was educated there—not a bad education, either. I learned to train wild animals. Perhaps you have seen me, and never guessed that years afterward you would meet me here. Why do you think Stephen Clavering offered to divide his inheritance with me? Because he knew of that wolf legend.

Because he knew that I could get a wolf—one that I myself had trained—and make the fairy story come true. No one else could have done that. Did we think of the judgment of God, then? No, we were planning. We left God out of it. We had to find a way to bring the wolf. Stephen did that, he brought it by water. I can't tell you how. I kept it here in a part of the great basement under this house where that poor weakling, Roger, never went. We had to plan for this night. Chloroform—that was my idea. Stephen struck him a blow on the head, too, and took him to the island, so that he should not come to himself and spoil everything."

She held up her hand.

"Listen! There is my child again—my child of the woods! Soon I am coming to you, my child! I led him through these woods at night like a dog. I knew how to make him howl, so that the coward upstairs would tremble in his shoes." She laughed. "Oh, it has not been such bad sport! But I felt all along that God was against us. I felt it when Roger began to fall in love with that poor, deaf-and-dumb fool. Now they'll be married. She'll have the fortune."

The howl came a third time. Its direction was different. It seemed nearer.

"We left the side door open!" Ted shouted, suddenly. He leapt forward, gun in hand; but the giantess barred his way. She caught his wrist.

"You can't stop my child!" she cried, in a frenzy. "He is the judgment of God! I starved him so he would kill Roger. He killed Stephen, instead. That was the judgment. Now he has tasted human blood. He must kill, kill, kill!"

Humberton dodged around her. In his mind was the picture of the open doorway upstairs, through which he had looked back and seen the deaf-and-dumb girl kneeling beside the bed of the man she served and loved. He seemed to hear pattering footsteps in the hall. If he could shut that upstairs door—

But before he could reach the hallway, Ted shouted to him. "Jump behind us, sir! Quick!"

Then a huge gray body, with red mouth and bared white fangs hurled itself into the room. The big woman turned. She pushed Ted back and stepped fearlessly to meet it.

There was a deep growl, and the sound of tearing flesh. She screamed once.

Ted fired three times. The two of them—the dying woman and the wolf—rolled over together on the floor. The wolf quivered—a long undulation of its lithe gray form. Then it lay dead.

CHAPTER SEVEN
FROM "A" TO "B"

THEY WERE back in the study at the Humberton Funeral Parlors, and it was ten days later. Both the tall necrologist and his driver wore new suits—badly wanted in Humberton's case, at least; and at the curb outside the parlors stood a new sedan, for which the need had been almost as pressing.

"The most unsatisfactory case I ever handled!" Horatio Humberton exclaimed, petulantly.

"Oh, I don't know," Ted Spang returned, soothingly, balancing himself with expert precision on the pile of books he was using as a seat. "You saved Roger Clavering's life. That's something—anyway he thinks so. And now he's off on his honeymoon with the girl. It's the old happy ending with bells on it for him."

"That is only the human element, Ted," Humberton declared, earnestly. "The solution of a case should be exact. It should leave no loose ends. And consider how many this one has left. How did the housekeeper know she was facing death that night? She did know it. She told us at the start that she would be dead by dawn. That may have been a premonition, or she may have intended to kill herself if fate had not forestalled her. But we don't know." He drew savagely on his long cigar. "That's my point. Why, we don't even know why the wolf was roaming about in the grounds. She may have let it out with deliberate intent. Or there may have been a mistake of some kind—a mistake for which she and Stephen paid with their lives. Then there is the interesting problem as to how Stephen Clavering—the distant cousin who was willing to murder for money—met this giantess, this mistress of the wolves. We don't know that, either. Roger Clavering couldn't tell me. Indeed, I told him far more than he told me. The case is finished, but from a scientific standpoint my work has been exceedingly ragged."

"I still maintain," Ted persisted, doggedly, "that when a fellow pulls down five thousand dollars for a job and saves his client's life, he isn't near so ragged as he might be. And at that, sir," he added, "those things you're crabbing about aren't important. The big mystery—the one that's got me walking tiptoe when I step out at night—is that crazy Clavering history. Here's Roger's father, his grandfather, and his great-uncle—all killed by wolves—all killed just before their fiftieth birthdays. There's Roger himself coming about as close to the same pleasant little finish as my nose is to my face. Coincidence? Coincidence my eye! You straighten that out for me, sir, and you can keep the rest, as far as I'm concerned."

The necrologist's rather austere visage relaxed a little. "You mean that, Ted?" he asked, hopefully. "Are you really so impressed by this family legend?"

"Why shouldn't I be?" the driver countered.

"Perhaps you should. Of course, you lacked my advantages. You didn't have long talks with Roger Clavering, while he was convalescing from his rather harrowing experiences. He's a pleasant little man, Ted, as you may have noticed—quite harmless, and the very one to be victimized by a polished scoundrel like his cousin Stephen. Now, let me ask you something. It is a wild country up there, isn't it?"

Ted nodded.

"Leaving out the time element—I mean the age at which they met their ends—is there anything especially hard to swallow in three members of the same family being killed by wolves in the course of years?"

"Well, no sir, perhaps not; but—"

"Tut, tut, Ted! I asked you to leave out the time element, but I can tell from your expression that you were about to drag it in. I have another question. Can you, without swelling your bump of credulity too much, admit that a wolf may have killed Roger's father just before he was fifty years old?"

TED DID not trust himself to elaborate, this time; he merely said; "Yes, sir."

"We progress. We have only two left to kill. Now, it will interest you to hear that as the result of close questioning on my part, I brought out from Roger Clavering the fact that although he had read the family history years ago, he has not read it lately until this year. Keep that in mind—it's important. But what is still more so is this—and I nearly had to psycho-analyze him to get at it-that until this year's reading he had never noticed the curious and dreadful coincidence of age. He had no doubt that it was there all the time, *but he hadn't noticed it.* And who do you think called it to his attention?"

Ted's eyes snapped with interest. "I could guess," he replied. "But go on, sir."

"It was Cousin Stephen! Of course it was Cousin Stephen. Stephen visited him about a year ago. When he left he borrowed the diary so that he might read it at his leisure. And when he returned the book, Cousin Stephen wrote Roger a friendly little note, pointing out that Roger's grandfather and his great-uncle had both been killed by wolves shortly before they were fifty, just as Roger's father had been!"

Ted stood up. The pile of books he had been sitting on collapsed but he paid them no attention. He said: "Boy, oh boy, oh boy!"

"Well, Ted, I had my microscope with me!"

The driver met his employer's eye. A slow grin spread over his face. "Yes, sir! And you examined the book?"

"Precisely, Ted—to find that Stephen Clavering had changed two important dates. The altered manuscript had Roger's grandfather and his great-uncle killed in the week preceding their fiftieth birthdays. The original did nothing of the kind! When I made that perfectly clear to Roger Clavering, he took hold of life again and really began to get well."

Ted sat in silence a moment, on another pile of books he hastily constructed. He lit a cigarette and still did not speak. His employer—all his ill temper cured—regarded him with a slightly quizzical, slightly triumphant gaze.

Ted's thoughts evidently came to a focus. He nodded crisply, and said; "I get it, sir. Cousin Stephen had one fact to go on—that Roger was coming to the age at which his father was killed. He started from that and worked up the rest. He meant to have Roger killed by the wolf while he himself hiked ten or twenty miles through the woods and boarded a train somewhere. Then he'd have shown up a few weeks later as next of kin. You and I would have been relied on as expert outside witnesses to prove that everything was regular. But here's one thing—how about the deaf-and-dumb girl? Wouldn't she have found a way to squeal?"

"Probably he counted on the housekeeper to prevent that," Humberton suggested. "He seems to have been quite certain of her loyalty to him."

"Maybe," Ted agreed. "All I know is, I'd have been nervous, in his shoes. That girl would have got him sooner or later, housekeeper or no housekeeper, or I miss my guess. Suppose we'd have shown up in the daytime? Wouldn't that have crabbed his game?"

"Now you're getting into remote possibilities, Ted," Humberton laughed. "Stephen needed darkness for his plan, of course. That was beautifully taken care of by the fact that the only train we could arrive on got in at night. I found, however, that just to make it doubly sure he had primed poor, apprehensive Roger with suggestions of a malign influence about the grounds—something in the nature of a supernatural wolf or 'werewolf'—which must not observe us getting in. Hence the signal light and the wild dash to the front door. Don't blame Roger too much."

"Blame him?" Ted retorted. "No one needs to sell me on the malign influence stuff. Or you either, I should think, sir. Didn't the wolf chase us to the door that very first night?"

HUMBERTON LEANED far back in his chair and gazed at his senior driver with a broad and benevolent smile. "No, Ted," he said, gently.

Ted was flicking off his cigarette ash against the edge of a book cover—a procedure which the extreme informality of the study rendered permissible. He stopped in the act to look his employer in the eye. "What do you mean, 'No?'" he demanded.

"You recall, Ted," his chief returned, evasively, "that the estimable giantess spoke of keeping her wolf in the basement? Also that it was she, according to her own admission, who both flashed the light and operated the front door on the night we had our race for life?"

"Sure I recall it, sir," Spang admitted. "That's what bothers me. If I knew she was out with the wolf—had him by a chain, maybe, like a dog—and they both chased us, then I could understand it. I guess she could have held him back so he wouldn't actually have caught us. He turned against both of them later, but he couldn't have been that way all the time. Yet on her own say-so, she was in the house. And this Cousin Stephen hadn't got back from the island, after taking Roger there."

"All true, Ted," his chief commended.

"Then you're not telling me the wolf didn't chase us? I thought for a minute that was what you meant."

Humberton's smile grew broader. "I mean exactly that, Ted. The wolf was chained in the basement."

Ted stood up again, with the usual result to his pile of books. "Now look here, sir," he protested, not without indignation. "You and I were in this together. I put it to you—wasn't the howl of that wolf getting nearer all the time?"

"No, Ted!"

"All right, then—am I crazy or am I crazy?"

"Neither, I trust." Humberton's tone was quiet and soothing. "I am willing to surmise, Ted, that possibly the lady regulated the volume of wolfish sound by opening and shutting a door. Or possibly not—I can't tell. And no doubt the amphitheater of trees behind us caused an echo sufficient to deceive our ears as to the direction of the noise. But, strictly speaking, I cannot allow that the wolf was getting nearer to us. On the contrary, we were getting nearer to the wolf."

"And all the time I was running you like hell we were going toward the wolf? Is that what you mean, sir?" Ted asked, with sudden illumination.

"Precisely. After all, it is as far from 'B' to 'A' as from 'A' to 'B!'"

Ted stared a moment at his employer, his expression a mixture of chagrin and wild hilarity. The latter won. He burst out laughing, and retrieved his cap from the book shelf where he had laid it when he came in. "All right, sir," he said, still chuckling. "I'll not ask any more questions. Not just now. You might prove there never was any wolf. I'm going out to polish the sedan before you tell me it isn't there!"

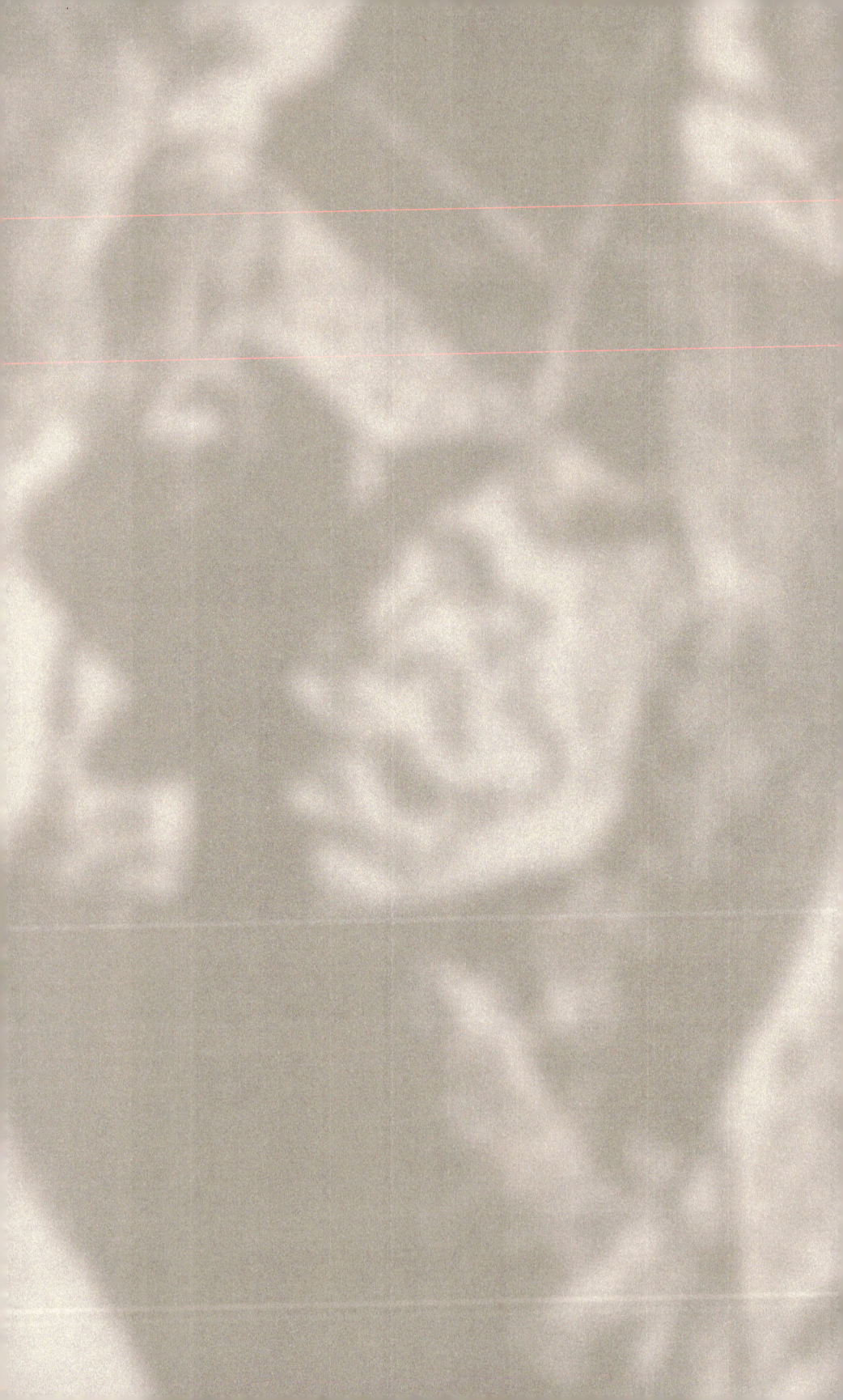

THE MILL OF HORROR

"I'VE SEEN DEATH!" THAT
WAS THE CRYPTIC PHRASE
YOUNG TRAHEY BABBLED AS
HE STUMBLED THROUGH THE
MORTUARY DOOR. AND DEATH
WAS WHAT THE UNDERTAKER-
DETECTIVE FOUND THERE IN THE
SHADOW OF THAT ANCIENT STEEL
MILL. FOR A MURDERER WAS AT
LARGE THAT NIGHT AND ONLY
HUMBERTON GUESSED HIS MAD
PLAN, KNEW THE SECRET OF THE
MANGLED BODY IN THE CRANE.

CHAPTER ONE
DEATH IN THE CRANE

POLICE DETECTIVE James Clyde growled, "Check!" and Horatio Humberton, smiling grimly, slid his queen across the chess board with a long, curving forefinger. He in turn said, "Check!" Then he leaned over the board to blow from it some of the droppings of Clyde's pipe, which were in the way of his next move. The ashes swirled a moment in the barely perceptible breeze. It was a stifling August night. Humberton had opened both the study door and the big front door of the funeral parlors, to make the game more comfortable.

Before the ashes settled again—before Clyde could make his next move—there was a sudden shuffle of feet in the narrow hall. There was a voice, too—high-pitched and agonizing. It screamed: "Death! Death!"

Clyde jumped to his feet, but he was not quick enough. A figure hurtled into the study, struck the table a glancing blow which slid the chess board to the floor, and with a low, moaning cry gripped Horatio Humberton by the throat. He went down, the intruder atop of him.

The detective nearly overturned the heavy table in his effort to round it without delay. He reached down into the shadows where the two were grappling, hooked two powerful hands under the jaw of the one on top, and with the same motion which wrenched him loose hurled him against a book case.

Humberton's assailant tottered. His eyes turned glassy. He slowly sagged to the floor.

Clyde did not wait to see what became of him. He sank to his knees beside his friend, and his hoarse voice revealed an amazingly gentle note. "Are you hurt, Ho?" he mattered, anxiously.

HORATIO HUMBERTON sat up, with a minimum of help from the detective. That brought his long face into the glow of the single electric bulb above the table. His thick spectacles had been bent somewhat out of shape, but he was calm.

"Did you think he was throttling me, Clyde?" he inquired, coolly.

The tall necrologist shook his head. Meanwhile, he was scrambling to his feet. "He was not attacking me at all, Clyde. His arms were around my neck, and he was sobbing against my collar. Surely you see what is wrong with him?"

Detective James Clyde gazed with new interest at the figure on the floor. What he saw was a slim young man— not much more than a boy, in fact—rather roughly dressed, who was certainly not violent now, whatever he had been. He was obviously unconscious.

Humberton stepped around the table and also looked down at their midnight visitor.

"Crazy?" Clyde suggested.

"I hardly think so. This boy has had an overwhelming nervous shock. When he burst into the room he was wild with fear. Your treatment was not precisely scientific, but perhaps it will quiet his mind as well as anything we could possibly have done. When he comes to himself, I hope he will be much calmer. Suppose you step into the morgue and get a dipper of water, Clyde, while I loosen his collar."

Clyde obeyed reluctantly. He did not enjoy stepping into the morgue. He made the errand as brief as possible, but when he returned with the water the eyelids of the youth on the floor were beginning to flutter. Humberton deftly slipped a book beneath his head to serve as a pillow.

"Never mind the water now, Clyde. We mustn't shock him more than is necessary. Ah, my boy—" He gently stroked the youth's forehead. "You are feeling better? Just lie there and recover."

But their caller's eyes opened abruptly to their full extent. He looked wildly into the faces bending over his. With an inarticulate cry he tried to struggle to his feet.

"What's that he says?" the detective demanded.

"Something about death." Since he seemed determined to rise, the necrologist guided him to a chair—the chair from which he had himself been catapulted.

For the first time, the reviving youth seemed to recognize him. "I'm all right, Mr. Humberton," he said, slowly. "Only you know—you know—I've seen Death."

"Easy, my boy." Humberton knelt in front of him, smiling into the thin, perturbed face. "Is that why you came to me? There is something you want me to do?"

"Yes. I've heard about you. I knew where you lived. I saw—" He shivered, stopped, then went on. "I saw Death—over in the field by the new mill. So I came to you. He's a big shadow. I saw him, I tell you—in the moonlight. I jumped in my car and came here. I saw—"

"Yes, my boy?"

"The man he killed is there in the field."

"What's that?" put in Clyde, sharply.

The youth's face turned slowly. He blinked up at the red-visaged detective. "It was a big shadow with the dead man under its arm. There's a crane in it, too."

"Crazy as a loon!" Clyde muttered.

He let his long legs down till he
was dangling outside the stairs.

"A locomotive crane. It's there in the field by the mill.
You think I'm making it up, but I'm not. You can get in my
car, and I'll take you there."

"Clyde, there is something back of this," Humberton
interrupted. "Suppose we go with this boy. Call Ted from

upstairs. No doubt he's playing solitaire in his room. You and he can go in my car. What's your name, my lad?"

"Melvin Trahey."

"I'll ride with you, Melvin. Mr. Clyde and my assistant will follow. On the way, you can tell me more."

IN A few minutes the chief of the Humberton Funeral Parlors rather regretted his decision. His visitor's car evidently was the result of a home remodeling job, through which an aged flivver had been converted into a racing model, with most of the temperament and double the speed of a broncho. But after they had rounded a score of city corners and had settled into the straightaway of a country road, he began to draw out the curious details of the thing the boy had seen—or thought he had seen—which had so shocked his soul.

Melvin lived alone with his father in a cottage near the site of the new mill, now half completed. There was a cemetery beyond the mill, but it seemed not to enter the tale directly. His father was asleep—drunk—and the boy had determined to go out and spear a few bullfrogs along the creek which ran through both cemetery and mill site.

"You eat them?" the necrologist inquired.

"Their legs," was the laconic reply.

It was still bright moonlight. The boy did not need to explain that he had been able to see quite a distance. He had speared half a dozen frogs when his attention was caught by a shadow crossing the field from the direction of the mill.

"What kind of shadow?"

"A big, black shadow. Like a man, but bigger. He was carrying something. I wanted to find out what it was, so I crawled on my belly through the grass. That was kind of slow. I sneaked up close to the crane, and—"

The little car lurched violently. Humberton snatched the wheel only in time to keep them out of the ditch. The boy was shivering convulsively, and sobbing.

"I can't tell you any more! I'll take you to the field, but you'll have to go in it and see for yourself! I won't go with you. You can't make me go!"

"Very well," Humberton agreed, soothingly. He still felt a little shaky, and kept a guiding hand on the wheel. "Perhaps you had better run along home to bed when you have showed us the field. No doubt I can find you in the morning, if I need you."

The new mill loomed up, a giant black silhouette against the background of shimmering moonlight. Opposite the field which separated it from the dirt road, Melvin Trahey pressed down sternly on his brake, and the little car squealed to a stop.

"See that thing out in the middle of the field?" he asked, in a whisper. "That's the crane. Good-by."

The Humberton sedan, Ted Spang at the wheel, pulled up just as Melvin Trahey's domestic racer rolled on. Clyde, who scrambled out first, walked forward with a swagger.

"You may not know it, Ho, but I'm one of the owners out here," he declared, expansively. "The Polished Iron Company! It's going to turn out iron sheets with a shine like the finest steel. Never been done before. Old Jonathan White invented the process, and croaked two months ago. Now his son, Walter, is carrying on and finishing the job of building. Then there's John Massow—ever hear of him?"

Humberton shook his head. The moonlight was so bright that Clyde could see the movement perfectly. They were coming to the barb-wire fence which shut the wide field from the road, and for a moment the detective was too busy squeezing through it for speech.

"Thought you might have heard of Massow," he went on. "But perhaps he's out of your line. He's a retired steel man—the big noise of Laurel Village, the suburb just beyond here. Has the biggest house in the village and the biggest vault in the cemetery—that little cemetery right over there. Also, the sugar behind this new mill is mostly his. He owns more than half of the stock, I guess, and young White has a quarter, and the rest was peddled out to the public. That's how I got my two shares. Hello! Maybe that's the locomotive crane the kid was raving about."

"It is. He said so before he left."

"Beat it home to recover, eh? Wish I hadn't socked him quite so hard. But he's all right—he could never have driven that way if he wasn't. Looks like fire still in the crane—fire in it at one A.M.! Can you imagine that?"

HUMBERTON DID not reply. Though his eyes were weaker than Clyde's, his inner perception was keener. There was something odd about the shape of the crane in the shimmering moonlight—something grotesque and unnatural. Ted, whose eyes and perceptions were both acute, gasped, and broke into a run. He easily outdistanced the others. But when he had reached the crane and gone on to the farther side of it, where he could see better, he shivered and turned away.

Almost at once he looked again. Ted never showed emotion for long. "It's a mess," he whispered.

His chief and Clyde came up. They looked in silence.

"Caught in the tackle—poor devil!" Clyde exclaimed, at last.

"I hope it got his head first," said the hearse driver, soberly.

"Notice his arms, Ho. Both in up to the elbows. That would look as if maybe his head was caught last—while he was still trying to fight his way out. What was he doing here? Lighting up a locomotive crane and trying to operate it at midnight!"

"You are not forgetting the boy's story?" Humberton prompted.

"About the big shadow that scared him? Don't tell me you believe in shadows that throw people into cranes! This shadow would have had to shovel a little coal first, too, and light up."

But the tall necrologist showed no answering grin. "Check suit—good quality," he commented, pinching between thumb and forefinger a bit of the fabric in which the pitiful, broken body was clad. "Whoever this may be, Clyde, it is surely not the workman who operated the crane. I should like to think this over a bit before we call the coroner. You recall the boy's evident state of terror. What do you think he did when he discovered the body?"

"He beat it," said Clyde, emphatically.

"So I should imagine."

Humberton was fumbling, very gingerly, with various levers about the mechanism. In a moment he found the one he sought, gave it a slight push, and instantly restored it to its former position. Clyde was mechanic enough to catch the meaning of his action.

"The power's shut off!" he exclaimed.

"Precisely. Yet if the boy bolted immediately after finding the body—"

"I get you, Ho! Look how this poor devil is ground up! It's a cinch *he* didn't shut off the power. And it's an equal cinch the boy didn't, I'd say."

The necrologist went on slowly and evenly, like a professor building up a proposition before his class.

"This crane ran long enough for the gears to macerate the body to a terrible extent—but not long enough to attract passers-by on the road by its grinding. I agree with you, Clyde that it was not shut off by the boy. His terror was real. But if not—"

He stopped, abruptly. Ted Spang had tapped him lightly on the arm. Ted was pointing down the field toward the cemetery, where a man running toward them had just vaulted the dividing wall. It was evident in the bright moonlight that he was a big man, but he ran like an athlete.

"Who is it?" he shouted, while still some distance away.

Humberton walked forward to meet him. "Who are you?" he countered.

"I'm John Massow. A boy got me out of bed. Said someone had been killed in the crane. Who is it?"

"Possibly you can tell," the necrologist answered, quietly.

The newcomer strode around the crane, to a spot where the moonlight beat pitilessly on what was in the tackle. So he came upon it rather suddenly. A shiver rippled through his heavy frame. He gazed a moment without speaking, then tottered, as if about to collapse.

Ted, who was watching as keenly as his chief, caught the big man and led him away. But in a moment, Massow recovered himself. Still in silence, he returned to the crane, and studied the body. He even examined the material of the suit, as Humberton had done. Suddenly he whirled furiously upon the three of them.

"What do you know about this? Why was the crane fired up at this time of night?"

"Maybe you can answer that," Clyde bristled. The detective, nearly as big as Massow, never relished being blustered at.

"How can I answer it? I was home, in bed."

"I think, Mr. Massow, we shall get further if you answer the one question which possibly you can," put in Horatio Humberton, soothingly. "We have driven out from town. The boy who roused you came to me first. I don't believe he knew who this unfortunate man is, and I am sure we do not. Can you tell us that?"

Massow stared from one to the other. "You don't know him?" he muttered. His hard, deeply lined face worked spasmodically. "But why should you? What's he got to do with you? The bottom falls out of the whole damned world for me, but that doesn't mean anything to you. I'll tell you who he is. You see this mill?" He waved an arm toward it. "He was the one man who could have finished it."

"You mean Walter White?" Clyde demanded.

Massow nodded.

"Why, I've got two shares of stock in this company!" the detective said.

John Massow's face ceased to twitch. A grim smile crossed it. "I'm sorry—you're out two hundred dollars," he returned.

CHAPTER TWO
CONVICT'S CUPOLA

THE DAY after the discovery of the mangled body in the crane, Horatio Humberton supervised four funerals and an embalming job. He had no time whatever for crime detection. But when leisure was available at about nine o'clock in the evening, he was glad to act as host in his study to a little conference composed of himself, Ted Spang, Clyde and John Massow.

Clyde had been busy all day on the case. He was eager to report results—such as they were.

"It *is* murder, Ho," he said, solemnly. "You know Sollerby, the coroner. He's a good doctor. Only a good one would have been able to get anywhere, the way the body was. He says Walter White was dead when the tackle crushed him. Killed by a blow on the head."

"You are sure of the identification?"

"I'll take responsibility for that," Massow put in, quietly. His deeply lined face, with sunken eyes beneath gray hair, set grimly as he spoke. "I went over him again this morning—in daylight. We haven't let his mother see him. He had a sweetheart, too—Betty Chanters. Of course we've kept her from him. At my suggestion, Clyde has brought in two other business friends of Walter's—men with strong stomachs who we thought could stand the sight. They agree that there's no mistake."

"Now we come to the queer stuff," the detective volunteered. "It looks as if we know who the killer is, Ho, though we haven't put hands on him yet. It's your yarn, Massow.

Tell it the way you did to me, this morning, before we staged our manhunt."

The retired ironmaster smiled, reflectively. "Perhaps you know, Mr. Humberton, that this mill of ours is not entirely new?"

The necrologist shook his head.

"Well, that's the case. We took over an older structure. Part of it, the old cupola, is still standing, a short distance from the newer portion. And I learned from Walter White a week ago that an escaped convict from the state penitentiary was hiding out in that cupola."

He paused, looked up under his shaggy brows at his attentive listener, and abruptly went on.

"Perhaps I'll be put in jail, before this is over, for keeping that discovery to myself, but I did—at Walter's request. He was a boyhood friend of White's, you see. Mr. White fed him. Walt used to come down at night a good deal, after everyone had gone, to stroll around the mill—said he could think better then than in the daytime. That gave him his chance with the convict, of course. I never saw the man very close, myself. He happened to show himself when I was there one night with Walt, going over things, or I'd never have known."

"And you think he committed this crime?" Humberton inquired.

"I do, for two reasons. Walter told me that this fellow was beginning to go crazy from the strain of hiding out. That's my first reason. My second is the murder itself. Why should anyone in his right mind fire a locomotive crane at midnight in order to grind up a body? It's an outlandish thing to do—not the act of a sane man, at all!"

Humberton looked at the detective. "What do you know of this convict, Clyde?"

"Everything, Ho, up to the time he broke loose. Nothing since, till I heard of this fellow in the cupola. He's Michael Burk. Killed his wife. Sentenced to the hot seat. Escaped a month ago, on his way to the pen—rotten work on the part of the bulls who were chaperoning him, if you ask me. White told Massow what Burk's name was, so that ties up."

The necrologist nodded, silently. He was a good listener.

CLYDE LEANED forward, to tick his various achievements off on his thick fingers. "Here's what we've done. We've shot his description and photo all over the state and all through Pennsylvania and West Virginia. That was done a month ago, but we're doing it over again. Mike is going to have plenty trouble making a getaway this time. Then we've gone over the mill—the old one and the new, what there is of it. I'll guarantee you, Ho, we haven't overlooked any place where he can possibly be. We found his hideout—a regular bed, right in the old cupola itself. There's a rope hanging down to the mill floor from the iron cupola platform nearby—left there by workmen who were moving out some of the junk, Massow says. I'll bet it made a slick way for Mike to slide to the ground pronto when he felt like it. But did we find Mike? We did not! He must have flown the coop last night."

"Then he should be caught soon. He will hardly get another hiding-place like that," the ironmaster commented.

"He will be caught—don't worry," Clyde declared, with professional pride.

"Mr. Massow, you said something last night which I should like explained." Humberton bent his thick spectacles questioningly on his visitor. "You hinted that since Clyde has two shares of your stock, he has lost two hundred dollars. That's what he paid for it, I understand. Does it follow that you are ruined by Walter White's death?"

John Massow nodded. "I am!" he said, bitterly.

"Why?"

"I'll tell you why. Our company owns the White patents, of course. They cover the machinery for the new process. But there's another angle—the chemical angle. In this process it means more than machinery—so much more that without it we are absolutely sunk. That secret died with Walter White."

"Surely you have it recorded somewhere?"

Massow grinned, bitterly. "If it were written down, I, being myself a chemist, could take the notes and go ahead. White's death, though a terrible personal blow, would not mean ruin to me. Unfortunately, the secret is not recorded."

"The old man was eccentric as the very devil, Ho," Clyde put in. "On top of that, I'll bet he was the world's greatest stock seller. You can believe it or not, and I consider myself hard-boiled, but I bought my two shares with the understanding that nobody was to know the secret of that plant except old White and his son, until the process was in production. Then you were to be let in on it, too, weren't you, Mr. Massow?"

"Not a minute before," Massow agreed.

HORATIO HUMBERTON, whose knowledge of business was as slight as it was encyclopedic in all that related to crime, or embalming, or the lore of funerals, nodded his acquiescence.

"We'll pass that," he conceded. "For reasons satisfactory to you and Clyde and the other stockholders, you let one man's life stand between you and ruin. He is dead. Our task is not to question your judgment, but to learn who killed him. Did you have another talk with the boy, Clyde?"

"Grilled him like a herring," the detective replied, moodily. "He's not any too bright, if you ask me. But he knows how to stick to a story, I'll say that for him. He saw a tall shadow come out of the mill with a dead man under its arm, and place the dead man on the crane. Then he beat it. From what he says now, I guess the nearest he got to the crane was half the length of the field away. That's his yarn. You couldn't get any more out of him with a stomach pump. After he dropped you last night, he did get a brain wave and go on to wake up Mr. Massow here, but that was the end."

"You consider him stupid, Clyde?" Humberton inquired, mildly.

"I'd give him ninety-nine and a half out of a possible hundred," the detective answered, with conviction. "He's weak-minded, that's what he is."

"I would hardly rate him much higher, myself. But stupidity and imagination don't go together. We can assume that the boy saw what he described, whether he interpreted it correctly or not. Now, Massow—"

He turned his near-sighted eyes owlishly upon the steel magnate, and it seemed then that he bent them inward upon himself, before speaking again; for he continued to stare silently and thoughtfully, as if John Massow were a specimen placed before him for examination. Massow fidgeted. He even looked slightly indignant. Ted Spang and Clyde, who knew the tall necrologist's odd ways, merely waited. They assumed that he was coming to a decision of some sort. So he was, and the nature of the decision astonished them thoroughly.

It was prefaced by an abrupt question. "You know the old cupola pretty well, Massow?"

"Why, yes—of course," Massow replied.

"That's fine!" Humberton smiled genially upon his guests. "Are you inclined for a little adventure, gentlemen? I have been sitting here, analyzing this strange occurrence in my mind, and I really believe I have the answer to it. You recall the shocking condition of the face and the hands of the unfortunate man in the crane? Well, you are undoubtedly correct, Clyde—it is murder. But I have my own ideas as to the murderer. You are sure you searched the old cupola thoroughly?"

"I am!" Clyde retorted, somewhat belligerently.

"Well—no doubt you did. But you made a mistake."

As his friend paused, Clyde was moved to a sharp rejoinder; but he refrained. He had learned to wait Humberton out.

"You made the capital mistake of searching in the daylight. This crime took place at night. The boy saw a shadow carrying the body—and shadows are things of darkness. With your permission, gentlemen, we will go out to the mill now, and search the cupola again!"

ON THE way out to the plant site Horatio Humberton said not a word. Such remarks as were addressed to him by his three companions were replied to by nods and grunts. But he came out of his silence to request that the car be parked at a spot on the road just opposite the location of the crane in the field, and he led the way with long strides to the scene of the tragedy. Though the moon was not yet up, and despite his nearsightedness, he seemed to find it without difficulty.

He did not turn on a flashlight to examine the crane. Instead, he walked around it several times in the dark, stopping at one point or another to stare at it or at the black bulk of the mill, looming at the farther side of the field.

"Were your construction crews working today?" he asked suddenly of Massow.

"I laid off everyone but the day watchman."

"And the night watchman?"

"He's over in the new mill, beyond the old one you see here. There's nothing of value in this part."

"How many men did you have in today's search, Clyde?"

"An even dozen, Ho," the detective answered. "I'm telling you, we did a good job."

But the tall necrologist shook his head, disapprovingly. "Too many. You could have done as well with four. That is all we shall use tonight. Massow, you know this old part of the plant. I want you to distribute us to the best advantage. But before you do—while we are walking over to the cupola—have you any explanation of the boy's bizarre shadow story? I should have asked you that before."

The iron magnate chuckled. "I know where he got the idea of the shadow, if that's what you mean. He's a Laurel Village boy, remember. I've lived in this village all my life. So did my father, my grandfather and my great-grandfather before me. This little community is old, and like most old places has its legends. The Shadow Ghost is one of them."

Clyde and Ted Spang closed in to hear. Massow noticed the fact, and laughed.

"I'm no story teller, boys. You can have this in two or three sentences. All there is to it is the murder of an Indian by a white man in Revolutionary times. This was a border settlement then, and a far more important place than it is today. The Indians came in force, and got their revenge by nearly wiping out the settlement. Some of the bodies in this old cemetery are without their scalps. This murdered Indian, by the way, is said to stalk around without his—the white man took it. He comes as a gigantic shadow, so how anyone can tell whether he has his scalp or not is beyond me. But that's the story."

"Does he kill—according to the story?" Humberton inquired.

"I forgot that. He does. Not often—not often enough for anyone to give a name to his last victim. He comes into the village and walks off with someone under his arm. Then that unlucky devil is never heard of again. There's your story. I suppose the boy saw this body in our crane, and within two minutes he was sure he'd seen the shadow, too."

"One more question—so far as you know, had the shadow ever before been seen in this field?"

"Now you come to mention it, I don't believe it has. It's a graveyard story—a typical one."

CHAPTER THREE
STAIRWAY TO TERROR

THEY HAD reached the high-arched entrance of the old cupola building. In the darkness the top of the arch was invisible. So was most of the building itself, except where a star or two peeped through dirty windows far up near the roof. Humberton drew the others close to him and spoke in low tones, as if the convict they sought might be watching within earshot.

"How many entrances are there to this building?" he asked Massow.

"Three. This one, another like it at the far end toward the new mill, and a little side door."

"Do you believe one of us should be stationed at each of those?"

"I suppose so." The iron magnate's voice was rumbling and discontented. "Mind you, I don't like this business, at all. That fellow's a desperate character. If he is still hiding out here—which I doubt very much—he might easily cut one of us off. There's plenty of junk lying around this place that would make weapons for him. You're the doctor, Humberton—we're doing what you say—but I'm not taking any responsibility for it."

"I will take the responsibility," the necrologist replied, evenly. "There are four of us. Where shall the fourth be posted?"

"There are flights of iron steps going up to the cupola— over a hundred of them. Someone should climb those. They lead directly to Burk's hideout which we found today. If he happened to be lying in wait, partway up, I wouldn't give much for the chances of the man who did the climbing. Suppose I take that assignment."

"I will take it," Humberton said, quietly.

"Why not give it to me?" Ted suggested.

No, Ted, with my nearsightedness I shall be safer where I have stair rails to guide me in the dark. Now, Massow, where will you have the others?"

The big man seemed to have accepted the inevitable. His voice became brisk. "Clyde, you're armed, and you were over this place in daylight. Besides, I guess you are more or less used to hand-to-hand fighting. Are you willing to climb up to the mouth of the cupola at the left of the other main door? You'll have to do some ticklish work over the girders, but I don't know a better chance of catching anyone who may be hiding up there."

"O.K.," Clyde agreed, curtly.

"You have a gun, too, Spang? Well, take the door straight ahead—the other main entrance. Cover all the ground around there. Keep your gun handy. Remember—he's a killer."

"Right," said the driver.

"I will run over to the little side door, to make sure it is locked. It was today— no doubt it still is. Then I'll come back here, and stand guard. I'm armed. Are you, Mr. Humberton?"

"I never carry a gun," the necrologist answered. "Shall we go to our posts?"

THE FOUR of them dispersed into the blackness of the old mill. But at the last moment Humberton put out a sinewy arm and imprisoned Ted's hand.

"Come with me, Ted," he whispered.

A moment later, he amplified the unexpected command.

"You will remain at the foot of the stairs, Ted," he said. "Don't bother about the other door. Keep your ears open for the least sound from above. Do you understand—the least sound?"

"I get you, sir," the driver concurred, also in a whisper.

"When you hear it, call to me. Call softly. At the same time, dodge to one side, so as to be under cover of the stairs."

"What kind of a sound will it be?" inquired the puzzled driver.

"I have no idea. Possibly there won't be any sound."

"But if there is, I yip." Ted concurred. "O.K., sir. Yip and duck. I've got it straight."

"One minute, before I go. Let me have your flashlight."

Ted's employer shot the thin white beam up the circularly winding flight of iron stairs. In another instant, he had shut it off again. It had been on so brief a time that anyone standing in the darkness and not expecting to see the light would hardly have noticed it at all.

"Ted!" Humberton's whisper was sharp and insistent. "What did you see when I turned the light on?"

"I saw the iron stairs, sir."

"There was no one—or nothing—on the stairs?"

"Not that I saw, sir. I had my eyes pretty well peeled."

"Remember, I am nearsighted. I must rely on you. Is there a hand rail on both sides, all the way up?"

"Yes, sir. I'm positive of that."

"That's all. Remain here."

He slipped the flashlight back into his driver's hand and at once started up. The darkness was thick. It pressed upon him, like some black, suffocating drapery. As he set his foot, silently but squarely, on one step after another, he seemed to be pushing the night aside—slowly forcing his way upward.

After half a dozen steps, he stopped and listened. There was the sighing of a breeze, far up among the ironwork traceries of the old mill; nothing else. He strained his myopic eyes downward toward where he knew Ted was waiting. Nothing was visible. Of course that was to be expected. Then he listened once more, intently. His ears were not like his eyes—they were keen. Finally, he continued his upward progress, but now he stopped at each step and again listened, his body taut, both sinewy hands gripping the stair rail.

At about the height of the twentieth step, he paused for a long while. He had been climbing so cautiously that no one on the ground or at the top of the iron staircase could have heard even the slight shuffle of his footsteps. But now he deliberately kicked the metal step, and uttered a deep imprecation, as if he had snagged his foot against it. His voice was subdued, but in the dead silence it was quite distinct.

He listened again, pressed closely against the hand rail. At last he heard a noise, from above. It was a very slight noise—hardly more than a ghost of a sound. Instantly, Ted's voice called softly from below. Humberton promptly slid his feet through under the rail, and let his long legs down until he was dangling on the outside of the iron stairs.

HIS ARMS had barely straightened to their full length when there was a crash from far up toward the head of the stairs. It descended, gathering volume as it came—the mighty clangor of iron smiting iron. As he hung there, waiting, something huge and swift pounded its way down the stairs with irresistible momentum; iron death for him had he been in its path. It had hardly gone past when he was on the stairs again, rapidly descending.

Ted Spang met him, partway up. "You're not hurt, sir?"

"No, Ted. I forgot to tell you not to call. Get to the door you were assigned to guard. Begin running this way when you hear the others coming. Don't turn on your flashlight."

Massow's voice came from somewhere in the darkness. "Humberton! Humberton!"

The necrologist did not reply; nor did he when Clyde's powerful bellow demanded: "Ho! Are you all right, Ho?"

Humberton, having reached the foot of the stairs at his leisure, deliberately picked out a spot in the dirt floor of the mill, and lay down. When running footsteps and a flashlight approached within easy hearing distance, he sat up and managed a rather convincing moan.

It was Clyde, almost incoherent with concern. Behind him came Massow, and still farther behind, Ted Spang.

"Are you hurt, Ho?"

"The breath was knocked out of me," returned the necrologist, weakly. "I shall be quite recovered in a moment or two. What was it? It whirled down the stairs and very nearly struck me."

Massow's light picked up the details of a heavy fly-wheel, now lying still and harmless. It had buried itself in the soft dirt, with the force of its impact.

"I guess he's up there," he declared, grimly. "He very nearly made us pay for going after him in the dark!"

"The dirty murderer!" Clyde let out a growl of honest indignation. "He's not going to get away with it! I'm starting after him right now with a gun in my hand, and I'm coming back with his body!"

But Horatio Humberton's voice recovered unexpected strength, for a man who had just been prostrated by the shadow of death passing by.

"You are going home, Clyde," he corrected with cold determination. "None of us must risk our lives any further tonight. We have demonstrated the important point—our man is hiding in the mill. If you missed him in the daylight, that was because you didn't search well enough. Come back tomorrow and do a better job. He has too big an advantage at night."

Clyde was reluctant. "What do you think, Massow?"

"I want to get him now. He killed my friend," replied the big ironmaster, curtly.

"Come, Ted. You and I will sit in the machine and wait till they join us," was Humberton's conclusion.

No amount of argument could move him—none ever could, when he had made up his mind. The result was that the search was abandoned for that night. They returned across the field, past the gaunt and silent bulk of the loco-motive crane.

A little beyond it, Humberton contrived to fall behind the others, and to link his arm into that of his mystified driver.

"Do you understand what happened, Ted?" he inquired, softly.

"Not any more than I understand Astronomy," was the emphatic rely.

"I am glad. You reassure me. Just at present, I don't want it understood too well."

"Tell me one thing, sir—just this one. I won't ask you any more. Was the murderer of young Walter White trying to kill you, too?"

The necrologist chuckled, under his breath. "Your ques-tion is not in quite the right form, Ted," he said. "I really can't answer it by 'Yes' or 'No.' I can tell you this much: that fly-wheel undoubtedly was meant for me!"

CHAPTER FOUR
FROM THE GRAVE

CLYDE DROPPED the necrologist and his senior driver at the Humberton Funeral Parlors, and sped on to get such sleep as he could in what was left of the night. Massow, he had already taken to his Laurel Village home. The front door of the parlors was ajar. Possibly they had left it so on their hasty exit. Ted, who was in advance, stopped at the threshold to ask a question.

"Was it an accident, sir?" he demanded. "That's what's eating me up right now."

"You mean the rather sudden descent of the fly-wheel?" his employer returned. "Far from its being accidental, Ted, I should say that it was partly planned by me—to the extent, at least, that I hoped for something of the sort if I was careful to lay myself open to it. Heavy chunks of iron are likely to be lying handy in old steel mills. I know now where we stand. All that is left is to find the motive."

"Does a crazy man need a motive?"

Humberton laughed. He, too, had delayed before entering the hallway, as if to have this colloquy out of the way first.

"No. Oh, no!" he assented. "But aren't you taking too much for granted, Ted?"

"Then he isn't crazy?" The driver whistled, softly. "This gets better and better! I should say that heaving that flywheel at you, when all he had to do was to stay hid, was more the act of a lunatic than of somebody in his senses— but you know best. Maybe White threatened to give him away. That would be motive enough for a desperate man, wouldn't it, sir?"

"I see a little coupé parked half a block up the street," Humberton said.

"Why, so do I," Ted stared, and darted a lively and interested glance at the half-opened door of the parlors.

"Everything's dark except our place," he whispered. "Someone parked up there, not being quite sure of our location, then walked back and went in. I'll bet he's in the study right now!"

"We will see," his employer returned, composedly.

"Let me go first," Ted said. He blocked the way, gave the door a quick push, then stepped behind the door jamb until he could see what was ahead. And at once, with a laugh, he gave way to his chief.

A girl stood in the light streaming from the study, at the far end of the hall.

"Mr. Humberton?" she inquired, a little nervously.

Horatio Humberton returned an affirmative and stepped into the hallway. The girl ran forward. She was tall and lithe. Her voice, quiet and restrained, had in it a suggestion of emotion which she was controlling with an effort.

"I am Elizabeth Chanters," she said. "You know? I mean—you know who I am?"

The necrologist took her gently by the arm, to impel her back to the study. "I believe so," he replied, gravely. "You are—the fiancée—

"Yes." She shot the word out, and went on rapidly, with a barely perceptible catch of the breath. "I didn't want to wait out in the car. I saw the door open, and came in. There was a light back here, so that was where I waited. It's all right?"

"Perfectly." He led her to a chair—his own chair behind the work table, which was the best place to sit in the cluttered study. "Come in, Ted. No doubt you have something to tell me, Miss Chanters. My associate, Mr. Spang, should hear it at the same time."

"I didn't come to tell you anything. I came to ask something. Do you know who killed him?"

"I expect to know, soon."

"I'm glad of that. You see, I expect to get news, too. Then we can check up together, and make sure the right man is punished."

HUMBERTON HAD remained standing, listening courteously, but also studying her face through his thick lenses. It was a softly contoured face, with large blue eyes, and crowned with naturally curling blond hair. The hair just missed being golden; the face just missed being shallow and a trifle silly in its expression. It was saved from both by what was probably a lately developed self-control in the presence of tragedy. She was a little girl grown up overnight.

The necrologist waited, still looking at her thoughtfully and sympathetically. Ted fidgeted behind him.

"It's hard for me to take things the way I should," she went on, with an oddly misplaced laugh. "I suppose that's because I'm only human, after all. Walter and I are Spiritualists. That's what I mean. We don't believe in death. So I oughtn't to grieve—especially after tonight. Only a short time before I started here, Mr. Humberton, a medium called me up and gave me a message from him. That's why I came here. I haven't the least idea who called—he said his name was unknown to me, and that it would make no difference, anyway—and I'm not quite sure whether the message is genuine or not. I want your opinion."

Humberton started. As a sort of side line to his studies in the wisdom of the Egyptians, he had gone rather deeply into psychic research. He never willfully missed an opportunity to investigate the subject. With a smile—much more engaging and human than the look of professional sympathy he had been wearing—he mechanically gathered a dozen large volumes into a pile from the number untidily scattered about the floor of the study, sat down upon the seat thus erected, and asked, cordially: "What was the message, Miss Chanters?"

"I was sitting by myself in my room tonight, Mr. Humberton. I wanted a message from him. Somehow I felt something might come through. I sat there with a pad on my knee and a pencil, hoping perhaps for automatic writing. You know what I mean?"

He nodded. Ted Spang, also sitting upon some books, listened with no less interest than his chief. Ted was skeptical by nature, but he had learned in the course of his years with Horatio Humberton that anything the tall necrologist regarded with close attention was likely to be worth the effort.

"There wasn't anything, though I waited a long time. But at last this telephone call came. It was from a man. He said he was a medium. He said Walter had been trying and trying to get through to me, and had finally done it by him. The message is—" She broke off. "You know the cemetery, near the field where he was found?"

Again Humberton nodded.

"That's the message. I'm to go out to that cemetery tonight—alone—before morning. He'll come through to me there."

"To the cemetery!" Horatio Humberton's nod was nearly one of satisfaction. "This is really very interesting, Miss Chanters. No doubt you would be afraid to undertake any adventure of the sort?"

"I'm afraid—of course." Once more the soft face tightened into almost unnatural firmness. "But if you think the call came from Walter, I'll do it."

Humberton glanced at his watch. "It is after two o'clock. You are willing to go out there tonight, by yourself?"

SHE NODDED, silently. He continued to stare at his quaint old timepiece as if it held the key to something far more important than the hour of night.

"What time did this call come through to you, Miss Chanters?"

"I can tell you that exactly. We live near St. John's Church, and just as I hung up the receiver, I heard the quarter strike. It was a quarter after one."

"And you came over here at once?"

"Almost at once. Father and mother had retired. I often sit up reading, long after they go to bed. I thought you could advise me better than they could, and it seemed to me, too, that I shouldn't alarm them. So, I just came."

Humberton smiled. "Will the telephone wake one of them, if it rings?" he asked.

"I suppose so—since I'm not there to answer it."

"Then I fear their rest is about to be disturbed. I will go into the office and call up your home."

Horatio Humberton had not been a funeral director for thirty years without learning how to soothe and convince other human beings. He returned rather soon to the book-cluttered study, and his lean face wore an expression of contented benevolence.

"I have had a pleasant talk with your father," he told his nervous visitor. "Without going into gruesome details, I have managed to set his mind at rest as to your absence from the house. He was very obliging. You may not be aware, Miss Chanters, that your father and I are members of the same lodge. I was able to supply a few points which satisfied him as to my identity, and he is willing to accept my pledge for your safety."

She rose. "Then I might as well start."

"Yes. You know the way?"

"Walter—" she choked a moment, but straightened her shoulders and went on—"often took me out to the mill. I've seen the cemetery. I'm to walk along beside the south wall until—until he comes to me."

"Very well."

They walked in silence to the front door of the parlors, the girl a little in advance. Then she asked: "Are you following me out there, Mr. Humberton?"

"I think not," the necrologist returned. "From what I know of psychic manifestations, the conditions laid down have to be observed very closely. Of course, I took the responsibility for your safety, but that was largely to satisfy your father. If you aren't willing to incur the risk, by far the best thing you can do is to call this off and go home."

"No doubt you're right." Her voice shook a little. "You haven't said so, but I gather you think this may be a genuine message from Walter, so of course I'm doing as he asks. Thank you—"

She hesitated a moment, then almost ran down the deserted sidewalk to her little car. But she had not yet reached it when Humberton shot a command at his faithful associate.

"Quick, Ted! Get out the car!"

"You're following her, sir?"

"Of course!"

Ted sighed, and disappeared.

HUMBERTON PLACED a restraining hand on Spang's arm. "Keep her car in sight, Ted, but don't let her suspect she is being followed."

"O.K., sir," Ted agreed, cheerfully. "That's not hard to do when I know where she's heading for." He slowed down to a steady pace, several blocks behind the rapidly moving tail-light ahead. "You had me going for a minute," he went on. "I couldn't figure how you'd ever let her go out there by herself. I suppose the idea is that if she knew we were close by she wouldn't act natural?"

"Precisely."

"Then that means you don't look for any real ghost? A real one ought to be able to sense for himself if anybody's around, I should think."

Humberton grinned at his inquisitive driver. They were now clear of the city and on the road to Laurel Village.

"I can't follow you in your analysis of ghosts, Ted," he said. "To me they have always proved an elusive subject. But I think you are right in wanting such information as I can give you. It isn't much. Let me ask you a question. Why was the body mangled so terribly in the locomotive crane?"

"Because the fellow that did it was crazy," the driver answered, promptly.

"Suppose, for the sake of argument that he was not crazy. Suppose that he was exceptionally keen. You saw the body. The face and the hands in particular were mutilated beyond all recognition. I doubt whether even Scotland Yard could get fingerprints from those hands. Now, what reason would a keen man have for doing that?"

Ted was an impulsive soul. When an idea struck him with force, he was likely to register the fact physically. He registered is now by suddenly treading the accelerator to the floor boards, so that the sedan jumped like a kangaroo, and Humberton's forehead just missed a collision with the wind-shield.

"Sorry, sir." Ted got his foot under control again. "That rather hit me between the eyes. But if the body in the crane was not Walter White, but somebody in White's clothes, where is White hiding out?"

"I don't know. I can't even be sure that the body is not White's."

"People have done that sort of thing to collect insurance," Ted persisted; but his employer's emphatic head-shake was visible in the moonlight.

"White apparently carried no life insurance. Clyde checked up on that in the course of his investigation. It seems that his family and that of Miss Chanters are both spiritualists. They go further than most members of the cult in holding that life insurance is not necessary, since the spiritual powers watch over man's welfare."

Ted whistled. "I'm glad my old man didn't feel that way," he said. "What with seven of us kids, my mother had her troubles as it was. But that leaves us where we started, shadow and all, don't it, sir?"

"Not quite, Ted, not quite. As for the shadow, I think we can safely assume that a body was carried from the mill. In the deceptive moonlight the man who was doing the carrying—a big man, by the way—became to the boy the giant shadow of the ghost legend." Humberton blinked about through his thick lenses. "Aren't we nearly there?"

"About a mile to go. The road bends around a clump of trees just this side of the graveyard."

"We'll park near the bend. Now Ted, follow me closely. We are dealing with a desperate man. It is quite on the cards that he may win. If he thinks he can safely kill me, he'll do it-for he knows that I suspect him!"

TED NEARLY stepped on the accelerator again, but restrained himself in time. "Who?" he demanded.

"Massow!"

"You're not kidding me, sir?"

"This isn't the time for that." Humberton turned his mouth squarely toward Ted's nearer ear, so as to be heard more easily. "When I was a young man, Ted, I had quite a flair for amateur theatricals. They told me I was good. I was better, however, as a critic. I had the faculty—and not every critic has it—of instantly distinguishing natural acting from the forced, artificial kind. Massow's acting at the locomotive crane last night was artificial. He tried to impress us with the idea that the finding of his partner's body was a tremendous shock to him. It was not a shock, at all. He knew perfectly what he would find there. I saw through him almost instantly. But—" the necrologist chuckled—"he, also, saw through me!"

"Saw through you?" Ted echoed.

"Saw that I suspected him. Perhaps I wasn't so careful as I might have been to keep him from seeing it. But in one thing I was careful, Ted—not to let him know that I realized suspicion of me."

"Sounds a little complicated, sir."

"More than a little, Ted. The whole business is weird and incredible. Perhaps the most incredible part of it to you will be the fact that I deliberately set the stage and gave him the chance to get rid of me, if he could—at the old cupola. I thought that a man capable of the atrocity at the crane might be capable of trying that. And he was! After we left him, he must have reached the top of the iron stairs by a route known to him but not to us. He's a strong man. No doubt he found it easy to dislodge that fly-wheel and set it at the top of the stairs. Then, of course, he returned to the mill floor by way of the dangling rope, in good time to come running up in the darkness to inquire about my welfare. He proved my reasoning for me, Ted. With me

out of the way he would have been safe—and he knew it.…
Here's the bend in the road."

"O.K., sir!" Ted neatly ditched the sedan among the
trees, and sprang out. The moon was not quite so bright as
it had been, but it served. They could see the coupé, parked
some distance ahead, opposite the cemetery.

Humberton also jumped out of the machine—a little
more gingerly. "Can you see anything of her, Ted?" he
inquired, anxiously.

"She's starting into the graveyard now. That stone wall
is on the far side of it," the driver replied.

"We must run. If anything should happen to her, I could
never forgive myself for exposing her to this. But it was the
quickest way to uncover his hand—and speed may mean
life or death."

"Shall I run ahead, sir?" Ted suggested.

"Yes, Ted. Cut across the field where the crane is, and
hide behind the wall. If anything happens, use your own
judgment. I'll join you as soon as I can."

Ted was off. Reaching the boundary of the large field,
he cleared the ditch, placed his hands on a post of the barb-
wire fence and vaulted that, then raced like a hare diago-
nally across the field. The tall necrologist, lumbering after,
soon lost sight of him. But Humberton continued at a
steady running pace. He eased himself through the fence,
and tried to be as noiseless as possible. It was no part of his
plan that Miss Chanters should know she was guarded.

CHAPTER FIVE
THE SECRET OF
THE CEMETERY

AS HUMBERTON neared the cemetery line, the moonlight brightened. He could see the girl. To his nearsighted gaze, her figure was vague, but he saw that she was walking very slowly—so slowly that he had time to reach the cover of the wall before she had come to its inner side.

"Don't breathe so hard, sir. She'll hear you," Ted cautioned, as his employer squatted down with him on the outer side of the low wall. Humberton received the suggestion in dignified silence, although several sharp rejoinders occurred to him. He did place one hand over his mouth, but continued to watch the slim figure of the girl as she slowly walked, within a few feet of them, toward the yellow disk of the moon.

The wall behind which they crouched had fallen into ruin in its middle portion, which left the cemetery for a hundred yards or more open to the fields at the side. No cover was possible there. They were able to keep even with the hesitant girl till this open space was reached, when Ted placed his lips close to his chief's ear and whispered again: "Shall I try wriggling along on my stomach so as to keep near her, sir?"

"The moon is too bright. We must wait here," Humberton decided.

"O.K., sir." She had moved beyond them, so Ted was able to speak with safety. "Notice that clump of trees over where the wall is built up again? She's walking right towards it. Can you spot anything queer about it?"

The necrologist strained his eyes, but at length shook his head. "I see nothing but the trees, Ted. They are very black in the moonlight. You must remember my nearsightedness."

"I can't be dead sure, sir," the driver went on, not whispering now, yet keeping his voice down carefully, "but I think I saw a light there, just a minute ago; a queer kind of a light. It looked pale, like the moon, but it wasn't the moon."

"You don't see it now?"

"That's the funny part of it: I do, and I don't. When I look right at those trees everything is dark, but the moment I glance away I seem to see the light out of the corner of my eye."

"Imagination, doubtless," Humberton commented, coldly.

Ted was silent, while the girl they were watching walked slowly—very slowly—toward the black clump of trees, with the moon behind them. She was sick with fear. That was manifest in each shrinking step. But she faltered on.

Ted quivered, suddenly, like a pointer dog that scents his quarry. He laid a firm hand on his chief's knee, and whispered, just above his breath: "Hear anything, sir?"

"I hear the wind among the gravestones," his chief returned.

"So do I. But this isn't the wind. I've been sneaking a glance or two behind."

"Something is following us?"

"Yes, sir," the driver answered.

"Our work lies ahead of us, Ted, not behind."

"O.K." Ted said, resignedly; but Humberton was not content to let it go at that. He gripped the young man's muscular arm, and spoke rapidly.

"Listen to me, Ted. I have let Miss Chanters go through with this thing because I suspect that a life is at stake, and this seems the most likely way to make Massow show his hand in time. I don't believe she is in any real danger. Yet she may be. She is walking very slowly, but in another moment or two she should reach the circle of trees. Then—"

"What then, sir?" Ted interrupted, excitedly.

"I don't know. She has been brought here for some purpose. Whatever it is it may be carried out then. If she seems in no danger, we'll not interfere. We'll merely follow. But there won't be time to talk about it. You'll have to use your own judgment."

TED NODDED. She was now so close to the trees that he wasted none of his powers in words. He was entirely concentrated on watching. The moonlight, reflected from the ground and from the shimmering tombstones, seemed a luminous stream through which she walked waist-deep. By contrast the point just ahead where her path plunged into the woods was like some black hole between the stars. She paused a moment before entering the blackness, and looked about her uncertainly.

Then she screamed, twice, and fell forward.

Ted was on his feet, and running, before the anguished tones of her voice had fairly died away. He reached the girl, and knelt beside her.

"She's all right, sir! She's coming round!" he shouted.

Then he leapt to his feet, and shot off between the trees. When Humberton came up to the girl, she was struggling to a sitting position.

"Don't try to stand yet," he cautioned, gently. "You are quite all right, Miss Chanters. We have been near you all the while. Can you control yourself enough to tell me what you saw?"

"I saw—I saw—" She broke off with a sob.

"You've been very brave. Try to hold up just a little longer. What did you see?"

"A dreadful face—all fire!"

"Walter White's face?"

"I don't think so!"

Ted was back. "Can't find anybody, sir."

Humberton gazed thoughtfully at his assistant. In spite of his advice, Miss Chanters was standing. She was even making an attempt to brush herself off.

"You have your gun, Ted?"

"Right here in my hand." Ted held it up for inspection.

"Can you use a revolver, Miss Chanters?"

The unexpected question seemed to have a composing effect upon her. Her voice was firmer as she answered: "I'm really quite good with one. Walter made it a kind of hobby. He taught me how to shoot

"That's very satisfactory." He calmly took the gun from Ted's hand. "I am going to ask you to do something to help us, Miss Chanters. If you aren't strong enough, please don't hesitate to say so, but if you are it will help greatly—greatly. I am giving you this gun. Do you feel able to return to your car alone, carrying it in your hand for protection, and to drive back to town by yourself? You have been the victim of a brutal trick, but I don't believe it will be attempted a second time, in the full glare of the moonlight."

She stopped, in the act of putting out her hand for the revolver. "A trick."

"There is no time now to explain. Can you do what I ask?"

"Yes," she answered, simply.

"Then here is the gun. Now, one thing more. When you reach home, call up police headquarters. Have them put you in touch with Detective Clyde. He is to drive out here at once. Tell him to bring a squad of men with him, but not to take too much time gathering them up. Will you do that?"

She hesitated. "Possibly I can find a phone somewhere before I get home. That would save time."

"You are not to stop until you reach home. I am responsible for you to your father, and I want you to promise me that."

She nodded, reluctantly. "Very well."

Humberton watched her until her figure began to blend with the broad sea of moonlight. Then he turned to his associate, and speaking more loudly and far more cheerfully than the circumstances seemed to call for, he remarked: "I fancy, Ted, we are in for an adventure. The gentleman we are hunting will be only too glad to hunt us, if he can do so at all safely. And we have no gun!"

TED SPANG was naturally bright and given to intelligent reflection, yet he had found more than one occasion during his service with Horatio Humberton when the eccentric necrologist had thoroughly mystified him.

He was mystified now. For after they had watched Miss Chanters reach the road in safety and drive off in her little car, Humberton remarked, pleasantly: "I love the moonlight, Ted. There is nothing more soothing than, a stroll on such a night as the present. Suppose we walk toward the middle of this beautiful old graveyard. I see quite a large building there, which no doubt is the vault of the Massow family."

He linked his arm in Ted's, and led the puzzled young man out into the moonlight. Once there, his whimsical mood vanished with startling suddenness, and he was serious again.

"Now that we are out of earshot, I can talk to you," he said, abruptly. "We suspect Massow. Very well! Why should Massow entice Walter White's fiancée out to this place. To kill her? I think not. If I had thought so, I never would have consented to her going. She screamed. Probably that was all he wanted. She had a peculiar, quite distinctive voice. No doubt anyone well acquainted with her would recognize her scream."

"Who'd be out here to recognize it?" demanded Ted, vastly interested. He began to walk faster, but his employer held him to a slower pace.

"I must have time to talk to you, Ted. When we reach the vault, our adventure resumes—unless my reasoning is all wrong. If Massow is hiding someone—someone who will recognize Miss Chanters' scream and be moved by it—what better hiding-place can he find than his own vault? But you asked me a question. You asked who would be hiding here."

"And I think you've made me see the answer, sir," the driver replied. "Walter White is the fellow who'd be hit hardest by the scream. I'll bet the guy in the crane was the convict. Massow killed him—or he died some other way—and dressed his body up in White's clothes. I see what you were getting at about the face and hands being smashed so bad. He did that on purpose, of course, so nobody would find out. But I still don't see—"

"Neither do I, Ted," Humberton interrupted. "I don't see what possible advantage Massow can get out of White's disappearance. But I am certain—almost certain—that White is in that vault. You and I are going to find out about that, right now!"

"Maybe he's laying for us in the vault," the driver suggested.

"Quite likely."

Ted laughed. His odd sense of humor was keenest in moments of danger. "What a mark! You and me standing out there in the moonlight—I hope he's afraid to shoot, because of the noise."

"Hardly," his employer returned, cooly. "The vault will muffle that."

He started around the corner of the stone building.

"Where are you going, sir?" Ted demanded, grasping his arm.

"I shall stand at the side of the door, as nearly out of range as possible, and try to get into conversation with the man inside. I shan't make an unnecessary target of myself. I promise you that."

CHAPTER SIX

THE MAN IN THE VAULT

TED RELEASED the lean, sinewy arm of his chief. Humberton walked to the corner of the vault, his worried associate just behind him. He halted exactly at the corner, where he could not be seen by anyone inside if the door chanced to be open.

"John Massow!" he called.

There was no response.

"Can you see if the door's open?" Ted whispered.

"It is."

"Then he's inside?"

"He has been inside, at least."

"Listen to me, sir. I've got the eyes of a cat in the dark. Start talking to him again. I'll slip around you and be in there while he's still thinking over what you say."

Ted's employer patted the young man's shoulder, affectionately. "There seems to be no other way, Ted," he agreed.

He raised his voice. "John Massow! You have one other chance, before the police come. I give you my word that if the man you have in there is uninjured—"

Ted's voice interrupted, from the interior of the vault. He had slipped past his chief so adroitly that the latter had actually not been aware of it. "Not a soul in here, sir," he reported.

"You are sure?"

"I felt all around in the dark, then flashed my light about. Half a dozen stone cases, with caskets inside of them, I guess—and that seems to be about all."

Humberton walked into the vault. Ted was playing the flashlight about, to prove the truth of his words. Stone, cold and damp, was all it showed—stone floor, ceiling, and walls; stone burial cases ranged at the sides; a house of the dead, bare and severe yet large, for the Massows in their day had been a family of importance.

The driver continued to move the ray of his flashlight from side to side. "He can't be in one of those stone cases," he suggested. "Not if he's alive."

Humberton snatched the light from him and directed it on the floor. "Stone!" he said, thoughtfully. "A stone floor.

Why is that necessary?" Suddenly he danced half a dozen steps—ponderous, heavy steps. "That's it, Ted!" he cried. In his excitement, he no longer kept his voice down. "You heard the hollow sound? The original vault is underneath this. The later vault was built above it. What better place to hide a crime?"

He swept the flashlight over the stones of the floor. They were ancient, covered with dirt. Dirt stuffed the crannies between them; old, fungus-caked dirt, festering with the growths of moisture and decay.

"There's a queer mark over here at the side," Ted offered. "Something seems to have scraped the floor in a sort of a half-circle."

Humberton looked. His nearsighted eyes had entirely missed the mark. Now they sparkled with interest. "Quick, Ted! Help me!" he exclaimed.

FOR A moment, Ted was mystified. His chief had laid hold of one of the massive stone burial cases at the side of the vault. Then the alert driver understood, and added his own strength. At first, nothing resulted. Soon, very slowly, the heavy receptacle began to move toward them.

"Careful!" Humberton warned; but it was he who had to be pulled aside by his assistant when the swinging burial case suddenly came faster and completed its arc. Ted took the flashlight, and shot a luminous ray into the yawning cavity. There were no steps, but some four feet below-they could see a clay floor. It extended on three sides beyond their line of vision.

For the last time that night, the necrologist delayed so as to take Ted Spang into his confidence. He put one long arm around Ted's neck, and drawing the young man's face close to his own, spoke into his ear.

"You are to remain on guard up here, Ted," he whispered. "I will take the light. Massow is somewhere about, I am sure. He may be standing in the darkness at the door to this vault, this very minute. If he follows me down, as I hope he will, get out into the moonlight and bring Clyde here as soon as he appears. You understand?"

"I don't like it, sir," Ted protested, earnestly. "Let me—"

But his chief brought him up short. "You are taking more risk than I am," he said, curtly. "He is armed, you are not. Don't fight him—simply keep out of his way."

He felt his way to the brink of the opening in the floor, and dropped. He landed on hands and knees. At once he looked up, to test the darkness of the crypt. It was so complete that he could see nothing of the rectangular hole through which he had just come. If Ted was careful, his chances would be good.

He moved cautiously several paces forward until he believed himself out of the line of vision of anyone standing at the brink of the hole and peering down. Not until then did he turn on the flashlight. Its beam struck against the wall at the farther end. Slowly, he swung it about, to make the circuit of the underground crypt. There were sealed burial cases against the walls, many of them, all rougher and cruder than those in the vault above; nothing else.

He started suddenly as a thought not connected with what he was looking at crossed his mind; and at that moment a barely audible hiss came from the black opening behind. Evidently some change had taken place in the upper vault. Ted was warning him.

BUT HORATIO HUMBERTON had a tenacious brain. Once a question had been raised in it, he was likely to press for an answer, in spite of danger. The question was: how could the air be so fresh? Until a minute ago, the underground crypt had been closed by the swinging burial case above it. Yet the air was good.

He began to peer behind the cases, between them and the stone wall. Then he had the answer. There was a wide opening in the wall, perhaps two feet high—an air shaft, connected with the surface, through which a current of air was coming. He shot the flashlight beam into the shaft. It had not traveled a yard when it flashed from the living eyes of a man. He lay bound and gagged, stretched out stiffly like a corpse, with his head toward the shaft entrance.

Humberton laid down the flashlight at the opening of the shaft and whipped out the keen, thin-bladed knife he always carried. The gag was thick and cruel. He had to cut carefully to remove it without injury to the bound man. But he had skilful hands.

"You are Walter White?" he demanded, as the thick gag fell away.

The man's lips opened and shut and his swollen tongue protruded. The pressure of the gag must have been sheer agony. But he managed to whisper: "Yes."

He struggled to say something else. Humberton's quick instinct caught it.

"Miss Chanters is not harmed in any way. Her scream meant nothing except that she was frightened. She is at home—safe," he volunteered.

"Thank… God!" They were hardly more than the hoarse shells of words, but the necrologist understood.

"I'll cut your cords," he said. "We must work fast. Don't try to talk."

"You will have plenty of time to do that," a deep sardonic voice interrupted, from the direction of the opening in the crypt ceiling; and at almost the same moment two things happened: light from a much larger and more powerful electric torch than Humberton's flooded the crypt, and Ted Spang landed lightly on the clay floor. John Massow, holding the torch, was looking down at them through the opening.

"I'm sorry, sir," the driver said, with real regret but no excitement in his voice. "I hadn't the least idea of getting caught this way. But he flashed his light and a gun on me, so what else could I do? I guess he'd been watching us all the time."

An amused laugh from the opening greeted this. "A good guess, Ted," Massow's voice agreed. "While you were looking for me after I frightened Betty with a little phosphorus, I had merely climbed a tree. I heard everything you said. I haven't been far from you since. Didn't know that, did you, Humberton?"

The necrologist straightened, and glanced toward the opening. "Not positively; I merely suspected it," he replied.

"Bluffing, eh? Let me tell you something, Humberton. If you'd known that, you'd never have trapped yourself here. Your only hope is Clyde. I heard you send for him. But it's half an hour's drive each way. That gives me forty minutes. Walk over toward your boss, Ted."

"Do as you are told, Ted," Humberton directed.

"Good." Massow suddenly landed in the crypt. There were six feet between him and Ted, and he kept his revolver carefully leveled from the instant his feet struck the clay floor. He was dressed as they had seen him earlier in the evening, but there the resemblance ended. He had appeared then a rugged, athletic businessman of the typical mill-executive type, though unquestionably larger and stronger than most. Now his lips were a thin line, he seemed to talk through clenched teeth, his eyes were narrowed and merciless. He was an adventurer, making the last, desperate move of a desperate game.

"I'll talk to you, Humberton," he said, setting his electric lantern on the floor so that it shone on the others but not on him. "You know who's there in the shaft?"

Humberton nodded, and Massow went on, speaking rapidly. "I killed the convict, Humberton. I had to. He attacked White and me. That meddlesome boy saw me carrying the body to the crane, after I'd fired up, but I'd already knocked White out and brought him here, after changing his clothes. What if I did torture him a little? Did he have to be so damned obstinate? If he'd been reasonable, I would never even have thought of telling him I was going to bring Betty out here and torture her, too." He laughed, harshly. "I made her scream, all right, didn't I, White? Humberton—you claim to know so much—you know what I want out of White?"

Humberton looked at him in the shadows behind the electric lantern, and half smiled. "The chemical secret of the process," he said, slowly.

"You're brighter than I thought. Look here, Humberton—I've got a right to that secret. Most of the money in this thing is mine. All I ask is the key. Half a dozen words! I'm chemist enough to recognize if it sounds genuine or not. Get White to tell it to me, here and now—give me your word, all of you, that you won't proceed against me. I'll let you go. If you don't—"

Humberton glanced toward the prostrate man in the ventilating shaft. He could see the dark, keenly conscious eyes, the cut swollen lips. The lips parted. White's voice was still thick, but intelligible.

"He's a liar," it said, with cold, unemotional contempt. "He means to kill us. You've never fooled me for a moment, Massow. You meant to kill me from the first—as soon as you had my secret. With me gone, you could buy the rest of the stock for a song. Then if you had the secret, you'd pretend to experiment and rediscover it. You're heavily in debt, but that would make you rich again. Am I right, Massow?" The thick voice rose, hysterically.

MASSOW STOOD in silence, his finger on the trigger of the gun. At last he said: "I'm giving you your chance, White."

"What chance?" the man in the shaft demanded, bitterly.

"Tell me your secret. Promise not to prosecute. I'll take your word for it, and let you all go."

Walter White laughed. It was an unpleasant laugh to hear. "Do you believe that?" he asked Humberton.

"No!" Humberton answered.

"All right!" Massow said, quietly. There was a change in his voice. It was cold and final.

"I've played the game and lost," he went on. "That's over." He shifted his gaze and looked steadily at Horatio Humberton. "If it's any satisfaction to you, Humberton, I'll tell you now that one of these bullets is for me. But none of you three will be watching when I take it."

He had been stepping backward slowly, so as to leave still more room between them and him.

"You first!" he said to Ted, in a sudden dry whisper.

At the word, Ted sprang like a cat.

But a streak of orange-red flame was quicker. The air burst with a roar.

Detective Clyde, his gun still smoking, dropped lightly behind the two of them. Ted had crashed into a man with a shattered wrist—a man who cursed as the weapon fell from his useless hand.

"You drew it rather fine, Clyde," Humberton remarked quietly.

"Sorry, Ho. Had to wait till I could get a bead on his hand. Against regulations to kill a man if you don't have to."

Now Ted Spang looked curiously at his chief. "Did you know all the time that Clyde was there, sir?" he inquired.

"I fear the answer is 'Yes,'" Humberton returned. "You know my unfortunate tendency to be theatrical, Ted," he went on. "That must be my excuse for not telling you sooner. When I left the room at the funeral parlors, ostensibly to call Miss Chanters' father, I telephoned Clyde, too. No doubt he was out here in the graveyard some time before we arrived."

Ted looked stupid—suspiciously so. "But you told the girl to telephone Clyde—when she was out here in the cemetery."

"A bluff, Ted," his employer explained, smoothly. "I wanted Massow to overhear me. And evidently he did."

The driver was silent, but Humberton could not resist the temptation to press the topic a little further. "You observed someone following us, near the old wall, Ted," he said. "Remember?"

Ted nodded.

"Well, that was Clyde!"

Ted broke his silence; broke it with a mischievous grin. "Yes, sir!" he agreed. "I'd have told you, only you didn't seem to want to talk about it. You see, he got his mug out in the moonlight—and I'd know Clyde anywhere!"

SECONDS OF DOOM

ONE AFTER ONE THEY TICKED
RELENTLESSLY PAST—THOSE
GHASTLY MURDER MOMENTS—
WHILE THAT MONSTER AT THE
SWITCH HELD A STOP WATCH
ON DEATH. AND ONLY HORATIO
HUMBERTON, THE MORTICIAN
DETECTIVE, STOOD IN THEIR
WAY. ONE LONE FIGURE PITTED
AGAINST DOOM.

CHAPTER ONE
"I KILLED HIM!"

MORTIMER TICH, whose riches distributed among a hundred men would have made them all exceedingly wealthy, stepped carefully from his limousine to the curb, turned up the collar of his overcoat against the biting night wind, and snarled a response to his chauffeur's remarks.

"None of your business whether I had a pleasant voyage or not! You're new, aren't you?"

"Yes, sir. The former chauffeur—"

"I didn't ask about the former chauffeur. He has no possible interest for me. To remain in my employment you will learn to answer questions instantly and accurately and otherwise to keep your mouth shut. Mrs. Tich knows I am in town?"

"Yes, sir," the chauffeur replied, intelligently profiting by his instructions.

"Is she staying up for me?"

"I believe so, sir."

"Why should I care about your beliefs? If you don't know, say so, say so! Tell her I'll be home some time tomorrow. I intend to spend the rest of the night here, where I can have a little peace and comfort. Well, why don't you bring in my grip, man, why don't you bring it in?"

The chauffeur brought it silently, and remained on the stone step behind his employer while the latter sputtered and fumbled for his key. It proved a large, old-fashioned key, just as the door it fitted was old-fashioned, as was the little one-story building itself, backed up to a skyscraper, like a dwarf against a giant. Tich got the door unlocked with some difficulty, then noticed his chauffeur.

"Why don't you put it down? Do you think I want you standing there like a stork? Put it down and get out. Get out, I say! Get out! I don't want you standing around!"

The man obeyed, hastily. Even so, he was not quite prompt enough. For the irascible voice squeaked a question at him as he was about to climb into the driver's seat.

"What's your name?"

"John Blake, sir."

"Irish?"

"Irish extraction, sir."

"I don't like the Irish."

With that, little Mr. Mortimer Tich, having pressed the electric-light button, slammed the heavy street door, bolted it on the inside, and looked about his office. The door might appropriately have been called an alley door, because that was what it opened on; and the office could have gone by any one of several names—laboratory, a den, or just a room.

TICH COULD afford to be eccentric. He could afford to be very eccentric. He was eccentric enough to own the mightiest structure in the city, and to keep back to back with it in the alley, the little two-room shack where he had started in business forty years before. He could have afforded any sort of office. What he had was a large, square room, with a roll-top desk—second-hand for forty years—some laboratory equipment and half a dozen chairs; also a

smaller room with a cot in it.
There was a palatial office in
the adjoining building where
he reigned as Chairman of
the Board of Tich Industries,
Inc., but he preferred the
shack.

He slammed up the roll-
top and sat down at it, his hat
and coat still on. It occurred
to him to roll a cigarette—he
always rolled his own. Something went wrong with the
rolling, however, so he flung
both tobacco and paper to
the floor. But instead of
swearing, he grinned. For his
thoughts had gone back to
the chauffeur and his indignant face, as it had been visible in the dome-light of the
limousine.

No doubt the man would
tell Sarah how he had been
treated—Sarah being Mrs.
Tich. She would know from
that that six months' rest had
not calmed Tich's nerves. He
didn't want them calmed.
Whose nerves were they?
They were his. If he started
out on a two-year trip around
the world on doctor's orders

His hand hovered above the switch.

(who was the doctor to give him orders, anyway?) he had a right to change his mind, hadn't he? He had a right to come back, hadn't he? He had a right to send his valet and his secretary packing, too, and come back alone. These were hard times. The fools wouldn't find any bed of roses to fall into.

He grinned, too, at thought of Sarah. Probably he would catch her at the very start of a social season. He'd spoil her social season for her! Nerves! A man has a right to his nerves, hasn't he?

Why hadn't he taken off his hat and coat? It was always comfortable in his office. He didn't need them on. The heat came from the Tich Building—his building. The janitor had orders to keep these rooms ready for instant occupancy, day or night. He took off the hat and coat and threw them on the floor.

Then he did a singular thing. It was the first decent thing he had done since reaching the city, and, oddly enough, it was to cost him his life before dawn. He picked them up again, carried them into the adjoining room where the cot was, and laid them upon a chair. Some lingering vestige of orderliness prompted him to do that. His mother had taught him, as a boy, to be orderly.

A button on the wall beside the cot controlled the outer-room light, which he had snapped on when he entered, by means of the switch beside the heavy alley door. He reached up and plunged himself into darkness. It was a warm, comfortable, homely darkness. Nothing like it on board ship, nothing like it in foreign lands. He felt glad to be back. Perhaps in the morning, if his secretary and his valet hadn't found jobs—

He woke again with the pleasant conviction that he had enjoyed a refreshing nap. It was still dark. Nerves? His nerves were as good as anybody's. He felt positively young. An hour or two of sleep had always been enough for him. He had meant to have a smoke. Of course he had meant to have a smoke. And he hadn't had it. The makings were on the floor in the outer room. He would have it now.

So he pushed the wall button, slid off the cot, and walked—a little unsteady with sleep—to the doorway of the outer room. He stood there a moment with his hand on the door post. His eyes traveled drowsily from side to side of the lighted office.

Suddenly he gave a violent start at what he saw. He quickly pressed with his foot a metal plate just in front of him in the floor.

Then his knees crumpled and he fell, almost exactly in the middle of the doorway, with a small round hole in his forehead.

MR. HORATIO HUMBERTON said, not without a touch of vanity: "And there, gentlemen, is my reconstruction of the crime, based on the indications found in Mr. Tich's room."

Horatio Humberton, known to the vulgar as an undertaker, but termed by himself a necrologist, and still more widely heralded as a student of crime, sat in the swivel chair at the roll-top desk in Mortimer Tich's office. Police Detective James Clyde, his chair tilted far back against the wall, had been listening to the manuscript his friend had just finished reading. So had Humberton's senior hearse driver, Ted Spang. Ted's attitude was in strong contrast to Clyde's. Not only were the young man's feet on the floor, but his elbows were propped on his knees, and his chin cupped in his hands. From this position he looked up brightly at his chief and grinned when the narrative came to a close.

"Pretty snappy finish, sir!" he commented.

"Did you write that all by yourself, Ho?" the detective demanded. It was Clyde's privilege, and the privilege of no one else, to call the tall necrologist by that familiar contraction.

"I did," was the rather curt rejoinder.

"Well, no offense. I didn't know you could write stories, that's all."

"This is not a story. I have merely put the coroner's findings and my own observations into story form. The result leads up as simply as possible from what we know to what we don't know—the manner of Tich's murder."

"I'm not saying a word against your yarn, Ho," Clyde observed. "It sounds good. But aren't you going a little too far in figuring we know all that? Take the dialogue, now—I mean between crabby old Tich and the new chauffeur."

"Practically verbatim, Clyde. The chauffeur, Blake, seems to have an excellent memory. Tich's remarks made quite an impression on him. In fact, he went so far as to assure me—not seriously, I trust—that if someone else hadn't beaten him to it he'd have taken pleasure in killing the old devil himself."

Clyde nodded. "Plenty felt that way. I don't know whether you keep track of labor troubles, Ho. We have to, more or less. I think Tich could have won any unpopularity contest in town. Just before he left for Europe he took care of a strike in his Middlington works by simply dismantling the place and shipping the machinery to other plants. Wouldn't talk with the strikers or compromise in any way. They walked out one day, and next morning the machinery was being loaded on cars. There's to be a conference tomorrow in his main office—here in the Tich Building. A lot of the big mugs are sleeping in the building tonight. They say old Tich has got the four top floors fixed up like a palace for guest suites. This pow-wow is so important even Tich being killed can't stop it. It's rumored they're going to slash wages to the bone, all along the line. He ordered it from Europe, or that's what they claim. Oh, he had something coming, all right. But that doesn't solve our puzzle. The door was bolted, remember. All the windows were locked on the inside. And no gun was found. What can we say about that? What—"

He jumped up suddenly at the sound of footsteps outside, and ran to the window near the cot, in the inner office.

"Visitors!" he exclaimed. "No, a visitor. Funny-looking. Not a reporter. I know all the reporters in this burg. About seven feet tall, more or less, built like a mummy. Go to the door, will you, Ted, and tell him to get the hell out of here?"

YEARS OF experience with Ted's character justified Clyde's reckless instructions. He knew the young man could be trusted to interpret them liberally. Ted's interpretation was very liberal, in fact. He opened the door and extended his right hand, in friendly greeting.

"Hello, Mr. Yoland," he said; and, turning to the detective, "This gentleman is a locksmith, Clyde. Does work for Mr. Humberton. I guess you use someone else, or you'd have known him."

Clyde's rejoinder was curious. He stepped forward—one step, to be exact. Then his right hand swung up, in a light-ning-like semicircle.

"Drop that gun and stick up your hands!" he directed, quietly. "I've got you covered!"

The tall man smiled with no trace of excitement, and did as requested. The revolver he had had in his left hand clattered to the floor. His hands ascended. Instantly, Clyde was at him, patting and feeling each pocket and suspicious protuberance, searching him thoroughly.

"All right, put 'em down," he said, when that routine was completed. "Take a Chair. I was going to throw you out, but I guess you can stay now. After awhile I'll give you a free ride. Where did you get that gun?"

The locksmith's thin, sallow face melted in an engaging grin. "Is that important?" he inquired, gently.

"How can I know if it's important till you tell me where you got it?" Clyde was facing him belligerently.

"Possibly Mr. Yoland means to imply, Clyde, that something else is more important than the gun's origin," Horatio Humberton suggested.

Before Clyde could respond to this, his prisoner nodded—a pleasant, casual nod.

"Thank you, Mr. Humberton," he acknowledged. "You took the words out of my mouth. I was about to suggest to this gentleman"—he smiled toward Clyde—"who I assume to be a member of the police—that the manner of my acquisition of the weapon I brought with me is not only unimportant but also obscure. I must have twenty-five or thirty similar ones in my little shop. I deal in second-hand firearms in connection with my business. The important fact"—he leaned forward, and his hands rose, eloquently—"the important fact, gentlemen, concerning this gun is that it killed Mr. Mortimer Tich!"

Sometimes Humberton's control of his official friend was little short of hypnotic. He managed now, without leaving his chair, and merely by a quick and significant turn of his head, to keep Clyde silent. Almost at the same moment, he nodded sympathetically to their queer visitor.

"And in whose hands did it kill Mr. Mortimer Tich?" he inquired, calmly.

Yoland shrugged his shoulders. "Do you need to ask, Mr. Humberton?" he demanded. "Would I come here to betray another? It was I who killed Tich. I claim no credit for the deed—a thousand would have been proud to relieve me of the honor—but I do ask you to recognize this"—he smiled impartially on all three of his listeners—"that I am one of the few in this city who had nothing personally against Mr. Tich. So far as I know, he has never harmed me. My act was entirely disinterested. I considered it better for mankind that he should not linger on earth. So I erased him."

"Think he's telling the truth, Ho?" Clyde burst out.

"Possibly," the necrologist replied.

CLYDE WHIRLED on the prisoner again. "All right, then. If you're telling the truth, go ahead and tell the rest of it. The first man who got here found the door barred on the inside. You weren't here, neither was the gun. How did you pull it off?"

"You know I am a locksmith? I think Mr. Spang explained that?"

"We know that. Go ahead," Clyde urged.

"You will understand, then, that the problem of getting into this building, when the door was not bolted on the inside, but merely locked, was no problem at all for me. In fact, I have had a key for months that would fit the door. And I have been watching for months for Mr. Tich's return."

"You mean you watched this office?" Humberton put in.

The prisoner's bright and very intelligent eyes met his for a moment. "I have watched many places. Last night's success was more luck than anything else. I chanced to see Tich get in at the station, and heard his directions to the chauffeur. So I followed—on foot. When I reached this place, everything was dark. It seemed that I had failed—he had gone somewhere else, after all. But I let myself in with my key. And I"—he flashed a smile at Clyde—"I bolted the door on the inside. There were certain things I wished to say to Mr. Tich; nothing personal, certain things on behalf of mankind—before I killed him. I did not wish to be interrupted. In case he should be in the building, after all, I wanted my opportunity to say those things, to grant him time for repentance, to which all men, however vile, have a right—you will appreciate my feelings. So I bolted the door."

"And then?" Clyde prompted, impatiently.

"Give me time. I looked about with my flashlight—in this room. He was not here. So I walked into the other room. There he lay, asleep on a cot. I gazed at him awhile. My light was full on him, but he slept on. At last I was ready. There was nothing in his face, even asleep, to make me wish to spare him. I made sure there were no weapons in his coat, which lay on a chair beside him, or in his desk. I turned on all the lights. Still he slept. So I called him."

He stopped. His quick, keen glance rested on the detective. "I should like to stand just where I stood when he came to the door of his bedroom. It will make the story clearer. May I do so?"

Clyde nodded. The tall man rose slowly. His trousers clung tightly to his legs, revealing the outlines of thighs scarcely thicker than his knees. He walked to the corner of the room farthest from the inner door, appeared to choose a spot very carefully, then placed himself there.

"This is about where I was. I waited for him here. Soon he came. He hesitated in the doorway, and I covered him with my revolver. I don't believe he saw me until that moment, for he gave a tremendous start. He was going to leap backward into his bedroom. I ordered him sternly to remain where he was or die instantly. He gave a little, choking cry. No other sound passed his lips until I shot him. That was not for fifteen minutes. I had been talking to him—telling him these certain things I wished to say. I could have told him far more, but the pleasure had to be cut short. Can you guess why? Because he had been clever enough to step on that plate in the floor, which summons help, and I had not been alert enough to see him do it. I heard a car draw up and someone jump out. Then I killed him."

HE PAUSED again and nodded toward the street door. "Mr. Spang," he said, "will you oblige? You are wondering—all of you—how I eluded capture. I am going to show you. Luckily, the hinges of that outer door remain intact. You can help me to demonstrate, Mr. Spang. With your permission, sir—" He bowed courteously to Clyde, then stepped into the corner by the door, back of the hinges. "Not everyone could do this. But I am very thin. Now, Mr. Spang, please open the door."

Ted did so, and could not refrain from chuckling. The door, swinging open, touched the wall at right angles to it. Ample room remained for the tall locksmith to conceal himself in the triangular space behind.

"There you have it, gentlemen," he announced, pleasantly. He seated himself again. "You see exactly how it was done. I merely concealed myself there when the officer snapped the bolt and opened the door. I waited until his investigation carried him for a moment into the next room. Then I walked away!"

"Why?" Clyde demanded, as he paused. "Keep on talking and tell me why!"

"You mean why I killed him?"

"No, I don't mean why you killed him. You've given a reason for that, and it's plenty nutty, but maybe it's straight. What I'm interested in is why you come here. Nobody tailed you. You walk in here on your own two legs and give yourself up. What's the idea?"

The tall man smiled. "No doubt you know something of Mr. Tich's character?" he queried.

"Who didn't? What I'm—"

"Patience, please—patience! If you knew his character, you are aware, too, that he stood for the most atrocious force in our social order—the exploiter of human lives. His death in itself is a fine thing. It cleanses a plague spot. But his death, properly advertised, can be a stupendous thing— an event which will blazon to the whole world the fact that his kind have had their day, that they can no longer fatten on human misery. You see?" His eyes glowed with enthusiasm. "When a cultured man—a sane man—gives himself up as I am doing, and glories in his deed, it will become front-page news in every country in the world. That is my answer to your question. I am merely making the most of what I have done."

Clyde shrugged his shoulders, and abruptly stepped to the telephone to call the wagon. So far as he was concerned, the case was over. But Humberton drew his chair up close to the eccentric locksmith.

"Mr. Yoland," he said, keeping his voice down, "do you care to tell me—in confidence, if you wish—why you have manufactured this story?"

The tall man met his eye without wavering. "My story is true, Mr. Humberton," he declared.

"Very well," the necrologist replied. "Ted, I think we shall be going. I want to sleep over this."

CHAPTER TWO

THIRTY MINUTES TO LIVE

B UT THAT night, in the privacy of his bedroom above the Humberton Funeral Parlors, Horatio Humberton found it impossible to sleep. He could not get the Tich murder out of his thoughts. He could hear the regular breathing of Ted Spang in the next room—Ted's nearest approach to snoring—but he himself lay on his back, staring wakefully into the darkness, and going over the incidents of the day. Something was wrong. It was something in the locksmith's story. What was it?

Suddenly, he had it. He threw his long legs out of bed, turned on the night light, and reached for the telephone which stood on a little table beside him. He dialed Clyde's number.

"Clyde," he called, eagerly, when a drowsy voice which he recognized responded, "am I mistaken, or is there a pistol range in the basement at headquarters?"

"Are you routing me out at two in the morning to ask me that?" the detective retorted, indignantly.

"Answer my question." Humberton's voice was excited.

"Well, there is a pistol range, Ho—"

"Then throw on your clothes and meet me at headquarters. Wait a minute—better still, call up the jail and have Yoland brought to the pistol range. We'll meet him there."

"Are you crazy, Ho—" the detective was beginning; but Humberton cut him short again.

"I've been crazy all day," he shouted over the wire. "Stark, staring mad. Unless there's time to make up for it, we're both disgraced for life. Don't wait to argue. Do as I tell you."

He slammed up the receiver, and at the same moment Ted Spang's cheerful tones floated through the half-open doorway from his room.

"Don't take time to wake me, sir," they said. "I'm half dressed already. I heard you phoning. I'll have the sedan down in front before you've got your pants on."

Humberton stepped to the door and looked in at his loyal assistant. What he had in his mind would not wait. It had to be told to someone.

"Ted," he said, "I remembered something. It came to me while I lay awake. Yoland was lying."

Ted was starting to lace his shoes. He glanced up with a grin. "Yeah?" he prompted.

"Either today or a year ago. We must find out which."

Leaving Ted scratching his head in bewilderment, Humberton returned to his own room, but he was by no means ready when his driver's crisp footsteps passed his hall door. In fact, though he did not wait to put on a collar and tie, he found his sedan at the curb, with the engine running, when he stepped out into the chilly night.

"Ally oop, sir!" Ted threw in the clutch and the car shot smoothly forward. "Think he's more likely to have been lying today?" he suggested as they gathered speed.

"Much more likely."

"Then it's dollars to doughnuts he was trying to keep us from stirring something up."

Humberton nodded. "Faster, Ted," he said, quietly.

"We're doing seventy, sir. I've been wanting to find out what this car has in her. I had the hearse up to eighty once."

"Clyde will be there before us. He has only half a block to go to headquarters."

CLYDE, IN fact, was standing on the sidewalk when they drew up. He ran forward and opened the car door. Contrary to Humberton's expectations, his tone was genial.

"Guess you tumbled on something, Ho," he said, explosively. "Anyway, it looks like it. Know what they tell me about this fellow, Yoland? He hasn't been to sleep—hasn't even tried to sleep. He's been standing by his cell door all night, listening."

"Listening?" the necrologist echoed.

"Don't ask me for what. I can't tell you. When I wanted to know why he didn't turn in, he said he was just restless. Restless my eye! They should have had sense enough to call me."

"You have him in the pistol range?"

"He's down there waiting for you. What's the big idea about that, Ho?"

But Humberton shook his head, impatiently. "Come!" he urged. "There may be no time to lose."

In the long, brilliantly lighted room in the basement of the big building they found the tall locksmith, conversing easily with the two guards who had brought him down. He looked up as Humberton and his companions entered. His normal smile had given way to a slight scowl.

"I am glad to see you, Mr. Humberton," he remarked. "You at least are not a professional policeman. One finds suspicion about the simplest matters in such an environment as this. Would you believe it, I have asked these gentlemen repeatedly for the time—since my own watch has been taken from me—and they have refused to tell me."

The necrologist started. For a moment he was silent. Then he glanced at his watch.

"Surely there is no harm in telling you that," he said, lightly. "It is now—" He stopped, and smiled at the expectant prisoner. "Wait! Some years ago, I conducted a series of experiments relating to the time sense in various classes of men. I found that the primitive type was more accurate than the person of culture. Permit me to experiment on you, Mr. Yoland. You are a man of considerable culture, I believe. Before I answer your question, tell me what hour you think it is."

In spite of his casual manner, a certain odd tenseness communicated itself from the necrologist to the others. No one spoke. They stared intently at the prisoner. His face was pale. His lips twitched nervously.

"I should say that it is about three o'clock," he said, finally.

"You have borne out my observations. A primitive man would have done better. It is actually"—Humberton paused, looking sharply through his thick spectacles at the prisoner—"twenty-three minutes after three."

THE THIN locksmith staggered backward a step. One of his attendants caught him. But he recovered himself almost at once, and bowed with old-fashioned courtliness.

"That is kind of you." He laughed. "Very kind, indeed! Such a little thing—the time of night—yet I was unable to procure it until you came! Now may I inquire why you brought me down here?"

"Certainly." Humberton turned briskly to the detective. "Clyde, will you let me have a thirty-eight revolver—loaded—similar to the one with which Mortimer Tich was killed? I want Mr. Yoland to engage in a little target practice."

"You want me to shoot a gun?" An instant change had come over the locksmith. His eyes were rounded with horror.

"That is it," Humberton confirmed, suavely. "Let me see—I fancy you were about ten feet from Tich. Now, we will place a target—"

"No, no! I can't! You can't force me to!" The words were screamed.

Horatio Humberton took the prisoner by the hand, and spoke to him quietly and gently. "Mr. Yoland, you are the man who told me, about a year ago, that although you were an expert in the repair of firearms, you could not yourself bear to discharge one. That fact seemed to have entirely slipped my mind, but it came back to me a while ago. You did not kill Tich."

Clyde had brought a revolver from a wall cupboard. He laid it down on a table at the side of the room, and came forward with a grin of interest on his round face.

"What's that?" he demanded.

The prisoner was calm again. "No, I did not kill him," he admitted. "What time is it now?"

Clyde was about to reply, but the necrologist forestalled him. "Exactly twenty-seven minutes after three," he said.

"Then I can tell you. Yes, I can tell—you can do nothing now. When I confessed to the killing, Mr. Humberton, you thought the case was ended. Believe me, it had only begun. Three minutes more—" He held up his hand. "Listen!" Do you hear something? No, not yet. Bauchmann will not be late; neither will he be one second ahead of time. You should have known Bauchmann. He is one of the greatest men in the world. Yet in less than three minutes he will be only a memory!"

"What's it all about, Ho? Let's get going!" Clyde cut in, excitedly.

Humberton stared at him coldly.

"Where shall we go?" he asked in a voice so low that the locksmith probably did not hear it. Indeed, their prisoner seemed rapt. His head was thrown back, his dark eyes shone with a feverish light.

"Don't you know?" Clyde sank his own voice to a whisper.

The necrologist shook his head. He glanced at his wrist watch again, and spoke slowly and distinctly to Yoland. "It is exactly half-past three," he said.

"Half-past three! Half-past three!" The locksmith shouted it exultantly. "The reign of tyranny is broken! The first great blow has been struck! Listen! Listen!"

"I fear listening can do no good, Mr. Yoland. This pistol range is sound-proof." Humberton was still speaking slowly. His eyes were fixed intently on the wildly excited locksmith, as if to weigh the effect of every word he uttered. He hesitated, then asked a deliberate question. "Is the thing you are listening for something that will be reported to the police?"

Yoland's face turned toward him. The mouth opened, in a dreadful, soundless laugh. Drained of blood, with eyes like burning lamps, it was more a horror-laden mask than a face.

"To the police?" he repeated. "Nothing that ever happened in the world will be reported sooner to the police! They know it by now. Good old Bauchmann does not fail. Go to a telephone." His laugh became audible. It was deep-throated and hoarse. "Your man at the desk knows, even though we could not hear!"

CLYDE, HIS face drawn with mystified apprehension, was about to slip out to a telephone. Humberton waved him back.

"I will go, Clyde," he said, firmly.

He was absent only a moment. When he returned, his mouth was grim. "The man at the desk cannot talk for excitement," he declared. "Tell me what has happened, Mr. Yoland."

"Nothing in all my life—" The emotion in Yoland's voice stopped him. He struggled with it, and went on. "Nothing ever gave me more pleasure than to tell you this. It is enough to have lived—for this moment. The Tich Building—" He choked again.

"Go on," Humberton prompted.

"The Tich Building is a heap of smoking stones and mortar. All the men in the guest suites—the men who came to the business conference—you thought they were great men. I tell you—" A sob cut off his breath, but he forced it back. "Bauchmann, who lies in dust with them, was a greater man than any. Bauchmann—"

"Can't we do something, Ho?" Clyde exploded, with agony in his voice. The even, rapt tones of the locksmith answered him.

"You can do nothing except to execute me when the time comes. Bauchmann and I have done this ourselves. There are no others. When the Social Revolution is complete, we shall have our reward. The historian of the future will not forget us. Bauchmann of the great soul and the inventive mind; Yoland, his humble helper, who deceived the police long enough for the mighty work to be accomplished! I tell you—"

Humberton interrupted. His hand, laid on Clyde's, imperatively signaled the detective to silence. "I don't understand, Mr. Yoland," he said, evenly. "Surely your story was not all false? You must have been present when Tich was killed?"

"When he was killed? Not only then, but for many a night before that. How do you think we carried in the dynamite, Bauchmann and I?"

"Ah, of course! You used his little office," the necrologist replied, with a smile. Clyde's eyes, searching his face, was puzzled and rather incredulous.

"His little office was invaluable! You see, he was gone for six months, so we had time." Yoland laughed, wildly. "We pried up the floor boards in the little building, and tunneled. Ah, Bauchmann handled that wonderfully. There'll never be another man like Bauchmann! We could lift the boards as we wished. They were fitted so well, with lugs setting into sockets on the under sides, that a regiment could have walked over them without suspecting anything. If Tich hadn't surprised us, he would have lived till; half-past three Bauchmann had a trap—"

Humberton looked at his wrist watch. He had been tensely but quietly listening until he had the information he needed. Now he exploded into action.

"Get an ax on your way out, Clyde. And a flashlight. Come, Ted! We still have half an hour."

Clyde stared at him, with open mouth. Horatio Humberton pushed him toward the door.

"Get those things!" he shouted. "Do you think I told him the correct time? It's exactly three o'clock!"

CHAPTER THREE

TUNNELS OF TERROR

T **ED WAS** first to reach the crisp outer air. He had raced out so fast that the man at the desk had risen with the half-formed intention of stopping him. Humberton was just behind. Clyde had delayed to pick up the ax and the flashlight, so both the others were already in the front seat of the sedan, with the engine running, when he threw himself into the back seat.

"Wait, Ted!" Humberton swung around to the big detective, speaking rapidly. "You'll have to get out, Clyde!"

"Have to do what?" Clyde objected, belligerently.

"The Tich Building is thirty stories. An explosion big enough to demolish that will wreck this entire section of the city. Run back into the station. Mobilize the newspapers. Have them phone the guest suites in the Tich Building, and every other available place in the neighborhood. Get the help of the telephone company itself, the hospital staffs—anyone who is awake at this hour. Rout out your police. Have them scour the district. Tell everyone you waken to come out without stopping to dress, and to run for his life."

"All that's in case you can't stop the explosion, Ho?" Clyde, too, spoke rapidly, but his voice was calm.

"Yes."

"O.K." The detective's big right hand reached over into the front seat, and gripped first Humberton's then Ted's in a lightning-fast squeeze. "Hope we'll meet again—here or somewhere. You'll find the ax and the flash in the back seat. There's my gun, too. So long."

The car leaped away from the curb like a released spring. For a moment neither Humberton nor his able hearse driver spoke. That brief leave-taking had been conducive to thoughtful silence. Then Ted, who had taken several corners with no regard for safety, leveled out at extreme top speed into a straight stretch, and chuckled, quietly.

"At that," he said, "I'd like to see Clyde with wings and a harp. He'd need an outsize in both of'em."

"The police won't be able to save themselves," his chief returned. "Whatever happens, they'll have to stick."

"Just what I mean, if we fail, it'll be us and them heading for glory together. Get the things out of the back seat, if you don't mind, sir. That'll save half a sec' when we stop."

Humberton did so. He nearly shot into the back seat himself, for Ted turned another corner at that moment. But a second turn, righted him violently. A moment more, and they were in the dark alley back of the great Tich Building. The tires slid in to the curb. Before they stopped, Ted slipped out to the street on the driver's side.

It was very dark. Ted waited for his chief. "Let's see your wrist watch, sir," he whispered, and Humberton held up the radium dial. "Ten after three. Do we go right in?"

"We may have to break down the door," the necrologist replied.

Ted strained his eyes up the stone steps. "Looks to me like it's open," he said.

They mounted the steps, and an inarticulate grunt from the driver, who was in advance, confirmed his surmise. He reached back for the flashlight. He already had the ax. In a moment, his hand stopped Humberton in his tracks. The glowing circle of the flashlight danced on the floor. It danced on the body of a man, too, lying on his face.

Silently, Ted turned the head to one side. "Murphy—one of Clyde's men," he whispered. "I meant to ask Clyde whether he had anyone on guard here."

"He's alive, but we can't wait." Humberton clipped the words short. "Study the floor, Ted—study the floor."

Almost at once, the driver replied with a subdued gasp of excitement. "Look here, sir!" he urged. "Look where Murphy's left hand is!"

A BOARD in the floor had been lifted, and apparently jammed down again. The prostrate policeman's hand was pinned beneath it. Blood still oozed from the broken flesh and stained the man's white cuff.

"Knocked out while the floor boards were up," the necrologist diagnosed, swiftly. "His hand was caught there when they were replaced. Now we know where to look. Pry up the boards with your ax, Ted, while I hold the light."

Ted attacked the job so vigorously that his employer had to caution him to quiet. The board which imprisoned Murphy's hand was lifted first. Humberton grasped it with his long fingers and helped jerk upward. It came away with the click of something especially fashioned for removal.

"Now the next!"

But Ted needed no more coaching. A second board came; a third and a fourth. He tried a fifth, and almost instantly gave up, with a shake of his head. "That seems all, sir."

"Flash your light into the hole. Careful! He's almost certain to be down there somewhere."

What they saw was a narrow tunnel, dug in the earth, just beneath the floor of the little old building. Humberton snatched the flashlight out of Ted's hand and gave him the revolver, instead.

"I will lead with the light, Ted. You follow, with the ax and the gun. You are the marksman. If you see anyone in the tunnel—anyone—shoot without hesitation."

"Right!" the driver agreed, curtly.

Humberton dropped into the tunnel. At another time he would have entered it rather gingerly, but seconds were precious. He had taken only one step forward when Ted landed lightly behind him.

Just before them, the earthy passage curved, at a spot which no doubt marked the foundation line of the little office building. The tall necrologist was able to walk, bent at a forty-five-degree angle. It was uncomfortable going, but faster than crawling. He hurried to the curve, stopped, and cautiously glanced around it. Nothing was visible but blackness. He reinforced his vision with the flashlight beam.

The tunnel sloped downward. For about twenty feet it seemed dug in clay as before, then a framework of planking appeared.

Ted whispered a suggestion. "That's where it starts under the Tich Building," he said. "I don't know much about it, but I guess the tunnel works around between piers."

Humberton nodded. He could feel Ted behind matching each step, sometimes actually treading on his heels. If any danger threatened, the adventurous driver wished to reach it as soon as his chief.

"Planks underneath, also," Humberton whispered back to him, in a moment.

"Think they're safe?"

"We must chance that."

Nevertheless, he tested the boards with his foot, and motioned Ted back while he did so. He kept a careful balance, with outstretched hands. The flashlight in his right hand glanced across the watch strapped to his left wrist. It was three thirteen. Just three minutes ago, they had entered the little building. Sixteen minutes remained.

"Come, Ted," he whispered.

THE PLANKING sounded hollow beneath their feet. They had advanced only a few yards on it when the driver caught his chief's arm. "Back, sir!" he warned. "It's sinking!"

In the same instant he flung himself back in the direction from which they had come, dragging Humberton after him. But he was not quick enough. They slid downward.

"Shoot, Ted!" Humberton directed, frantically.

The same thought had occurred to both. If they were going to destruction, perhaps they could still get the man who was sending them there. That would prevent the greater horror—the explosion. Two orange-red bursts of flame, which had not waited for Humberton's word, burned past his head. The roar of Ted's gun was stupendous. It tore the silence to shreds, and tortured their ear drums. As the stillness closed in again, they found themselves sprawling in soft earth, somewhere below.

Someone was speaking to them, from the place they had quitted so violently. It was a guttural, metallic voice, cold and even as steel.

"I am Bauchmann," it said. "You forgot, my friends, that the tunnel curves again. Or perhaps you did not know. You could not possibly injure me with your bullets. I am here, safe. I have even rigged an electric light from the building supply, so that the monster, Tich, pays for my convenience."

A hoarse chuckle followed; and suddenly the voice became gentle. "You are not injured?" it inquired. "It was not my purpose to cause you suffering."

"No," Humberton answered. He could hear Ted's whispered confirmation behind him.

"I am glad. You have your light?"

"I just found it in the dirt, sir," Ted informed his chief.

The man in the darkness above them must have had sharp ears. He replied: "That is well. It is terrible to die in the dark. You are in some abandoned workings. Before the Tich Building was erected, several of the smaller structures about here had central heat. That passage was used then. I am sorry that you must be killed, for I have no quarrel with you. You have yet several minutes. I shall not strike till half an hour after three o'clock."

There was a slight pause. Then the metallic voice said: "Good-by, my friends! I shall be the first to die—the first of many."

"One moment, Ted." Humberton listened to the diminishing footsteps above them. "Give him time to get away, then turn your light upward."

"Right!" Ted's voice was as cheerful, and nearly as calm, as if he had been officiating in his usual capacity at a funeral. But its tone changed a little when he flashed the light above his head. "Not a chance!" he declared.

Humberton could see that for himself. They must have dropped at least fifteen feet into the soft earth. Far above them, the planking still sagged—the trap they had fallen through—no doubt a trap cunningly arranged for exactly such an occasion.

"This passage extends both ways," the necrologist said.

"How much time?" Ted asked, quietly.

"Not quite ten minutes."

"Come on, sir."

He started running. Humberton followed.

Suddenly, Ted stopped. "Planking!" he announced. "Up to the ceiling! This end of the passage has been boarded up."

Humberton glanced at the heavy boards, as Ted's flashlight revealed them. "It must lead under the Tich Building," he said. "Well break through, Ted. Now!"

THEY RUSHED the barrier together. The boards held. They rushed it again. The third time, it gave, where the wood was cleated to the roof of the passage. They crashed through, on their faces. The fallen boards crashed beneath them.

Ted flashed his light. "Caught! It's a blind alley, sir!"

"They wouldn't board up a blind alley," his chief objected.

"Can't help it," Ted shrugged. "Wait a minute—you're right, sir. Here's an opening at the left. I never saw it. We'll make this yet!" He caught Humberton's eye, and laughed. "We'll make it just in time to be blown up with the rest of the town, eh, sir?"

"Listen!" Humberton whispered.

A voice was calling; a rather hoarse and thick voice, with poor carrying qualities. "Mr. Humberton!" it was saying.

Ted answered with a lilting halloo. His high-pitched tones seemed to echo and reecho indefinitely.

"Right through this left opening!" he exclaimed, almost at the same moment. "That's where he is, I think. There's a light."

The bearer of the light appeared. He was a short, squat man, carrying an enormous lantern, which swung in time to his leisurely steps. Its yellow glow, escaping through holes in the lantern top, disclosed that he had a bald head and an extremely small white mustache, perched in the center of his broad face.

He began talking as soon as he was able to see them. "Well, I must say this is a pleasure, Mr. Humberton, sir. Mr. Clyde said I might do well to look for you. I'm the night watchman, you know, sir—Tich Building. Mr. Clyde says the police are backing you up through that little building, but, thinks I, I'll come down these old, little-used passages—"

"Your name?" Humberton interrupted.

"Titherington, sir. I—"

"Titherington, your building is to be blown up in exactly six minutes. The man who intends to do so is in a passage somewhere above this. We fell through—he set a trap for us. The police cannot possibly reach him in time. You must show us a way."

At the first sentence, the watchman's mouth had opened. It wobbled aimlessly for a moment. Then it snapped shut abruptly. "Six minutes?" he jerked out. "Yes, sir! I know where he'll be. You can't make it in six minutes. But come on."

He ran, wheezing, with the little jumps of a man long out of training. They turned a corner—another—another. Sudden light dazzled them. It was only an electric bulb, high in the ceiling of the last passage. A row of huge, shining switches were ranged beneath it on the wall. The old man's breath choked in his throat, but he forced himself to talk rapidly.

"See that hole—high up in the wall? It's an old drainage pipe." He nodded at Humberton. "You're thin. You're the only one of us thin enough to crawl through it. You'll find your man at the other end, I think. But you can't do it in six minutes."

Ted started to say something, and stopped. Part of what the watchman said was plainly true. No one of them but Horatio Humberton—tall and thin to the point of emaciation—could be certain of entering that hole.

The necrologist spent possibly five seconds in thought; and even that brief space of time was not passed in idleness by the others. Ted used it to slip revolver and flashlight into his chief's pocket. Old Titherington, with one sage glance at the height of the drainage pipe opening, dropped to his hands and knees and motioned to Ted. Instantly the driver caught on. He mounted to the platform afforded by the old man's back, and made a step for Humberton with his clasped hands.

No one had said a word; but when an upward shove and a tremendous boost from Ted had fairly shot his employer into the opening of the pipe, Humberton heard a remark from the spot he had just left.

"Good-by, sir!" Ted was saying.

CHAPTER FOUR

SPLIT-SECOND STUFF

HUMBERTON'S LARGE hands pressed the slippery surface of the pipe with a grip which did not slip. His sharp elbows reinforced them at an angle, and added leverage. His bony legs, like the driving rods of a locomotive, pushed him rapidly forward and upward. He fairly wriggled through the pipe.

Soon the vertical angle increased. Gravity was stacking the cards against him. Worse yet, a scum of slime on the inner surface caused his hands, his elbows, and his knees to slip together. He began to slide back. Just ahead, there was a dim lightening of the thick blackness. He was nearing the end of the pipe. Yet his chances of getting there were poor.

Clawing and struggling, he slid back half a yard.

Another minute of intense struggle to regain the ground he had lost, and at last he reached a second bend. Just beyond it was a luminous disk. It looked like the moon. It was the end of the pipe. At the bend, the pipe straightened again to the horizontal.

Humberton stopped—only inches from the end. He heard something, as soon as the noise of his own progress ceased—a queer, sing-song muttering. He saw a square, low-ceilinged room, piled high with canvas sacks. He inched forward a little more, and looked into the face of a man.

It was a great, bushy face, with an enormous brown beard and small blue eyes. The man was clad in overalls. The eyes were not looking at him. They were fixed on a watch, held open in the palm of the man's hand, and illuminated by the rays of an incandescent bulb, swung from a beam of the ceiling. He studied the watch with profound intensity, kneeling the while with his other hand on something which at first Humberton could not see. Then a shift on the part of one of them brought that, too, into sight. It was an electric switch—a knife switch— screwed to a board. Wires attached to it ran toward the pile of canvas sacks.

The handle of the switch was upright. The right hand of the man hovered above it. His forefinger barely touched the black rubber knob at its tip.

As he waited for the watch to tick its final seconds. The bearded man sang, softly. That was the sound Humberton had heard. His voice, guttural and deep, sometimes rose into a low-pitched, wild melody, but more often sank to a bass growl. He swayed as he sang. His finger, trembling above the switch, seemed at the point of throwing it into contact from sheer tremor of nerves.

Very slowly the tall necrologist wriggled from the pipe. He was hardly a yard from the man. If the intent eyes lifted from the watch, he meant to fling himself forward. If the finger started to close down on the switch handle, he would do so.

He got clear. But his right foot, in dragging out of the pipe, struck its edge. The bearded man glanced up. In that instant, Humberton remembered that he had a revolver in his pocket. Within the pipe, he could not possibly have brought his hand down to pull it out. Now there was no time. He had remembered too late. He threw himself at the man, caught the menacing right wrist in a feverish grip, and they rolled over together.

Even as he fell backward, the man laughed. "You are Humberton?" he said. "Now we fight it out, *hein?* I knew of that pipe, but I thought no one could be thin enough to come that way. We have yet nearly one minute. You are ready?"

WITH A sudden burst of strength, he broke loose, and in the same movement dove for the switch. Humberton caught his other wrist, and doubled it behind him into a hammer lock, with some added feature of his own which no wrestler could have named, and they again tumbled backward together.

"You are quicker than I thought!"The bearded face broke into a grin—a rather disquieting grin, since it was so entirely unexcited. "Quick—yet not strong. Let me show you."

Humberton felt the muscles tighten slowly under his fingers.The powerful left arm began to force itself free. He threw every ounce of his own strength into the struggle. The bearded man grinned again, and with a quick twist wrenched himself loose.

"We die together! The time has come!" he shouted.

He was clear. One creeping step—he did not wait to stand upright—and his hand began to close upon the switch.

Humberton had been thrown sideways. He twisted. It was really only a partial twist of his thin body—just enough to permit his long fingers to brace themselves against the other's hips. He straightened then with the leverage of a catapult. The bearded man, with a guttural curse, rolled completely over and beyond the switch, and brought up against the farther wall.

Humberton snapped the switch back beyond the vertical. It had nearly closed. Then he drew the revolver from his pocket.This time he remembered it. He meant to shoot.

"Do not shoot, please!"

The necrologist stared in astonishment. His companion was sitting against the wall, smiling. He had put his hands up, but now he lowered them slowly.

"Perhaps you believe me when I say I have no weapon of any kind—none but the little electric switch. I would not wish to be humiliated to die by a bullet—I who have expected to die with a thousand others in a cataclysm which shall shake the social order. My watch is before you on the floor. Perhaps you will oblige with the time?"

Humberton glanced at it—without, however, altogether taking his gaze off the bearded man. He answered: "Three thirty-one."

"Ah, it is a pity! The great moment has passed, and the workers of iniquity still live. What do you mean to do with me? May I ask that?"

"I shall hold you here until help comes," the necrologist replied, curtly. He hoped it would come soon. No doubt Clyde would find a means of bridging the gap where the trap of boards had been sprung. But it might take time.

"What is it that is said in the Bible?" The bearded man sat and looked at him composedly. " 'My help cometh from the Lord?' You may find your help, Mr. Humberton, from a source unexpected, like that. The time—once more?"

Humberton blinked at him, with mild astonishment. "It is now three thirty-three," he returned.

"What matters it—the time? You think that? I can tell so by your face. I must explain. Soon even for that will not be time. You see to my right? It is a door. It leads to another passage which you will never see. It is secured on the other side, this door, with a heavy wooden bar. Had you my strength even, and hours to spare, I think you could not break down that bar from this side. I dropped it, then I came here by still another passage which I know. You see the door?"

The necrologist nodded, silently. He had not noticed the door until it was brought to his attention. It fitted snugly into the opposite side of the room. Something in the quiet smile of the man who sat near that door, under the threat of his revolver, disturbed him. He wished Clyde would come.

"You see the door—yes. But you cannot see my helper beyond the door. If you listen closely, you may hear him. Will you do me that favor, my friend?"

HE HELD up a hand for silence. Humberton listened. A faint ticking came to his ears.

"You heard? He has been waiting there, this helper of mine, moving, ever moving, yet still. Why does he wait? Because he knows that I would rather throw the switch with my own hand. But there is the chance—always the chance—that something will interfere; maybe someone with a gun. Then I cannot throw the switch. The time again—if I am not too much trouble?"

Slowly, Humberton answered. He was staring at his companion with a growing feeling of horror. "It lacks a minute and a quarter of three thirty-five," he said.

"Then I must tell you quickly. This helper is a little clock. You guessed that? He is connected by wires to these bags. At three thirty-five—" He smiled. "Can you guess that, too? Can you guess what happens at three thirty-five?"

The necrologist was silent.

"I see you have guessed." The bearded man's eyes shone feverishly. "At that moment he closes the connection. And we have our explosion, after all! Be brave! You will not know when it comes!"

Humberton tried to speak. No words came forth. He merely continued to stare at his companion and at the closed door. The man opened his hairy mouth again, with a cavernous chuckle.

"You think maybe you can crawl back into the pipe? Then the great explosion will not touch you? Let me tell you, my friend. This building—how high is it? Thirty stories? These bags will blow those thirty stories to dust.

You and me, too, my friend. This mighty building—little you and me—we vanish together. What will be found where we were? Only a big hole—and much dust!"

He paused. A curious, twisted grin flickered on his face. "You think yet that you can escape?"

Humberton shook his head. He had no words. His mind was in a fog. Through the fog he saw his triumphant tormentor and the barred door, behind which the tiny clock was ticking.

"That is well," the bearded man commended. "Now let me tell you a joke. This is a great—a magnificent joke! You will die laughing at it—*hein?* That little clock outside the door, it is wired to the current supply of the Tich Building. That is the joke. He pays—Tich pays—for the destruction of his own so fine building! But the joke will perish with us—a pity, my friend!"

He stopped again. His eyes were shut in a silent laugh of intense amusement. Humberton listened in the silence. The ticks of the little clock, faint but clear, beat on his brain. The words of the bearded man beat on his brain, too. They were important. Something, deep in his mind, shrieked to him that they were very important. They meant life or death. But he could not think. The fog wouldn't lift.

"How long now, my friend?"

Humberton glanced at his watch. "Fifteen seconds," he answered, dully.

The bearded man leaped to his feet, with a hoarse laugh. "Prepare yourself, then! The hour is at hand!" He snatched the watch up from the floor. "The seconds! The precious seconds of life! I will count them!"

His arm began to rise and fall.

"Ten seconds!" he shouted.

"Nine!" He roared with wild delight.

"Eight! Eight, my friend!"

Something thundered in Humberton's mind. The fog had lifted. He heard again the words he had been struggling to grasp. *"The current supply... of the Tick Building!"*

His voice soared suddenly in a shriek—he would not have recognized it as his own—a shriek which hurtled down the iron pipe.

"Ted! Throw off all switches!"

The counting went on. It had not stopped.

"Five!"

"Four!"

The heavy bass broke—but did not pause.

"Three!"

Humberton watched the dangling bulb. Its glowing filament meant death. Unless it went out....

"Two!"

"One!"

The light flickered—was sucked out. They were in darkness.

For a moment he sat perfectly still. Then a half-sob escaped him. He could not hold it back. He snapped on the flashlight.

He directed it at the bearded man's bewildered face, and covered that face with his revolver.

A POLICE car, containing Detective Clyde and his friend, Horatio Humberton, pulled up in front of the Humberton Funeral Parlors. Ted was not in it. At least half an hour had elapsed since Clyde's man had taken Bauchmann into custody. Several times, Humberton had inquired about his driver. Each time, he had received an evasive answer.

"Clyde," he said, firmly, "I insist upon knowing what has become of Ted. Unless you tell me, I shall return at once to the Tich Building."

Clyde cleared his throat, with vast embarrassment; but just then a second machine stopped behind them, and his manner at once became cheerful. "Here he is!" he shouted, joyfully.

Humberton stepped to the curb, and looked at the other vehicle. "That's a fire truck," he exclaimed.

"Sure it's a fire truck."

"You tell me Ted is in there?"

"They're taking him out right now," Clyde replied, with conviction.

But that statement was not strictly correct. True, two firemen were helping Ted from the front seat of the "hook-and-ladder"—for such the vehicle was—but he was descending largely under his own power, and indeed he seemed to spurn their good-natured assistance. Perhaps that assistance was rather too broadly good-natured for his taste. Ted walked with a limp. He passed them with considerable dignity in spite of it. He appeared about to enter the parlors. He had spoken to no one.

"Ted!" Horatio Humberton exclaimed.

"You can keep your kidding till tomorrow. I'm not feeling good," the driver returned, without turning his head.

His chief overtook him. "Ted, I insist on knowing what has happened to you," he said, earnestly.

For the first time, Ted glanced at him; but it was a cold glance.

"Get it from Clyde or the firemen," he returned, curtly. "Get it—and write a story about it if you want to."

With that, the door of the funeral parlors slammed behind him.

"What was it you used, boys?" Clyde inquired of the firemen. "A block and tackle?"

"Just a rope," one of them replied. "We hitched it on to his legs and pulled."

"Now, look here, Ho—" Clyde evidently had taken the burden of explanation on himself, though reluctantly. "Ted wouldn't stand by and twiddle his thumbs while you were having a life-and-death fight, would he? You know Ted better than that."

"There was nothing else for him to do."

"Of course there wasn't. He realizes that better than you do—now. But he thought maybe, by squeezing like the very devil, he could get through the pipe, and be in on the scrap."

The necrologist nodded—a nod of enlightenment.

"Oh," he remarked.

"Well, he was mistaken."

The two firemen nodded, too. Then they climbed back into the truck.

ABOUT THE AUTHOR

DO YOU remember when Dr. Coué came over from Europe a few years ago with his singular formula for well-being: "Every day in every way I'm getting better and better?" And the amazing furor which swept the country in the wake of the good doctor? We were always a bit dubious and skeptical as to just how efficacious his method might be. Possibly it had its worthy points but at the first faint traces of even the most minor sort of indisposition we hustled up to our family physician for some of his old-fashioned, orthodox treatment. And it didn't include any magic mumbling of a catch phrase either.

We believe that the same general rule is applicable to the building of a magazine. We could sit here and reiterate the obvious fact that every month in a dozen different ways *Dime Detective Magazine* gets better and better. We know it to be true but merely saying so over and over again wouldn't go very far toward keeping up the good work. It takes more than that. A lot more. Plenty of the good old-fashioned, orthodox treatment, in fact, to supplement the catch phrases.

And the treatment in this case consists in going after the best writers in the market; getting them to outdo even their own previous efforts in furnishing new mystery and thrills for the ever increasing army of loyal *Dime Detective* readers; and making each issue one galaxy of exciting detective action from the front cover to the back.

This month we are proud to introduce a new master-mystery author to the readers of *Dime Detective* in the person of J. Paul Suter, whose splendid hair-raiser, "The Angel of the Damned," opens the issue and is illustrated on the cover. He writes from his home in Youngstown, Ohio to tell us something about himself and his unique necrologist-detective, Horatio Humberton.

Since you asked me—my gosh, was it a week ago, and here I am only just replying?—for information as to where that tall, gaunt person with the thick glasses, Mr. Horatio Humberton, came from, I have been casting about in what I optimistically term my mind to find out whether I know, myself.

The result is appalling. For several years I have been writing about Humberton, and suddenly, as the result of your query, I find that I never realized who the man really is. I realize it now. And I am rather alarmed. For it has come to me that, in all essentials, Ho Humberton is a highly respected banker of my acquaintance, who never conducted a funeral nor tracked down a murderer in his life.

To be sure, the banker doesn't wear thick glasses, and he doesn't smoke long, black cigars, and if the embalming of the dead is a hobby with him he certainly keeps that fact a profound secret from his friends; but it is he, nevertheless. If he *were* a necrologist—if he *did* dabble in detective lore—he would be Humberton.

Do most of your writers plot their stories out in advance, so that they know just where they are going, from first word to last? I wish I could. My method is so unscientific that it becomes laughable. The murder mystery comes to me first. I get to wondering about it—what a heck of a thing for someone to do!—why should anybody pull off a killing like that?—who did it, and why, in the name of common sense? I wonder, without arriving at any conclusion; and then, some fateful evening, I sit down to the typewriter, throw Humberton onto the job, and let him do his stuff. As the story progresses, I begin to sense who the murderer is. Sometimes I am right; but more often, I find toward the end of the story that someone I did not suspect is the real criminal, and then, of course, I have to go back and do a lot of rewriting.

That, it seems to me, is about the hardest way to write a detective story. I know a lot of easier ways, but with me they don't seem to click. If I can tell in advance who did the horrid deed, the story is more than likely to be a flop.

As for my personal tastes, if they are of interest to anyone, I play volley ball and pitch horse shoes (doing neither very well), I believe in ghosts and am profoundly interested in all sorts of psychic phenomena. I like to read all manner of books, with a slant toward ancient Egypt. I don't drink or smoke, but I do over-eat—with the result that I have to diet, every once in a while, to keep the old waist line below my chest measurement. Also, I am inclined to "reach for a sweet," and you know what that does.

Married; five children, and about three thousand books. Wife can write much better than I, but she doesn't know it. Consider myself pretty nifty at humorous writing, but the editors don't. Turn out a few ghost stories each year. Do most of my writing at night, all alone, in a downtown office building. Have had the family train the Graflex on me a time or two, so you are likely to see a picture of me shortly. If it doesn't seem good enough for publication, let me know, and I will send a snapshot of my brother-in-law. He has "it."

Thank you, Mr. Suter. We appreciate your letter and hope to hear more from you in the near future.